**Praise for the
Pennsylvania Dutch Mystery series**

"As sweet as a piece of brown-sugar pie . . . Magdalena is so likable." —*Booklist*

"The series' popularity is rising like sticky bun dough. . . . [The] key to Myers's success is her main character." —*The Morning Call* (Allentown, PA)

"Deadly games, food, and fun . . . fast-paced, tongue-in-cheek . . . zany humor . . . a funny and entertaining read . . . [by] a wise and perceptive writer." —*The Rocky Mount Telegram* (NC)

"With her sassy wit and odd habits . . . Magdalena is a delightful main character." —*The Champion Newspaper* (Decauter, GA)

"Had me constantly laughing. . . . Life would never be dull with [Magdalena] around. . . . A wonderful book with skillful writing and I highly recommend it to everyone." —I Love a Mystery

"Broad, sometimes self-deprecating humor, nonstop action, off-the-wall incidents, and idiosyncratic characters result in clever entertainment." —*Library Journal*

continued . . .

Custard's Last Stand

A PENNSYLVANIA DUTCH MYSTERY
WITH RECIPES

Tamar Myers

A SIGNET BOOK

SIGNET
Published by New American Library, a division of
Penguin Group (USA) Inc., 375 Hudson Street,
New York, New York 10014, USA
Penguin Group (Canada), 90 Eglinton Avenue East, Suite 700, Toronto,
Ontario M4P 2Y3, Canada (a division of Pearson Penguin Canada Inc.)
Penguin Books Ltd., 80 Strand, London WC2R 0RL, England
Penguin Ireland, 25 St. Stephen's Green, Dublin 2,
Ireland (a division of Penguin Books Ltd.)
Penguin Group (Australia), 250 Camberwell Road, Camberwell, Victoria 3124,
Australia (a division of Pearson Australia Group Pty. Ltd.)
Penguin Books India Pvt. Ltd., 11 Community Centre, Panchsheel Park,
New Delhi - 110 017, India
Penguin Group (NZ), cnr Airborne and Rosedale Roads, Albany,
Auckland 1310, New Zealand (a division of Pearson New Zealand Ltd.)
Penguin Books (South Africa) (Pty.) Ltd., 24 Sturdee Avenue,
Rosebank, Johannesburg 2196, South Africa

Penguin Books Ltd., Registered Offices:
80 Strand, London WC2R 0RL, England

Published by Signet, an imprint of New American Library, a division of Penguin
Group (USA) Inc. Previously published in a New American Library edition.

First Signet Printing, January 2004
10 9 8 7 6 5 4 3 2

Copyright © Tamar Myers, 2003
Recipes copyright © 1990 by Linda Zimmerman. Reprinted from *Puddings,
Custards, and Flans: 43 Easy Recipes from Old Favorites to New Creations.*
Published by Clarkson N. Potter, Inc.
All rights reserved

Ⓟ REGISTERED TRADEMARK-MARCA REGISTRADA

Printed in the United States of America

For F. Jay Ach, with my deepest gratitude

Acknowledgments

Special thanks go to Linda Zimmerman for allowing me to use recipes from her wonderful book *Puddings, Custards, and Flans,* published by Clarkson N. Potter, Inc., 1745 Broadway, New York, New York 10019.

1

I much prefer Hernia to Intercourse. Or Lancaster, Pennsylvania, for that matter. Hernia has Amish and Mennonite ambience out the wazoo, but it has yet to be discovered by tourists.

My full-board inn, the PennDutch, is the only game in town, and it has only six guest rooms—actually five, now that I've taken in a foster child. My establishment caters to the rich and famous, who come here to do the staring, and not to be stared at themselves. My favorite guests are Babs and Brolin, Brad and Jennifer, Mel and his wife, Julia—well, you get the picture. Even Presidents have stayed under my roof, and despite the fact that I'm a Mennonite woman of high moral standards, one even tried to stay in my bed. The only guest I really want to entertain, and still haven't had the privilege to do so, is George Clooney. That's why I was thrilled to the soles of my size eleven shoes when his shiny black limousine pulled into the gravel driveway of my converted farmhouse.

It was the largest limousine I had ever seen. I mean not just long, but high, like an SUV. In fact, forget SUV. The only thing that set this vehicle apart from an RV was the rounded roof and darkened windows. While I may have been shocked, I wasn't surprised. No doubt a good-looking man like George traveled with a bevy of buxom bathing beauties, each with their own consortium of hairdressers, makeup artists, and the like. In fact, it wouldn't have surprised me if they all were on horseback inside that motorized monster.

What did surprise me was that only three people emerged, and none of them was George Clooney. The first person to exit the limo stood at least seven feet tall. He lumbered around to the side and opened a door. Out popped a woman who, although comely, was certainly not worthy of George Clooney. The last to exit had silver hair and a tan acquired in the tropics. I judged him to be about sixty. He looked more like the actor George Hamilton than George Clooney, but alas, he was neither.

This mature man was obviously in charge. He approached first, his manicured hand extended, his capped teeth blinding in the September sun.

"Colonel Custard," he said, in a charming Southern accent.

I loathe the medieval custom of shaking hands. It was originally intended to show that one was unarmed, but now it serves as the number one conveyor of the common cold. Much better, I think, to fold one's hands like the Thai people and bow. But when in Hernia ... so even though I didn't know this man from Adam, I did like the Hernians and pumped the proffered paw.

"Magdalena Yoder," I said in my quaint Pennsylvania accent.

The porcelain grin widened. "You've got quite a handshake there, ma'am."

"I grew up milking cows." I gave his hand a final squeeze, one guaranteed to drain the last drop from the most recalcitrant bovine. With George Clooney due to arrive any minute, it was time to dispatch the interloping trio. "How can I help you, Mr. Custard?"

He gave me the once-over. "I don't think you'll be needed, thanks. Ivan here"—he nodded at the giant chauffeur—"can handle the luggage."

"Excuse me?"

"The sign out by the road says PennDutch Inn, am I right?"

"That is correct, and I am the proprietress."

"Then I'm at the right place."

"Perhaps so, but you're definitely here at the wrong time. The entire inn has been booked for George Clooney—the actor." I clapped a hand over my mouth. Sometimes it feels good to let the horse out of the barn *before* closing the door.

Colonel Custard didn't seem the least bit impressed. "You don't say?" He reached into an inner pocket of his three-piece suit and removed a snakeskin wallet, which, I might add, matched his shoes. From the classy billfold he extracted a slip of paper. "I have the confirmation number right here. Thirty-three, thirty-two, thirty-three."

I gasped. Those uninspiring numbers are actually my measurements, and I give them out as confirmation numbers only to a select few. You can be sure I never explain their significance to the recipients.

"How did you get that number?" I demanded.

"I believe it was you who gave it to Ivan over the phone when he made the reservation."

"But that's impossible. I distinctly remember speaking to George Clooney's personal secretary."

"What did he sound like?"

"Like a cross between James Earl Jones and an enraged bull." I meant that kindly.

The colonel nodded again at his chauffeur. "Ivan, say something."

"What do you want me to say, boss?"

There was no need for him to say anything more. The ground was shaking from the vibrations of the deepest voice I'd ever heard.

"B-but that's impossible. Over the phone you identified yourself as working for George C."

The colonel turned to his employee and frowned. "Ivan, I've told you many times not to pull that stunt." He turned back to me. "My name *is* George C. It's Colonel George Custard. I apologize for the confusion."

Ivan, whose head was half the size of Massachusetts, hung his noggin in shame. "Sorry, boss."

Neither of them was half as sorry as I was. For two weeks I'd been mending my panties and darning holes in my socks, and I was a happily engaged woman, for crying out loud. Well, there was nothing to be gained by pouting. And an empty room—make that five empty rooms—was not going to enrich my coffers.

"Come on in," I said.

The woman in the trio spoke up for the first time. "Shall I bring my pots in now, or wait until we've checked in?"

"Pots?"

"Forgive me," the handsome colonel said. "Please allow me to properly introduce my staff. You have already met Ivan Yetinsky, my chauffeur and right-hand man. Now allow me to introduce my personal cook, Miss Anne Thrope."

"Your cook?"

The young woman stepped forward. "I hope you have an institutional-size stove. One of good quality."

I stared at her, not quite comprehending. "My stove?"

"It isn't a wood-burning stove, is it? I've never cooked on one of those."

I can only take comfort in the fact that it is the dimmest bulbs that often burn the longest. "It's a gas stove, dear, and you won't be cooking on it, I assure you."

The charming Colonel Custard flashed me a smile that forced me to squint. "Miss Yoder, Anne always cooks for me."

I smiled back, although my mellow yellows didn't even cause him to blink. "Not here, she doesn't."

"Perhaps something can be arranged."

That got my attention. I may be a simple Mennonite, but I am an astute businesswoman. I even offer my guests something called A.L.P.O.—Amish Lifestyle Plan Option—whereby they get to experience the Amish and Mennonite work ethic by helping out with chores. Of course they pay extra for the privilege.

"What sort of an arrangement?" I asked.

"How does a thousand a day for run of the kitchen sound?"

"Make it two grand and you've got yourself a deal."

He grabbed my hand again and, instead of pumping it, held it tightly. I won't deny that enough electricity passed between us to cook Sunday's roast.

"Miss Yoder, I think you and I are going to get along very well."

I shut my eyes altogether for a second, and then opened them wide. Against the blank screen of my lids I'd already begun to undress this man, a total stranger. Not that it's okay to undress a man, mind you, unless he's your husband—and then what's the point? Please understand that I do not normally engage in such wanton behavior, but there were enough phcromones wafting between the colonel and me to make a mummified Pharaoh moan. The sooner I hustled their bustles into the inn, the sooner I could get out of that charged situation. Maybe run some errands.

"Welcome to the PennDutch Inn!" I cried.

Although the next few days promised to be lucrative,

they were not going to be easy. Keeping my distance from the charismatic colonel was going to be the least of my problems. When she heard that I had agreed to let another cook into her kitchen, my own cook was going to go ballistic.

2

"Ach!" she squawked when she heard the news. "Then I quit!"

Freni Hostetler is a stout Amish woman who dresses in black and wears a white bonnet indoors. A pair of wire-rimmed glasses perch precariously on an almost nonexistent nose. To look at us—I'm tall and thin, and flat as a carpenter's dream, not to mention that my shnoz deserves its own zip code—you'd never guess that we are cousins. Cousins of a sort. Our family tree is so intertwined that I am, in fact, my own cousin. Give me a sandwich, and I constitute a family picnic.

"You can't quit," I said.

She stared at me through lenses dusted white with cake flour. "I will not have that woman in my kitchen."

"It's my kitchen, Freni."

"Yah, but it is my denomination."

"I think you mean 'domain,' dear." Pennsylvania Dutch, not English, is Freni's first language.

"Whatever, Magdalena. I will not share this kitchen."

"I'm not asking you to share it, Freni. I'm simply suggesting you take a short vacation."

"Ach! So now you want to get rid of me?"

Besides being my cook, my kinswoman is also my friend. She is my departed mama's age. When Mama and Papa met a premature death, squished in a tunnel between a milk tanker and a truck full of Adidas shoes, it was Freni and her husband, Mose, who acted as surrogate parents to my sister Susannah and me. I no more want Freni out of my life than I want to get rid of my shadow.

"Freni, you have three little grandbabies that you claim you never get enough time to play with. Take that time now. Just for a few days. Now go home and enjoy yourself."

"Ach! To enjoy yourself is a sin, Magdalena!"

"I didn't mean that way," I wailed. "Just go home and relax. Your job will be waiting for you as soon as this eccentric bunch of guests leave."

Freni is like a stubby little milk cow, or a two-year-old. Take your pick. You push one way; she pushes back. You pull; she pulls. Now that I had given her permission to take a few days off, she had no interest.

"Better I should stay around to keep an eye on things. You don't want she should break your pots and pans, yah?"

"She brought her own, dear."

Even through the curtain of flour I could see her dark beady eyes assessing this information. "She brought from home?"

I shrugged. "She's a professional cook—not that you aren't too, dear. Anyway, no doubt she has these high-tech gizmos that cook without water, or whatever. I'm sure our stuff is safe."

"Then I stay."

"I beg your pardon?"

"So maybe I learn from this woman, yah?"

Freni, like myself, was born knowing everything. We started forgetting a few things around age twenty, with a slow progression in memory loss since then. We are not about to learn anything new, that's for sure.

"Freni, you will just be torturing yourself."

She crossed her stubby arms. "So?"

There was no point in arguing. Until the colonel and his entourage left, there would be two cooks in the kitchen. One would actually prepare food; the other would skulk about, clucking like a pullet who had just laid her first egg.

I must say that although Miss Anne Thrope didn't seem to particularly care for people, she certainly knew her business. This was the tastiest meal I'd had since my last trip to Pittsburgh. Never mind that I couldn't pronounce the names of all the fancy dishes, or even identify many of the main ingredients.

My culinary limitations are partly Mama's fault, and partly Freni's. Both women held strongly to the belief that there were four important food groups: meat, sugar, starch, and grease. Fruits and vegetables fall into a secondary category, suitable for garnish but not essential for nutrition. If served by themselves, vegetables must be cooked to the consistency of mush.

I've long since given up trying to convince Freni that cheese is not a fruit. To her, the hard-to-classify foods (eggs and dairy products) take on the category of the food with which they are commonly served. Because I insist on a slice of cheddar with my apple pie, cheese has become a fruit. By logical extension, macaroni and cheese is also a fruit dish.

At any rate, after serving us, Miss Thrope retired to the kitchen to rejoin the clucking Freni. Ivan Yetinsky, I was told, would eat his meal up in his room. That left just the very handsome Colonel Custard and me—and my daughter, Alison.

Well, Alison isn't really my daughter. She's the foster

child I mentioned before. It's a long story that would bore you to tears, but the gist of it is that I was once briefly married to a bigamist named Aaron Miller. This wasn't my fault, you understand. I was duped. Anyway, he ran off to rejoin his legal wife up in Minnesota. After a year he returned, not to reconcile, but to dump off his twelve-year-old daughter. The girl, whose very existence was news to me, was too much for Aaron and his *real* wife to handle.

Being the dummkopf that I am, and probably doomed to forever be as barren as the Gobi Desert, I agreed to take the child in for a year. This decision came at a great personal sacrifice; Alison is highly allergic to cats, so I had to get rid of Little Freni, a purebred Siamese given to me by my latest suitor. A cat for a kid. Was it worth it? you ask. Well, the kid has driven me so far up the wall I now have footprints on the ceiling. But she's been a blessing as well. I'm forty-six years old, yet if I die tomorrow, I will have lived a hundred years. Who can ask for more than that?

Although I am engaged to be married to a wonderful man, it was still fun to pretend that Alison and the colonel and I were a nuclear family. What did one call a colonel's wife anyway? A colonel*ess*? I'd certainly settle for Your Ladyship.

"Please pass the fancy-schmancy carrots, dear," I said. The orange roots, which had been doctored up with some incredible seasonings, were midway between Alison and George C. I held my breath to see who would respond to my request.

Alas, it was Alison who picked up the bowl. "These things are hard as rocks. I like Auntie Freni's better."

"Mind your manners," I said, but couldn't suppress a grin. I knew from experience that Freni would be in the kitchen with her ear pressed to a glass. I widened the grin into a friendly smile. "So, Colonel, what brings you to this neck of the woods?"

Before answering, he patted the corners of his mouth with a genuine poly-blend napkin. "I'm here on business."

"Really? But Hernia has no businesses—outside of my inn, a small grocery, and a feed store."

"Ah, but soon that's all going to change. And that's why I'm here."

"There's some kind of yucky sauce on this meat," Alison whined.

I gave her a loving glare. "How is it going to change, Colonel?"

"Do you know the Jonas Troyer property at the end of Main Street?"

"Yes, what about it?"

"I purchased it last month."

"Get out of town!" In retrospect, I should have meant that literally.

"Your inn was all booked up then, so I had to stay in Bedford. Used a rental car so as not to garner attention."

Bedford is the nearest city, and while it is twelve miles away, it may as well be twelve hundred. The Good Lord Himself could be staying in Bedford and we'd never know it.

"But I didn't even know the Troyers were in the market to sell."

The colonel winked. "They weren't. I made them an offer they couldn't refuse. They've decided to retire to Florida."

"And you'll be moving here?" My fiancé is everything I could want in a man, but in the event he turned out to be a bigamist, it would be nice to have a backup.

"Maybe—I haven't decided. Fortunately I have enough good people working for me that I could work out of my home in Louisville."

I will be first to admit that I am easily distracted. "You said business. What kind of business?"

He dabbed his mouth again and took a sip of ice water. As a faithful Christian, I don't serve my guests wine. The colonel had brought his own, but I had insisted he keep it in the limousine.

"I plan to build a five-star hotel," he said.

"What?"

"I've been to Lancaster County many times, Miss Yoder. I know what a draw the Amish are for tourists. But in my opinion that area has become overdeveloped. Just too many tourists and urban refugees. I've done very careful market research and concluded that Bedford County contains some of the best Amish ambience in the world. Your charming Hernia, of course, is the epicenter. I think the time has come to capitalize on that, don't you?"

Through the wall I heard the crack of Freni's glass hitting the floor.

"But you can't do that!" I cried. "It will ruin Hernia."

He cocked his silver head in amusement. Suddenly he didn't seem at all handsome.

"I'm not building another Amish World," he said. "This is a very small, but tasteful, hotel that will cater to the elite. The crème de la crème, so to speak. They know how to deport themselves."

"You mean like *my* hotel?"

"Not quite. My hotel will be a five-star operation."

"But I have Hollywood stars—well, usually."

"Yours is an inn, Miss Yoder. Custard Suites will have one hundred well-appointed rooms and all the best amenities, including a spa."

"But you'll be stealing my guests!"

"I don't think so. You draw mostly from the celebrity crowd, don't you?"

"Babs has class. You can't get any more elite than that."

"Yes, but I'm talking about real thoroughbreds. The Cabots, the Vanderbilts—"

"Haufta mischt!"

"I beg your pardon."

"That's Pennsylvania Dutch for horse manure."

He looked taken aback. If only he'd taken himself back to Louisville, or wherever he came from.

"Why do you find this so upsetting?" he asked.

"Because you're going to put me out of business, that's why."

"Miss Yoder, I've already explained that we're not competing for the same customers. Your quaint little inn can just keep chugging along as usual."

"It doesn't chug! Why, I'll have you know I'm booked solid for the next year. You only managed to get in by lying."

"That was Ivan's doing, not mine."

"Maybe, but you're a snob. Thoroughbreds indeed."

"I'm a snob? You're the one who is in love with Hollywood."

If the truth hurts, mumble something even more hurtful. That is, of course, *not* the Christian way. But I can't be true to my faith all the time.

"Why, I doubt if you're even a real colonel," I said.

"I am. I'm a Kentucky colonel."

"Like Colonel Sanders?"

His face hardened. "What about you? Are you a *real* Mennonite, or is this some little charade you put on for the benefit of your guests?"

That shocked me to the toes of my heavy cotton hose. I patted my organza prayer cap.

"Of course I'm a real Mennonite. My family has been either Mennonite or Amish for the last five hundred years."

"Well, you could have fooled me. I thought Mennonites were supposed to be a kind, peaceful people."

"We are."

"Maybe most are. But you, Miss Yoder, have a tongue that could slice Swiss cheese."

Alison, who'd been watching this discourse intently, jabbed the air with her fork. "Hey, you can't say that to my mom."

My heart burst with sinful pride. She may not have sprung from my loins, but she was as faithful as any daughter. At least when the attack came from the outside.

I flashed Alison a smile. "Colonel Custard," I said, "I feel it is only fair to warn you that I fully intend to inform the citizens of this community of your diabolical plan to destroy their way of life."

"I don't intend to destroy anything. But if you think you can stop me from getting a building permit, you're too late. I've already got it."

I gasped. "Melvin Stoltzfus! That miserable, menacing mantis who poses as our mayor."

Colonel Custard nodded. "He was actually a very pleasant man. I think I'll offer him a job in—"

I didn't stay to hear the rest of his sentence.

In addition to being mayor, Melvin Stoltzfus is our Chief of Police. This is only a temporary condition, mind you, due to the unfortunate incarceration of our previous mayor. But that is another story. Hernia is such a small community—just over two thousand souls—that a lot of its administration is done by consensus. While the mayor does have the power to issue building permits, if there is the potential for controversy, he or she must run the proposal past the town council. The council is composed of the owners of the top three businesses, which, incidentally, are the cornerstones for Hernia's tax base. And the PennDutch, I might add, provides the town with its single highest source of revenue.

When I was a year or two younger, and in a rebellious phase, I bought a sinfully red BMW. I now drive a very modest, and Christian, Toyota Camry. Pressing the pedal to the metal I arrived at Melvin's bungalow in less than ten minutes. I prayed for patience for another full minute and, finding it not forthcoming, decided that the Good Lord must have intended for Melvin to get a good scolding.

Before going further I must explain that the man is also my brother-in-law. He is married to my younger sister, Susannah, who is nothing like me. Whereas I still cling to the faith of my fathers, my sister's apple not only fell far from the tree, but it rolled into another orchard altogether the day she became a Presbyterian. Although I have not been able to confirm the rumors that members of this denomination bathe in beer, my sister has confessed that she has personally had sex while in a standing position, an activity that is bound to lead to dancing.

At any rate, I marched to their door, rang the bell several times, and when no one answered, I tried the knob. The door swung open easily, and just as my sister was putting a dog down her bra. Perhaps I should explain this as well. But what can I say other than that Susannah, who lacks a discernible bosom, carries a pitiful pint-size pooch named Shnookums around in her undergarment as ballast? The miserable mangy mutt— Shnookums, not Susannah—usually goes undetected. This is due to the fact that my baby sister eschews conventional clothing, preferring to drape herself in fifteen feet of filmy fuchsia fabric.

"It was feeding time," Susannah said. For the record, she doesn't nurse the critter, but feeds him the most expensive dog food on the market.

"How come you didn't answer the door?"

"I had to finish burping him first, Mags. You wouldn't want him to have gas, would you?"

"Where's Melvin?"

"He's taking a nap."

"Well, go wake him."

"No can do, Mags. He left strict orders not to be disturbed."

"Then I'll wake him. It's after supper, for Pete's sake. This is no time to be napping."

"Mags, I wouldn't go in there if I were you."

"I'm not afraid of him, Susannah."

"I know that. But"—she giggled—"my iddle-biddle Sugar Buns always sleeps naked."

I clapped my hands over my eyes. The last thing I wanted was to see my nemesis au naturel.

"Melvin," I hollered, "nap time's over!"

There was no response.

"Rise and shine, Mel! Your chickens have come home to roost and I'm the biggest hen of them all."

Still no repsonse.

"I'm counting to three, Melvin, and then I'm coming in. Even if it means plucking my eyes out afterwards."

Being rather fond of my peepers, I counted all the way to thirty. In English *and* Spanish. I was going to try it in French when the bedroom door opened. My hands still covered my eyes, but I spread my fingers just wide enough to see if there was anything I might find offensive.

Although what I saw didn't cause me to pluck out my peepers, I did close them tightly. But of course I got a good gander first. Melvin was naked from the waist up, with only a sheet to shield his unmentionables from my prying eyes. Trust me, Melvin's bare torso was bad enough. His skin had the color and texture of tapioca, and his chest was no bigger around than a loaf of bread. My theory that Melvin was really a giant praying mantis had finally been confirmed.

"What's so damned important, Yoder?" he demanded.

"You shouldn't swear, Melvin. Not around my baby sister."

"This is my house, Yoder. I can do what I want."

I decided to move right along from what he shouldn't to what he *couldn't* do. "Melvin, you know you can't issue a building permit that the town council wouldn't approve of."

Melvin's eyes move independently of each other. His left eye focused on my face, while his right eye focused behind me, presumably on Susannah.

"The colonel's in town?"

"So you do know this man! Melvin, what on earth were you thinking?"

"Revenue, Yoder. That's what this town needs more of—revenue."

"But it will ruin Hernia."

"Don't be so stupid, Yoder. This is the twentieth century. This is progress."

"It's the twenty-*first* century, Melvin. And there's enough so-called progress everywhere else on the planet. Hernia doesn't need any."

"What's the matter, Yoder? You afraid you can't compete with the big boys?"

Nothing hurts like the truth, but I tolerate pain well. "There isn't going to be any competition, Melvin. That's what I came to tell you."

"You know that according to our bylaws, once a permit has been issued, it can't be revoked, even by your stupid little town council."

"That's true," I said. "But also according to our bylaws, it can be revoked by a community referendum."

In a rare moment of ocular coordination, both his eyes bored into mine. "That's insane. A referendum means ballots. That's going to cost Hernia money, not add to our revenue."

"I'll pay for the ballots."

"Idiot!"

I could have called him a name as well, but what's the point in having large feet if you can't think fast on them? "I'm calling a town meeting tomorrow night at Beechy Grove Mennonite Church. Be there, or be square."

I turned on my long but narrow heels and strode from the room. The fact that I fumbled with the doorknob did not mar the impact of my departure.

Unfortunately I was still in a snit when I got home. A calmer Magdalena would have been more patient with the man waiting for her on the back steps.

3

"Gabe! Good heavens, you nearly scared the daylights out of me."

"That's because it's nine p.m., Magdalena. There's no daylight left."

"Very funny. What do you want?"

I didn't mean it to sound the way it came out. Gabriel Rosen is my fiancé, even though he hasn't gotten around to buying me a ring yet. He's also a handsome Jewish doctor from New York City, one who decided to retire early and create a new life for himself writing mystery novels on the farm opposite mine. We have been engaged for two months, and are planning a spring wedding.

Because I will not abandon my faith, and Gabe has no interest in being a Mennonite, ours will be a mixed marriage. My pastor, Reverend Schrock, seems to have no problem with this. After all, Jesus' mother also married a Jew. If only Mrs. Schrock would be as open-minded. As a pacifist, she cannot publicly espouse the idea of burning me at the stake. In private I know she's been stocking up on kindling. But since she's convinced I'm going to burn in Hell anyway, she may as well spare herself the effort.

Gabe has the face of an angel. A deeply tanned, dark-eyed angel with curly black hair. He looked fondly at me.

"Magdalena, I just came by to say good night. Maybe even steal a kiss or two if you're in the mood." Gabe knows I won't go further than first base until after we're married. And since there's not much of a second base for him to reach—well, he's lucky I even agree to leave home plate.

"I'm sorry, Gabe. It's just that I'm really—well, peeved."

"You said a dirty word." He laughed and kissed my forehead.

"I did not!"

"Easy, babe. I'm on your side, whatever it is."

"*It* is Melvin."

"What's he done now? Use city funds to purchase an ice plant in Greenland?"

"Worse. He's sold us out to the tourists."

"How do you mean?"

I grabbed Gabe's hand and pulled him off the porch, in the direction of the barn. "I didn't get a chance to tell you, but the entire inn has been booked by this guy who calls himself Colonel Custard. Turns out he bought the Jonas Troyer place and plans to build a five-star hotel. He even has a professional chef."

"Get out of town!"

"That's what I told him, but he won't budge."

"Deny him a building permit. You're on the town council."

"That's where Melvin comes in. He already gave this guy the green light."

"Holy shoot!" Gabe has modified his speech since knowing me. "There's got to be something we can do."

"*We,* dear?"

"Magdalena, we're a team now, right? Besides, I love this town just like it is. That's why I moved here. I don't want to see it overrun by tourists in polyester shorts with disposable cameras."

"According to the colonel, this will be an elite crowd. Linen shorts and Nikons are more like it."

"Well, I don't want that either. Don't worry, babe. We'll think of something."

"I already have."

"That's my girl. Care to share?"

I told Gabe about my plans for a town meeting. The first thing we needed to do was to get out the word. We divided all the blabbermouths in town between us, and then he went home to call his share, and I went in to call mine.

Before leaving he gave me a kiss on the lips.

My calls went as well as expected. Ninety-nine point nine percent of the folks on my list were properly outraged. In a peaceful town like ours, outrage can manifest itself as a soft sigh, especially when coming from those of Mennonite heritage. The Amish don't have telephones, but Gabe had promised to get the word out to a few of the key elders the first thing in the morning. Perhaps this should have been my job, since I was raised among the Amish and can call virtually all of them kin. But the hunk from the Big Apple was glad for an excuse to visit our most reclusive citizenry.

The .1 percent of the people who didn't respond as expected was my very own pastor's wife. Before I go further, allow me to stress that Lodema Schrock is an anomaly among my people. Only once have I been compared to her, and the comment stung like a cloak of nettles. Can I be blamed then for saving that call for last?

"Do you know what time it is?" she growled.

"Why, yes, I do," I said pleasantly. "May I speak to the reverend?"

"Did somebody die?"

"No, but this is extremely important."

"If nobody's actually dead—"

I could tell she was about to hang up. "The whole town is about to die."

"What? Has there been a terrorist threat?"

"Not a terrorist threat, but a tourist threat."

There was a moment of silence. "The reverend has asked not to be disturbed, Magdalena, unless it is an emergency. You tell me what this is all about, and I'll decide if he needs to be wakened."

There's no point in pussyfooting around with a Rottweiler. Instead of a bone, I threw this one a juicy steak.

"This hotel magnate is in town and he wants to—"

"Build a five-star hotel?"

I gasped. "How did you know?"

"I was raking leaves this morning when he stopped and asked me directions to your place. He's a very nice man, don't you think? Very handsome."

"So is the reverend, dear." There was no reason I should be the only one to feel guilty for having found the cunning colonel so charming.

Lodema has selective hearing. "I think that man is just what this town needs, don't you?"

That gasp depleted the room of oxygen, leaving me temporarily light-headed. "You're not serious!"

"Magdalena, this is a chance for us to do our Christian duty."

"Our what?" I couldn't believe what I was hearing.

"Our witness to the heathen, of course. Here in Hernia everybody goes to some kind of church—well, except for your boyfriend, who is you-know-what."

"You mean Jewish."

"Whatever. Magdalena, I know you think I'm prejudiced, but I'm not. I'm just worried about his soul. Which brings me back to all the tourists this new hotel would bring. A lot of them do not belong to churches, or belong to churches of the—uh—wrong persuasion."

"You mean Catholic now, don't you?"

"Magdalena, you won't find the word 'pope' in the Bible, you know."

"It might be." I will confess that I am woefully ignorant of other folks' customs and beliefs. But—and I realize this may be terribly unchristian of me—I prefer to leave the saving of souls to the Good Lord Himself. My job, I believe, is to live a life that exemplifies love. Trust me, this is hard enough.

"Magdalena, are you quite through?"

"No, I still need to speak to your husband."

"Well, I'm afraid that's imposs—"

I could hear her protest while the reverend wrestled the phone from her hand. A door slammed before he got on the line.

"Sorry about that, Magdalena. You know how Lodema can be. But then, we all have our crosses to bear, don't we?"

"Amen to that. Look, Reverend, did she tell you about this Kentucky colonel who thinks Hernia is a living museum, and who wants to capitalize on that fact?"

"No."

I offered up a silent prayer of thanksgiving before giving Reverend Schrock my spin on the story. He didn't once interrupt me.

"So," I said, "you can see how this will forever alter our peaceful little community, and that's why I want to hold a town meeting, and our church is the best place I can think of."

"I agree."

"What?" There hadn't been a second of hesitation.

"Do you want to give me a list of names, Magdalena? I could start calling right now—or do you think I should wait until morning?"

"Uh—"

He laughed. "Or have you already called everyone and told them the meeting is at the church?"

"Guilty," I wailed. "I'm sorry, I really am."

"Don't be. You did the right thing. Now get some sleep. I have a feeling you and I are both going to need to be of sound mind."

I hung up, as my pastor directed, but a sound mind for *moi*—well, that was simply out of the question.

If there is no rest for the wicked, as Mama used to say, then I must have been very bad when I was a little girl. I mean, I don't remember being particularly naughty in my adult years. Even as a teenager I was the model of Mennonite moderation.

At any rate, because the colonel had rented my entire top floor, Alison had been moved downstairs and into my room. When I got into bed I found her on my side. Since I generally sleep alone—definitely a mixed blessing—both sides of the bed were mine. To find the urchin sprawled across my entire space, reading a supermarket tabloid, was at the least unsettling.

"Try to draw your gangly frame in a bit, dear," I said kindly. "You're lying about like a canister of spilled pick-up-sticks."

She scooted to the right three inches. "Hey, Mom, did ya know that most of them Hollywood movie stars are really aliens from outer space?"

"Doesn't surprise me a bit." I love the fact the girl calls me Mom. Odds are she is the only child who ever will. Even if Gabe and I married tomorrow, I would be unlikely to bear a child. There are but a handful of authentic Chinese restaurants that can serve eggs older than mine.

Alison read while I removed my prayer cap and undid my practical bun. Then, like Mama had always insisted, I brushed my hair a hundred strokes. When it came time for me to change into my cozy flannel nightgown, I disappeared into the bathroom.

The second I emerged, Alison whooped, much like I do when I spot a quarter on the sidewalk.

"Hey, it's not that bad," I protested. The gown was as pure and white as the driven snow, just like I was before I married that bigamist Aaron. I'd been planning to wear a similar gown, only pink, on my wedding night to Gabe.

"You look like a granny," she said. "Like in 'Little Red Riding Hood.' "

I decided to humor her. "My, what a big nose I have."

"Yeah, it is kinda big and pointed." She paused. "But I seen worse."

"Thanks—I think. Now scoot your cold little tootsies over so I can get into bed."

She did so without complaining, and didn't even complain when I said a rather lengthy prayer. There was, after all, a good deal to pray about, what with our very way of life on the line.

I turned off the light and we settled in. It was, I thought, going remarkably well. Sleep alongside the urchin actually seemed possible.

Just as I was dozing off, half thinking and half dreaming of Gabe the Babe, I heard the most annoying sound. At first I thought it was a mosquito that had gotten into the room, which didn't seem possible, given that it was mid-September and we'd already had a hard frost. My second thought, as the noise grew louder, was that a prankster—possibly my Gabe—may have taken it into his head to mow the lawn in the dark of night.

Then it hit me. The racket was coming from the child in bed next to me. Who knew that a twelve-year-old girl could snore like a middle-aged man?

"Roll over, Alison. Your snoring's about to bring the rafters down."

The child didn't budge, nor did the snoring abate.

I poked her in the ribs with an index finger. "You shake the plaster off the ceiling, dear, and you're helping with the repairs."

I may as well have been speaking to the dead. Drastic times call for drastic measures, so I poked her with the sharpest thing I had.

"Ow!" She popped to a sitting position. "Whatcha do, Mom? Stab me?"

"My nose doesn't feel too good either."

"So why'd ya do it?"

"You were snoring like a banshee. Be a dear, and roll over, will you?"

"No problemo." She turned on her side. "Hey, Mom, now that we're both awake and all, can I ask ya something?"

"Sure." Anything to shut her up so I could get back to sleep before the Babester inserted himself into someone else's dream.

"Well, I was thinking," she said, "that I wouldn't mind it too much if you drove Jimmy and me on our date, on account his mom's gotta work Saturday night and they only got one car."

The child may as well have dumped a bucket of ice down my flannel nightie. "Date?"

" 'Course we wouldn't expect ya to hang around the whole time. Ya'd get bored anyway, right? Hey, I got it! Why don'tcha just let Jimmy borrow your car? Then everything would be cool."

"Jimmy can drive?"

"Of course. He's seventeen, Mom. What do ya expect?"

"To wake up and find this is all a bad dream."

"So you're okay with that, right?"

"In a pig's ear. Let me get this straight. Are you trying to tell me, dear, that you want to date a seventeen-year-old? And what's more, you want me to be your chauffeur?"

"Hey, Mom, ya got a hearing problem, or what?"

I switched on the light. "Definitely what. I can't believe we're even having this conversation. In the first place, twelve is too young to date—and a sixteen-year-old? Does his mama know about this?"

Her eyes narrowed as her lips protruded. "He's seventeen, not sixteen."

"And that makes it better?"

"He's a senior, Mom. How sweet is that?"

Words seldom fail me. This time was no exception.

"What kind of high school senior would date a seventh grader? A warped one, that's what. One who wants to take advantage of her."

Alison's face turned the color of my nightie. "Jimmy loves me!"

"Loves?" This was the first I'd even heard of this fledgling romance, and already the *l* word was being thrown around.

"Well, likes. It's the same thing, ain't it?"

"One likes pizza, dear, but—"

"You're just jealous!"

"Me? Of what?" I was genuinely mystified, because even Alison finds Gabe attractive. For an "old man."

" 'Cause you didn't have a boyfriend when you were my age."

That was certainly true. Skaggy Maggy, the less charitable called me. The memory of that still stung, but I was not jealous of a twelve-year-old's boyfriend.

"I am not jealous, dear. And what I said goes. You are not dating, and you certainly are not dating a seventeen-year-old."

"Man, that's so unfair." Her face went from regular-nightie white to wedding night pink. "Jimmy is the only man I'll ever love. How dare you keep us apart?"

"There will be others, dear. Trust me."

"I hate you!"

"I beg your pardon?"

"You heard me! I hate you, hate you, hate you. I wish I'd never come here."

"Alison!" I didn't know what else to say. Even the crustiest curmudgeon can be cut to the quick.

"Well, I do hate you. And your nightgown sucks."

I turned out the light. For this I gave up my beloved kitty? Little Freni might have puked in my shoes and shredded my drapes, but she had never shredded my soul. Who needed this? And from the stories I heard from friends with teenage children, it only got worse. Maybe I should rethink this whole custody thing before I got into it even deeper. But with a heart full of hurt, it was hard to think.

Perhaps in the morning I would have a clearer head. If Alison really hated living with me, maybe it was best she return to Minnesota and the ampler bosom of her real mother. But that wouldn't be the case, would it? The judge up there had made it clear; either the girl stayed with me, under my strict supervision, or it was off to reform school for her.

Alison, who'd made her painful point, went straight back to sawing wood. I, on the other hand, tossed and turned all night. If I'd had a load of dirty laundry in bed with me, instead of a snoring girl, I might have gotten something done.

As it was, I crawled out of bed the next morning with eyes like unlanced boils, and a headache the size of Montana. I've had days that started better.

4

———————

A fretting, flailing, frantic Freni is a fearsome thing. When I entered the kitchen that morning, preceded by my headache, my elderly kinswoman was on me like white on rice.

"Ach!" she squawked. "Liquor! Liquor!"

My first impression was that a very large parrot, or maybe a clever crow, had been released in the kitchen. Finding only a flapping Freni, and Anne Thrope, I breathed a sigh of relief. Bird claws can wreak havoc on even the most tightly pinned bun.

"It's only champagne," Anne muttered through scarlet lips.

Now I understood Freni's agitation. My hackles were hiked as well.

"I told the colonel he had to leave his wine and stuff in the car. He should be grateful I didn't make him pour it out."

"But Colonel Custard always has champagne with his eggs Benedict."

"Not in this house, he doesn't."

In a move meant to challenge me, Anne poured some

of the bubbly brew into a tall, elegant glass. She set the liquid sin on a breakfast tray and smirked.

"Get rid of that stuff now," I said. Whenever Mama used that tone on me, I moved so fast I flirted with time travel.

"Make me," Anne said.

As long it was my house, there was no need to make her do anything—not when I could do it myself. I strode over to the kitchen table and snatched the vile beverage from the tray. With only a second's hesitation I dumped the champagne into the sink. I had to taste it first, you see, to make sure it really was champagne, and I wasn't just getting my chain yanked. Trust me, it was the real McCoy.

Anne bypassed the daggers and shot me butcher knives. "The colonel is going to be angry."

"Serve him some apple juice. I doubt if he'll know the difference." To test my theory I drained the few drops left in the bottom of the glass. So there was a slight difference, but still, the color was almost identical.

"You serve him the apple juice," Anne said with a toss of her head. For a supposedly accomplished chef, she was acting like a teenager.

I called her bluff. "I'd be happy to take the tray up to him. I have some news I need to deliver along with it, anyway."

"Uh—you can't go upstairs."

"Says who?"

"The colonel rented the entire upstairs floor, remember?"

"Indeed, I do. But this is my inn, and I go where I like. Besides, someone has to clean the rooms."

"Ivan will do that."

Never look a gift horse in the mouth, even one with lips like cherries. I don't mind stripping beds, but cleaning toilets is the pits, as my sister Susannah would say. Sometimes I long for the days when all we had was an outhouse. It was a six-seater, the largest outdoor commode in the county. Papa's theory was that the family that sits together—but I digress.

"Then summon His Majesty to the dining room, so that I might serve him his morning repast."

She sauntered off while Freni fumed. As for yours truly—well, there is no use sighing over spilled champagne, not as long as I wanted to remain a Mennonite. I dumped the remainder down the sink.

Freni poked me with a finger the size and shape of a prune. "Good thing I stopped her, Magdalena, yah?"

"Indeed."

"So, you going to give these Englishers the ho-hum, right?"

"You mean heave-ho, dear." As I mentioned before, Freni's mother language is Pennsylvania Dutch, a dialect of High German. As is the custom of the Amish, she refers to anyone other than an Amish person as English, even if said person is straight off the plane from China. After all, Freni's ancestors, like mine, arrived in this country almost three hundred years ago, when the English were the majority of white settlers.

"So, you will throw them out?"

"No can do. They're registered guests."

"But they broke the rules, yah? With this liquor."

"Strictly speaking, I don't think champagne qualifies as liquor—although of course it's still not allowed."

"Ach, Magdalena, this is no time for word games. This man wants to ruin Hernia. Are you just going to sit and fiddle your thumbs while Nero burns?"

"Absolutely not, dear. He'll get his comeuppance. In fact, tonight the colonel and his crew are going to hit the road."

"Ach! You will make for them a car accident?"

"Don't be silly, dear. That would be against the law. No, I've got something quite legal up my sleeve."

Freni's eyes glittered behind lenses as thick as the

bottoms of Coke bottles—well, back in the day when they were made of glass. "What is it, Magdalena?"

"Why don't you come and see for yourself? Do you and Mose have plans for tonight?"

"Mose?"

"Your husband, dear. Fifty-five years, isn't it?"

"Fifty-three. Yah, my Mose and I come. What time do you want we should be here?"

"Not here. Seven thirty at Beechy Grove Mennonite Church."

"Ach!" Although we are cousins, and my religion gave birth to hers, Freni has rarely visited my church. The last time, I believe, was for my parents' funeral.

"It's not a service, dear. It's a town meeting. All of Hernia will be there. In fact, go home right now and start telling your friends. Tell everyone you know."

Freni frowned. "At your church, Magdalena, do you have graven idioms?"

"I beg your pardon?"

"Like the Catholics."

"Ah, images! No, dear. No statues of any kind. Unless you count Wilbur Neubrander, who hasn't cracked a smile in forty years."

"Always the jokes, Magdalena." But the frown had fled, and I could tell she was getting excited about the evening's event. Good entertainment is hard to come by in Hernia.

The colonel's eyes flashed under neatly trimmed brows. As displeased as we were with each other, there was still enough electricity passing between us to power a small generator. Later, in the privacy of my room, I would slap my own face for having even entertained lascivious thoughts about the man who planned to destroy our town. And me an engaged woman!

"Miss Yoder, I still don't see how any of this is your business."

"Hernia is my business. You should be grateful I even told you about this meeting."

"Why *did* you tell me?"

"Because I believe in playing by the rules. You, on the other hand, sneaked into town on your previous visit like a thief in the night."

"Everything I did was legal, I assure you."

"But not ethical."

"That," he said, flooding me with more pheromones, "is a matter of interpretation." Trust me, if his share of the pheromones had been water droplets, I would have had to dig out my bathing suit. Fortunately it was a modest one-piece deal, in black, with an attached skirt. But a worldly man like him probably wore one of those Speedo things—I gulped for air.

"What happens tonight won't need any interpreters. You'll be hitting the road, buster. Sayonara, as they say in Japan."

He had the temerity to smile. "I've always liked a woman with attitude."

"Attitude? Colonel Custard, I assure you, I have not yet begun to fight."

"Miss Yoder, if you somehow manage to screw up this deal for me, you can bet I'll sue."

"Sue away!" I cried. "You'll just be wasting your time and money. Once the people hear—"

I was interrupted by a thump above my head. After delivering her message, Anne had returned to the kitchen to torture Freni. That meant the noisemaker upstairs was Ivan, something that came as no surprise.

"Is that big galoot rearranging my furniture?" I asked, not unkindly.

"Huh?"

"Didn't you hear the thump?"

"I'm afraid I didn't."

As if on cue, Ivan obligingly dropped something else. "There it goes again!"

The colonel shrugged. "Whatever he's moving, I'll make him put it back."

"You do that. And if there's been any damage done to it, or the floor—well, then we'll see who sues."

He displayed his caps in what I suppose was meant as a smile. "We could be friends, Miss Yoder, you and I."

"When geese wear shoes." I strode from the room. One minute longer and I would have drowned in my own lust.

Before leaving for the town meeting, I buttoned down the hatches. That is to say, I gave Alison strict orders to finish her homework, told her where and how to call me in an emergency, and then locked the chicken house for the night. My hens are free-rangers, but every evening at dusk they come back to the coop to roost. I lock them in for their protection, not from two-legged thieves, but from foxes and raccoon. It isn't even a proper lock that I use, but a bolt through the hasp. Nonetheless, it is an important nightly ritual, and a necessary one if I hope to maintain a flock.

Although I was the first to arrive at the church, I wasn't alone for long. No-sirree-bob! I may be a bad fiancée, undeserving of the Babester's affection, but I am a darn good organizer. Even if I have to say so myself. By seven o'clock that evening the carriages began to arrive—both horseless and horse-powered. At half past, when the meeting began, the parking lot of Beechy Grove Mennonite was jammed, and there were cars and buggies parked for a quarter of a mile up and down the road in both directions. The sanctuary, which theoretically holds three hundred people, was packed so tight head lice had to stay outside.

Most, but not all, of the people who sat up front were members of my church. Directly behind them sat members of the First Mennonite Church, our more liberal sister congregation. Behind them sat the Baptists and

Methodists, then the Presbyterians, and finally the handful of folk who attend the church with thirty-two names. By and large the Amish did not sit, preferring to stand along the walls. Gabe the Babe, incidentally, graced the front row, right next to Lodema Schrock. To be sure, the Schrock was shocked by my hunk's chutzpah, and was practically sitting in her husband's lap to avoid the possibility of physical contact with someone of the Hebrew faith. Short of making a scene, however, there was nothing she could do about it.

The town council was seated on the dais, where the pulpit normally stands (our church does not have an altar in the liturgical sense of the word). As president of the council, not to mention chief organizer of the meeting, yours truly was seated dead center. On my right sat Sam Yoder, the manager of Yoder's Corner Market; on my left, Elspeth Miller, owner of a feed store, our town's only other business. Curiously absent was my brother-in-law, Melvin Stoltzfus, our less than illustrious mayor and Chief of Police.

From my favored position I had a bird's-eye view of virtually everyone in the room. Although I had been watching the door like a hawk, there was no sign of the colonel or his staff. Perhaps he'd come to his senses, and they were back at the inn packing.

My ancestors originally came from Switzerland, and at the appointed hour I stood and delivered my spiel. The audience was properly horrified by the scenario I presented, and some of them who hailed from nonpacifist traditions—particularly the Methodists—seemed eager for blood. Well, maybe not literally, but emotions were running high. In fact, in the space of ten minutes I'd been able to whip up so much energy that I briefly considered running for political office.

"Are we all in agreement?" I said in finishing. It was a rhetorical question, of course.

"I don't agree at all," someone said.

5

Pear and Ginger Custard

Apples also work well in this recipe.

1½ pounds ripe Bartlett
    pears, peeled, cored,
    and cut into pieces
¼ cup sugar
1 cup heavy cream or
    half-and-half

4 tablespoons grated fresh
    ginger
4 large eggs, lightly beaten
1 teaspoon unsalted butter
Garnish: 8 slices candied
    ginger

Put the pears and sugar in a medium saucepan. Cook slowly for about 5 to 7 minutes, or until the pears are soft. Set aside to cool. If the pears yield an excessive amount of water while cooling, drain before pureeing. Puree in a processor or food mill, then put in a mixing bowl. You should have about 1½ cups.

Scald the cream with the grated ginger in a medium saucepan. Remove from the heat and let the ginger steep for 15 minutes.

Reheat the cream just until it begins to bubble around the edges. Slowly stir ¼ cup of it into the eggs. Stir the mixture into the remaining cream and strain into the bowl with the puree. Whisk together to mix thoroughly. Pour into 4 buttered ½-cup ramekins, filling each about three-fourths full.

Preheat the oven to 350° F. and bake in a bain-marie for 40 to 45 minutes, or until a knife inserted near the center comes out clean. Chill for several hours. Unmold if desired and garnish with candied ginger.

SERVES 4

6

I whirled in astonishment. The comment had come from Sam Yoder, who, as a fellow council member, should have been backing me one hundred percent. Sam, incidentally, is a kissing cousin on my daddy's side, and although we've never actually kissed, it's not for his lack of trying.

"I beg your pardon?"

Sam stood and without as much as a "please" or "thank you" snatched the microphone right out of my hand. "I think you've understated the problem, Magdalena."

"Excuse me?"

"This hotel will not only ruin Hernia, but the entire county. Next thing you know they'll be widening Route 96 down from Bedford, and you know what that means."

"I do?"

"Strip malls, that's what. Laundromats, automobile dealers, pizza parlors, and video stores. The sound of clopping hooves will give way to the screech of tires and the roar of motorcycles. How many hitching posts do you think Blockbuster will install in their parking lot?"

It took a bit of energy, but I retrieved the microphone. "Sam, dear, the Amish don't rent videos, but your point is well taken. Okay, now that we all understand—"

"Drugs," a voice in the pews said.

I scanned the audience. The voice was familiar and came from somewhere near the back.

"You wish to speak?" I asked.

In slow motion a lanky man unfolded himself and rose from his pew. I recognized him immediately as Reverend Richard Nixon of the First and Only True Church of the One and Only Living God of the Tabernacle of Supreme Holiness and Healing and Keeper of the Consecrated Righteousness of the Eternal Flame of Jehovah.

If the reverend grew a beard, he'd be a dead ringer for Abe Lincoln. I'm not quite old enough to have heard Lincoln speak, but I imagine Reverend Nixon sounds like him too.

"Miss Yoder, members of the council, and citizens of Hernia, and Bedford County in general—"

"Get to the point, Rev," Elspeth Miller whispered.

The good man could not hear her and plowed on. "As Samuel Yoder just said, the hotel will bring unnecessary development, which will in turn invite a flood of urbanites, and in their wake, the drug dealers will surely follow. Then we will undoubtedly see an influx of harlots and ladies of the night, and the next thing you know there will be a bar opening on Main Street."

"How soon?"

I recognized the impudent youth as our town's sole Episcopalian. " 'Wine is a mocker and beer is a brawler,' " I said. "Proverbs, chapter twenty, verse one."

There were mutters of approval and a smattering of applause. I smiled in triumph.

"Now then—" I began.

" 'Wine that gladdens the heart,' " he said. "Psalm one hundred and four, verse fifteen."

" 'Do not get drunk on wine, which leads to debauchery.' Ephesians five, verse eighteen."

" 'Come, buy wine and milk.' Isaiah fifty-five, verse one, second half."

The muttering grew louder, some of it possibly in his favor. Unfortunately, I'd run out of wine quotes. Oh, what humiliation, to be bested in a Bible-quoting contest by an Episcopalian—even if he did quote from the New International Version, and not the King James, which everyone knows is the translation from which the Good Lord Himself reads.

"Moving right along," I said, my face as red as any drunk's, "the reason I called this meeting is because we can revoke this outsider's building permit with a referendum. All we need to do is get this petition signed"—I reached into an otherwise empty bra and withdrew a sheaf of papers—"and we will have put a moratorium on Colonel Custard's building permit."

"Which would be wrong! Even a sin!" Lodema Schrock had leaped to her feet and was poking the space in front of her with an index finger. Perhaps she was seeing bubbles where I saw nothing but hot air.

"Lodema, dear," I said with admirable restraint, "the chair hasn't recognized you yet. You need to ask permission to speak."

"Then you didn't recognize any of the others, because no one else asked permission."

"Can I help it if they don't play by the rules?"

"Rules, schmules." Lodema jumped away from her chair with the agility of an aerobics instructor. She turned to face the crowd. "We're all Christians in this room, are we not?"

"I'm not." The Babester was smiling.

Lodema was clearly not amused, but she wasted no time in getting back on track. "We are supposed to be lights unto the world, right? To put our lights on stands for all the world to see. Well, how can we let our lights shine on the world if we never have contact with it?"

A low rumble emanated from the perimeter of the room and rolled inward. The Amish much prefer that their lights glow discreetly within the confines of their community. The less contact with the world, the better.

The last thing I wanted was for the Amish, who comprised at least a quarter of the folks in attendance, to bolt en masse. So you can imagine my gratitude when I saw Herman Middledorf, our high school principal, wave his hand.

"The chair calls on Herman!"

"Permission to speak?"

"Granted."

"That's no fair!" Lodema looked like she wanted to ride her current of warm air right up onto the stage and punch my lights out. As a good Mennonite she would not have actually done so, but I was relieved nonetheless when Reverend Schrock reached out a restraining arm and pulled his wife gently back to her seat. Believe me, there was going to be an extra bill or two in the offering plate come Sunday.

"Speak," I ordered Herman. There was no telling how long my pastor could keep his wife under control. He's not had a good track record.

Herman Middledorf has slicked black hair and glittering ferret eyes. Think Hitler without the mustache. He toyed with his clip-on tie as he spoke.

"What Reverend Nixon said, what Sam Yoder said—they're both right. These outsiders will have children, and I guarantee you're not going to want these kids learning alongside yours." He paused and when no one, not even Lodema, objected, he seemed to gather courage. "Tattoos and piercings, that's what these new kids will bring. Do you want your children turned into colorful pincushions? I rest my case."

Alison arrived on my doorstep with rings in at least

three places where the Good Lord did not intend for there to be holes. You can be sure the holes are empty now.

"And a good case it is," I said quickly.

"Here, here," Elspeth Miller cried. She may as well have hooted. The woman barely comes up to my chest, and wears enormous horn-rimmed glasses. Every time I see her I'm reminded of an owl.

I smiled benevolently at the tiny thing, although personally—and this is terribly unchristian of me—I loathe her in my heart of hearts. Well, maybe "loathe" is not the right word after all. That would definitely be a sin. No, it's more like disdain mixed with pity. Elspeth, you see, was a husband-beater. Beat her husband, Roy, regularly. The poor man had to walk around in long-sleeve shirts in the dead of summer or, if the lacerations were to his face, skip work altogether.

You may find it strange that an itty-bitty bird of a woman could beat up a man, but there is a reason in this case. Roy is a true Mennonite, a pacifist through and through. It pains him to slap a mosquito, much less raise a hand to defend himself. Elspeth is not of our faith. She is a Lutheran, born in Germany. This is not to imply that Lutherans or Germans are necessarily violent. I know plenty of peaceful folks in both categories, but unlike Elspeth Miller, none of them had an honest-to-goodness Nazi storm trooper for a father. At any rate, after years of putting up with her abuse, and praying that she would change her ways, Roy up and left. Nobody seems to know where he went, but for his sake, I hope it was New Zealand.

"Elspeth, do you have anything else to say?"

The woman wastes no love on me either. "Only that you move this meeting along, Magdalena. Pass that petition around."

"Yah wohl," I muttered. I dangled the papers over the edge of the platform. "Any volunteers?"

The first woman out of her seat was Wanda Hemphopple, owner of the Sausage Barn. A liberal Mennonite, Wanda lives in Hernia, but her business is all the way up by the interstate. That's the reason she is not on the town council. I have been known to say prayers of thanksgiving that this is the case. Although I love eating at the Sausage Barn—much to Freni's consternation—learning to love Wanda is a lifelong project, and I have just recently reached middle age.

Wanda snatched a couple of papers from my hand. "I have to agree with Elspeth. You do prattle on, Magdalena."

"Moi?"

"You should have been a senator. Then you could filibuster."

"Why, I never!"

"Which is probably why you can't stay married."

"I could have stayed married if Aaron hadn't been a bigamist."

She signed her name at the top of the petition while she spoke. "A lot of my customers are single. If you like, I'll keep my eye out for a good man."

"I've got a good man, thank you very much, and he's sitting right there!" I pointed to Gabe.

She shuddered, which in her case was a dangerous thing. It was Wanda who invented the beehive hairdo back when the Good Lord Himself was just a boy, and I don't think she's washed it since. Like the Tower of Babel, Wanda's do strives to reach the heavens. Should Hemphopple's tower topple, Hernia could be obliterated by an avalanche of dandruff and assorted vermin. Rumor even has it that the U.S. military has been begging Wanda to travel to various hot spots in the world and let down her hair. I did not start that particular rumor, by the way. I merely passed it on.

"Magdalena, you don't mean that guy from New York, do you?"

"I most certainly do."

She shuddered again. "You really ought to reconsider."

"Why? Because he's Jewish?"

"Don't be ridiculous. I have nothing against his faith. It's because he's a writer."

"What's wrong with that?"

Wanda cocked her head to give me a disbelieving look, and the gargantuan cone of hair tilted perilously. "Because writers tend to be mentally unbalanced. Mystery writers in particular. I read somewhere that ninety-eight percent of them are nuttier than a PayDay."

I breathed a sigh of relief. "He's not an official writer, because he doesn't have anything published yet."

"That doesn't matter. It's the fact that he wants to get published. What kind of person expects to get paid just because they have a good imagination? Egomaniacal weirdos, that's who."

"Weirdo alert!" I cried. The Babester had gotten up and was headed our way, no doubt to rescue me.

Gabe and I both felt the meeting was a success. The four petitions sent around the room garnered 536 signatures. That doesn't count the big "NO" that Lodema scrawled across the tops of three of the papers.

After my sweetiekins dropped me off, I went straight inside to check on Alison. The girl was supposed to be studying for a math test the coming morning. I have only a small black-and-white TV, which I keep stored in the attic ever since reruns of *Green Acres* went off the air, so I knew that wouldn't be a problem. But the telephone—that's harder to control than my tongue at a coffee klatch. Sometimes I think the child has it glued to her ear.

Sure enough, when I stepped into my kitchen, there she was with the receiver pressed to her head. What's more, she didn't look the slightest bit guilty. How was I *not* to feel that I had failed as a mom?

"Alison!"

"No, I'm not making this up," she said. "I saw it with my own two eyes."

I took a deep breath and prayed for patience. It is my least-answered prayer.

"How would a certain young lady like to have her allowance docked?"

She hung up without even saying good-bye. "Mom! Ya oughta seen him! He was the grossest thing I ever saw. He was big and hairy, and boy did he stink."

My heart sank. "You had that Jimmy character over here while I was gone?"

Alison howled like a leashed hound with a fox in front of its nose. "Jimmy? You say the dumbest things, ya know that? No, it weren't Jimmy, silly. I'm talking about Bigfoot."

"Excuse me?"

"Ya know, like in *Harry and the Hendersons*. Only this one was real."

I still didn't have a clue as to what the child meant. "Your reference eludes me, dear. Please elaborate."

"Man, are ya, like, stupid, or what? Bigfoot, Sasquatch, the Abominable Snowman. Ya know, those big apelike creatures that everyone *knows* exist, but the government likes to pretend they don't, on account they'll scare the crap out of people. Just like with the aliens."

"Oh, that." I have glanced at the supermarket tabloids from time to time, but only while in the checkout line. I feel it is my right for having been made to wait. "Alison, dear, those stories are just the figment of someone's imagination. There is no such creature."

"Ya calling me a liar?"

"I'm saying you are mistaken. Perhaps it was a shadow or something. Where did you see it?"

She pointed toward the kitchen door. "I was studying for my test, and suddenly I smell the worst thing ever.

Like a dead skunk or something. So I go to the door to look out and I see this thing—and it *was* Bigfoot—come out of the chicken house. And I'm like, holy shoot." (Alison used a slightly different word.) "So I call Uncle Melvin 'cause he's the police chief and all, only he wasn't home, but I left a message anyway, so then I called Jimmy, and he's like, 'I'll be right over if I can,' and then you come barging in."

"Jimmy's coming *here*?"

"Yeah, if he can get his mom's car to start. She even had to hitch into work today. Jimmy thinks it's just a clogged fuel line or something like that—"

"Alison, sweetie, did you say the chicken house?"

"Yeah. Ya turning deaf or something on me, Mom?"

I brushed aside the cheery gingham curtains that cover the glass portion of the door and peered into the darkness. It was like looking down my well. It took a second for my peepers to focus.

"The door to the henhouse is open!"

Alison grinned. "What did I tell ya! Believe me now?"

I am not afraid of things I know for a fact don't exist. And *if* there really was such a creature as Bigfoot— well, I'd give him what for. There was no way his tootsies could be anywhere near as big as my size elevens. While mine is a peaceful sect that doesn't condone violence, that ban applies only to mankind. The Bible very clearly encourages us to subjugate the beasts of the field—just not drive them to extinction—and surely Bigfoot, assuming he even existed, was a beast. I grabbed the heavy-duty flashlight I keep by the door, quite confident that whacking Sasquatch atop the head was not a sin.

"Hold the fort, dear!" I cried and sailed out into the night.

7

The door, as I've stated, was open, and there was a faint odor of skunk in the air, but inside the coop nothing appeared amiss. The hens blinked at me from their perches, and I counted sixteen of them, just like I was supposed to. The fact that there was no rooster was due to the unfortunate visit a month ago by a coyote that was directionally challenged and ended up in my yard instead of a California suburb. Chanticleer, may he rest in pieces, put up a brave but futile fight defending his harem. I heard the ruckus before it was too late, and the conquering canine escaped with just the carcass of my courageous cock.

At any rate, satisfied that there was no big hairy beast lurking in the shadows, I closed the door for the second time that evening. Something was fishy all right, but it didn't have anything to do with any mythical beast. Some *person* had undone the latch of my henhouse, and I had a sneaking suspicion who that might be.

I was halfway back to the inn when a car came barreling up my driveway, spraying gravel every which way. Thank the Good Lord I'm as thin as a rail and was able to turn sideways and avoid most, but not all, of the missiles. Petrified as I was, I could still feel the pain as a petite pebble pinged my protruding proboscis.

I waited patiently for the nincompoop behind the wheel to get out, before letting him have it. "Melvin Stoltzfus! I could sue you, you know."

He flashed his badge. "Police business, Yoder."

I might have done something distinctly unchristian with his badge, had not the passenger door opened. Out popped Zelda Root, Melvin's sidekick and Hernia's only other police officer. She's a short thing with enormous breasts, no hips, and matchstick ankles. In other words the poor woman is shaped vaguely like the dearly departed Chanticleer—except that he had only one breast, and she has almost no feathers. But few people ever notice Zelda's intriguing physique, not if they get a gander at her head first. Her bleached hair is short and worn in spikes, like greasy porcupine quills. As for her face—don't get me wrong; there is nothing inherently homely about it. The fact is Zelda applies her makeup with a trowel, making even Tammy Faye seem like a minimalist. For years there were rumors that Jimmy Hoffa was alive and well and living in Hernia, disguised by layers of Maybelline. For the record, I have long since confessed that sin.

"Zelda," I said to the more reasonable of the pair, "let me venture a guess. You're here because an imaginative young girl called in to report that she'd seen Bigfoot."

"Magdalena, you saw it too?"

"No, dear. I don't normally see what doesn't exist. Would you like to come in for a cup of hot chocolate before you turn around?"

Zelda teetered forward on platform shoes that were clearly not regulation. "But they do exist."

"You're damn right," Melvin said, nodding so hard I thought his head was going to snap off his scrawny neck and roll back down my drive. "Tell her, Zelda."

"Well, my uncle Barney up in Maine was on his annual deer-hunting trip with some buddies of his. One morning Uncle Barney wasn't feeling very well, so he stayed back at the camp while his buddies went off to hunt. Suddenly this big hairy thing rushes into camp and tries to—uh—well, it tries to mate with my uncle. Fortunately one of the hunters had forgotten his cap, and returned just in time. He was able to scare it off by shooting his gun in the air."

I gasped. "Was the beast male or female?"

Even though it was dark, and Zelda's war paint as thick as ever, I could tell she was blushing. "Male," she whispered.

"Oh." That ruled out Veronica Stucky as an explanation. The big gal, as hirsute as any I've known, had a reputation for being the aggressor in her relationships with men. One day, about ten years ago, she left Hernia to become a logger up in Maine. To my knowledge, no one here has heard from her since.

"So you see, Yoder," Melvin said pompously, "Bigfoot does exist."

"I've got one at the end of each leg," I said.

"Very funny, Yoder. Now, if you don't mind I'll be interviewing the eyewitness."

"I do mind."

"It doesn't matter. This is police business."

"But she doesn't even have an attorney!"

Melvin ignored me and started for the house.

I might have tackled him, or at least punched him gently behind the knees, had not Zelda attempted to lay a comforting hand on my arm. The woman has fingernails so long she's been banned from airplanes, and I could feel the claws right through my sweater.

"Let him go, Magdalena."

"That mantis is a menace. I won't have him interrogating my daughter."

"She isn't your daughter."

"Well, she's my foster child. It's the same thing."

"Hmph." Zelda's eggs aren't as old as mine, but she doesn't stand much of a chance of becoming a biological mother either. Not as long as she carries a torch for Melvin, who is happily married to my sister. "Look, Magdalena, if you try and stop him—well, you know my Melvin."

"He isn't your Melvin, dear. He's married to Susannah."

"That's only temporary, Magdalena. Besides, Alison seems like the type who can hold her own."

That was certainly true. Alison didn't particularly like her foster uncle, and I'd seen her give that twit tit for tat on more than one occasion. It might be fun to watch them bump heads again—but alas, on the Bigfoot issue, they seemed to be on the same page.

"He has five minutes," I said. "Any more than that, and I'm cutting off his allowance."

I wasn't joking either. Although our parents left the farm, now the inn, to both Susannah and me, it states in their will that I am financially in charge until the time my sister achieves emotional maturity. The woman is now thirty-six, and she still receives a monthly allowance. Of course she shares it with Melvin.

"Good call," Zelda said, before clopping off in her platform shoes to find Melvin.

I had every intention of eavesdropping on the Bigfoot conversation, but halfway back to the house my eye caught a glimmer of light emanating from Mr. Custard's parked limo. You can bet your bippy I decided to check it out. One might think this was none of my business, but whatever happens on my property is my business. And suppose I was wrong about Bigfoot? What if it was hiding in the limo and decided to take it for a spin? I doubted if the creature had had drivers education class once, much less twice like me.

As I approached the extravagant car, the light extinguished but my curiosity did not. I have knuckles that can cut glass, so I rapped gently on the tinted window.

"Come out, come out, whoever you are," I cried cheerily.

A back door opened a crack. "Busted, am I?"

"That depends on who you are. If you're a seven-foot ape man—"

The door opened all the way and the overhead light came on. I was both relieved and disappointed to see that it was only Colonel Custard.

"Care to join me?" he asked. He held up a bottle of wine and a half-filled glass.

"I don't drink. You know that."

"I meant for a little conversation."

"I'm a happily engaged woman, Mr. Custard."

"Believe me, Miss Yoder, I have no designs on you."

"I beg your pardon!"

"It's nothing personal, you understand. It's just that I don't have time for women in my life right now."

"You mean you're gay?"

"To the contrary. I consider myself to be highly heterosexual. There was a time, in fact, when I—well, a gentlemen doesn't tell, does he? Let's just say they numbered in the hundreds."

"Scoot over, dear."

He obliged and I slid into the softest leather I'd ever felt. "Ooh," I moaned.

"Smooth, isn't it? That's because it's the foreskin of a whale. Got the idea from Ari Onassis. He had barstools made of the stuff for his yacht. Of course I wouldn't dream of further endangering whales, so I made sure these foreskins came only from whales that died of natural causes."

"Yuck!"

"Don't worry. They were freshly dead whales."

"Colonel, aren't you afraid to be sitting out here alone with Bigfoot on the loose?"

"Bigfoot?"

"That's why the cop car is outside. I'm afraid my charge, Alison, has taken her imagination on a ten-mile hike. Claims she saw the critter by the henhouse. The odd thing is the henhouse door *was* open, and there is a strange smell outside."

"The smell," he said, "belongs to the dead skunk up the road. I believe a car hit it earlier this evening." He cleared his throat. "Miss Yoder, how did my lynching go?"

"What?"

"The meeting you called. Have the townspeople let loose their hounds? Are they traipsing through the woods as we speak, with lit torches? Or is it going to be tar and feathers?"

"Well, now that you've brought it up, I see no harm in telling you that we got more people to sign the petitions than I even anticipated. I'm afraid, Colonel, there is going to be a referendum, and ultimately your building permit will be revoked."

He swished the contents of his glass—which emitted a rather pleasant odor—and drained it in one gulp. "You're a remarkable woman, Miss Yoder. In another place and time, you and I might have made beautiful music together."

"Is it too late for just one note?" I asked. Then I slapped myself. Gently of course. But gosh darn it, was I so repulsive that a man who'd bedded hundreds of women wouldn't even pick up his bat and stand at home plate?

He chuckled as he poured himself a refill. "Don't get me wrong. You're quite a handsome woman, Miss Yoder."

I patted my bun and its organza covering. "I am?"

"Most certainly. If I didn't have other distractions— well, you wouldn't be safe sitting here."

I kept the smile on the inside of my mouth. "Distractions such as ruining my hometown?"

"My hotel won't ruin it, in my opinion, but you already know that. My distraction is a disease. Melanoma. Have you heard of it?"

"Skin cancer, right?"

"Yes. It's the most dangerous of the three common types and can be fatal if not diagnosed early."

"And yours wasn't?"

"Unfortunately not. I spent a lot of time unprotected in the sun when I was a boy, growing up on a farm in Kentucky. Had some terrible burns. Got a little sensible in later years but neglected to take my skin seriously. Then about two years ago a mole on my abdomen began to change shape and grow. Sort of bicolored, it was. Well, you know how most men are about seeing a doctor. Anyway, to make a long story short, I've had three painful surgeries since then. After the last they thought they'd gotten it all and I was in remission. But just last week I found out it's back and spreading with a vengeance. In fact, it's in my liver now."

"So you're drinking!"

"Why not? I'm going to die anyway."

"But—"

"Miss Yoder, I can anticipate your next question. Why would a dying man want to build a five-star hotel in a nowhere place like Hernia?"

"I wouldn't have used the word 'nowhere.' "

"Touché. But the answer is, this hotel is my last hurrah. You see, Miss Yoder, I'm a rich man, but my money has all been made in the stock market—mostly investing in hotel chains and restaurant franchises. Don't get me wrong; even with the bear market of late, I still have plenty. But I have nothing concrete to show for it. Before I leave this planet—or shortly after—I want there to be something real. Something with my name connected to it."

"How about an orphanage in India? Or a prosthetic center in Cambodia?"

"Those things are good—wonderful even—but un-fortunately, I happen to be a selfish man. I want to leave behind something really classy. Something legendary. A five-star hotel in this quaint little town—I can see that on the cover of *Architectural Digest*. You might say this venture is Custard's last stand."

"Well, it isn't going to happen."

He sipped his wine. "So I've been told. Miss Yoder, mind if I ask you a big favor?"

"You want me to share my faith?" Maybe I couldn't badger Gabe the Babe into seeing the light, but with a dying man I stood a chance. It was for his benefit, of course, not mine. He was the one who needed to avoid Hell, and the Bible says it is never too late to repent. Okay, so there was a small, maybe infinitesimal, part of me that wanted to convert this man so that the Good Lord would put another star in my crown. But is that such a bad thing to want?

He laughed. "No, I'll pass on that. Every religion I can think of is filled with hypocrites."

"But that's only because we're human. God isn't a hypocrite. And I'm just barely one."

"I happen to think you're refreshingly honest, Miss Yoder. No, the thing is, you see, neither Miss Thrope nor Ivan know my cancer has returned. So anyway, I have a doctor's appointment in Pittsburgh tomorrow, and I plan to go in by myself. I've already told my staff they can have the day off, which, of course, leaves them with-out a car and no place to go or nothing to do."

"There are plenty of chores," I sniffed. "Either of them ever milk a cow?"

He laughed again. "You're a hoot, Miss Yoder, you know that?"

"Flattery will get you nowhere." I rubbed the soft leather seat beside me. "So what is the favor you want, Colonel?"

"I'd like you to show them a good time."

"I beg your pardon! Just because I was an inadvertent bigamist—"

"What I mean is I'd like you to show them the local sights. Maybe take them out to see an authentic Amish farm. I'll pay your A.L.P.O. rate."

"Well—"

"Double it, in fact."

"What *I* was going to say is there's a nice little hiking trail along Slave Creek I could show them—I don't hike personally, you understand, as it uses up unnecessary heartbeats from the stockpile the Good Lord gave me at birth—and then afterwards I could take them up to the top of Stucky Ridge for a picnic lunch. As for the visit to the Amish farm, this isn't like some other places where they have models open to the public. Our Amish are very private. But I suppose I could ask Freni if she and her husband, Mose, would mind giving your staff a brief look. Just don't count on her saying yes. I don't think she cares for Miss Thrope."

He nodded. "Anne isn't much of a people person. So, we have a deal?"

"Deal." I slid over the leather, which didn't feel nearly as soft on the way out. I should have been happy for the extra moola the impending field trip would bring, but I felt more like a goose was walking over my grave. Quite possibly this one was wearing shoes.

8

Rumors are like chicken pox. They pop all over the place and demand attention. If you scratch them the slightest bit, they spread even faster. Alison's Bigfoot rumor spread like the pox in a fifth-grade classroom. When I woke up the next morning there were half a dozen reporters camped on the front lawn.

Having played hostess to the stars, I am a veteran in dealing with the paparazzi. My approach may be unconventional, but it works for me. Give them what they want, I say, because they're going to make it up anyway. One might as well have a little fun.

"Good morning, ladies and gentlemen," I said, appearing at the door in my best broadcloth dress and whitest organza cap. My brown brogans, by the way, were polished shinier than any apple. "The rumors you've heard are absolutely true."

Magically the six reporters tripled their ranks and within seconds there were microphones crowding my face. I smiled pleasantly.

"Not only was Bigfoot seen on this property, but"—I paused for dramatic effect—"she, and it was definitely female, was caught cavorting in my barn with a certain Melvin Stoltzfus."

There were gasps, both of disgust and of delight. No one seemed to be astonished. Apparently, either you believed in the beast, or you didn't.

A woman I recognized from the *National Intruder* shoved her mike within millimeters of my mug. "Did you see this yourself?"

"Heavens, no! But I've heard from a reliable source that this is true." Strictly speaking, this wasn't a lie. I had told myself that story while getting dressed, and under normal circumstances I am a very reliable source.

"Who is Melvin Stoltzfus?" someone called from the back of the pack.

"He's Hernia's Chief of Police," I said and proceeded to spell his name.

"And your name, ma'am?"

"Lodema Schrock. Miss Yoder asked me to speak on her behalf." Okay, that was an out-and-out lie, in that I was actually bearing false witness against my neighbor. Melvin, incidentally, I consider a relative, not a neighbor. In either case, I planned to repent fully the moment the reporters left.

"Miss Schrock," the woman from the *National Intruder* said, "can you give us any more details?"

I pretended to remember. "Well—I'm sure you'd find this out anyway, so there's no harm in telling—apparently this isn't the first time Miss Bigfoot has done the horizontal hootchy-kootchy with our Chief of Police. I think the hairy harlot might be pregnant."

More gasps. By now the more reputable journalists were edging toward their cars, but the woman from the *National Intruder* and a young man from *Outrageous* inched closer.

"Anything else, Miss Schrock?" Miss National Intruder demanded.

Alas, I found myself unable to hold out for a private repentance. A wave of guilt washed over me like fumes from the skunk, which, by the way, was still lying on the highway.

"I lied!" I wailed. "I'm not Lodema Schrock; I'm Magdalena Yoder."

Mr. Outrageous scribbled furiously. "How many personalities would you say you have, Miss Schrock? And is this Stoltzfus guy one of them?"

"Definitely not!"

Miss N.I. shoved her microphone so close to my lips I could taste the metal. "Which one of your personalities slept with Bigfoot?" She happened to glance at my shoes. "Or are *you* really Bigfoot, and that's a disguise?"

When the going gets tough, the tough go shopping, but there isn't any place worth dropping bucks at in Hernia, unless you're in need of cattle feed or day-old bread. Feeling utterly desperate, with my bony back literally up against the wall, I grabbed the broom I use to sweep the porch. I certainly did not intend to hit anyone with the broom, merely to brandish it in a threatening manner. Can I help it that my palms were sweaty and the worn wooden handle slipped from my grip? Well, you would have thought the young woman from the *National Intruder* had been walloped.

"Did you see that?" she cried, her voice rising to decibels only a Chihuahua can hear. "She tried to kill me!"

"I did not," I wailed. "Besides, you can't prove it."

"What about all these eyewitnesses?" the wench hissed.

There, you see? I had no choice. To shut the woman up, and avoid an expensive lawsuit, I gave her an exclusive interview in the kitchen. I told her that I was indeed the legendary Bigfoot, masquerading as a mild-mannered Mennonite maid. Yes, I said, I had to shave my entire body every day, a process which took a good three hours because I was still fairly new at it. There were only a handful of us left, the rest still roaming the wooded mountains of southern Pennsylvania. I missed my hirsute family terribly, I said, and was seriously considering returning to the wilds. Then, after making the reporter sign a paper terminating her rights to sue, I posed for a few photographs.

That seemed to satisfy the juvenile journalist and she left, eager to post her story. The other reporters, sensing she was on to something, trailed her like bloodhounds after a dripping steak. I had the feeling I hadn't seen the last of them, but I took advantage of the lull to whisk an oblivious Alison off to school. Then I turned my attention to my charges for the day.

Just as I had expected, Anne Thrope and Ivan Yetinsky were not ideal tourists. Anne found fault with everything, beginning with my car, which apparently wasn't fancy enough for her. She wanted to take the limo, which was still parked in my drive, but of course we couldn't. Although I must say I was tempted to tell the colonel that if he wanted to run into Pittsburgh, we either had to exchange cars or else that roll of duct tape I keep in my kitchen junk drawer was going to find a new use.

Ivan didn't mind the make of my vehicle, but it was a chore getting him to fit into my Toyota Camry. Fortunately I had a clean spade hanging in the toolshed, and was able to use it much like a shoehorn. Getting Ivan extracted was going to be much harder, but he assured me he had a strong bladder and didn't need to get out again until we returned home. If the man was willing to see Freni's farm from the backseat of a Japanese car, that was his business, but as we left the driveway he kept trying to look behind him. Fearing he would rip the overhead upholstery, I had to reprimand him as if he were a small child.

Once we were on the road, I thought things would go

smoother, but Anne continued to criticize everything she saw, and Ivan the Terrible actually fell asleep. I didn't know which was worse, to hear my hometown run down by Miss Anne Thrope, or hear Ivan snore while I tried to elucidate the finer points of Pennsylvania Dutch customs.

Anne took forever to hike the Slave Creek Trail, if indeed she hiked it at all. For all I know, she hoofed it back to the PennDutch and caught a few z's.

I know Ivan did. He continued to snore so loud I had to sit on a log fifty feet away with my hands over my ears.

As for the picnic up on Stucky Ridge and the visit to Freni's farm, they were a complete waste of time. If only that's all they were. Freni took umbrage when Anne not only pronounced the Hostetler farm primitive, but turned up her nose at a jar of homemade preserves my elderly relative gave her. Freni, bless her heart, threatened never to work for me again if this was the sort of guest I was going to subject her to. Ivan behaved with Freni, but he spilled so many things on himself during the picnic that when we returned to the PennDutch, he was able to slide out of the backseat without any help. You better believe that Colonel Custard was going to have to pay for some new upholstery.

And speaking of the colonel, the man had somehow managed to make it to Pittsburgh and back, *plus see a doctor,* in just over five hours. The round-trip journey into the city takes me four and a half hours. Either the crafty colonel had pulled a fast one on me and decided to stay at the inn, *alone,* or that behemoth of a limo of his was capable of sprouting wings.

Whatever. Miss Antisocial and Mr. Slippery went upstairs, while I headed straight for my private bathroom. My new philosophy, formed while I schlepped the ungrateful duo around, was that when the going gets tough, the tough take a bath. I figured I had just enough time for a long relaxing soak before Alison came bursting into the house from school, since she normally takes the bus back. Baths, I've discovered, are where I do my second-best thinking, and I had a lot to think about. Ever mindful of my modesty, lest Alison get home early, I locked the bathroom door.

I had just removed my sturdy Christian underwear and had one toe in the water when I felt the house shake. My first thought was that it was a tornado. I'd lived through one of these devastating storms, but I'd been fully clothed then.

"Please, Lord," I begged now, "just let me get my clothes back on, and you can blow the entire house away. Take me too, if that's what you want. Just don't let the rescue workers find me naked."

Believe it or not, during those few seconds I managed to get fully dressed. They say that a room without windows is the safest place to be during a storm of any kind, and my bathroom definitely doesn't have any of those. So, you see, there was no place for me to go. I sat on the throne, the lid closed, awaiting my fate. If the pearly gates opened, I was at least dressed and ready.

But the tornado, which should have been just wind, now had a voice. "Miss Yoder, are you in there? Miss Yoder, can you hear me?"

"Yes, Lord." Funny, but God sounded a bit like a woman. Who knew?

"Miss Yoder, open up! It's a matter of life and death."

I flew from the pot to the door. Why the Good Lord didn't have the archangel Gabriel bust down the door was beyond me. But who am I to argue?

Yes, I fully expected to meet my Maker on good terms because as a woman of faith, I am assured of my salvation. What I did not expect was to come face-to-face with Miss Anne Thrope.

"What?"

"Well, it's about time, Miss Yoder. I've been pounding on the door until my fists are sore."

It took me a second or two to shift gears. "I was in my bath, if you must know. And guests are not allowed in my room without permission." To get to my bathroom, the crabby interloper had to tromp right through my boudoir.

"I didn't have time for civilities. Something terrible has happened upstairs. You need to call 911."

"Uh—that would be Melvin, our Chief of Police. Why? What's happened?"

"It's the colonel. I think he's dead."

I was upstairs in less time than it took to pull the drain plug. I've had other deaths at my inn, and they've never been anything but trouble.

Sure enough, lying on his back on the floor of my largest guest room was Colonel Custard. He looked remarkably peaceful, I thought, despite the fact that he was quite clearly dead. Murdered, in fact. I know—I'm no doctor, but I could see the neat round bullet hole in his forehead, and the gun lying beside him on the floor. Had it been suicide, there would have been a much nastier entrance wound.

Besides, in a corner of the room hunched the monstrous Ivan. The slippery hulk was weeping bitterly, his tennis racket–size hands barely covering his face. What other evidence did I need? I strode over to the victim, bent, and with the hem of my skirt scooped up the gun.

Fortunately, I had recently installed phones in the guest rooms (I'd held out for years). I dialed Melvin just as Miss Thrope thundered in the door.

"Did you call?" she gasped.

"I'm doing that now." Why hadn't the frenzied woman called 911 herself? Unless she felt incapable of giving directions to the PennDutch. Well, that was certainly silly. In these parts, no directions are needed.

"Hernia Police," said a cheery voice on the other end of the line. "How may I help you?"

"Zelda? Magdalena here. I've had a bit of trouble at the inn. Is Melvin there?"

"Magdalena, it's not another murder, is it?"

"How did you know?" I wailed. "I don't have *that* many!"

Zelda sighed. "So it is a murder. Well, as it happens, my sweetiekins has the day off and took that wife of his into Bedford grocery shopping."

"His wife happens to be my sister Susannah, and Melvin is not your sweetiekins."

"Hmph. Do you want me to call the hospital so they can dispatch an ambulance, or do you want me to come over?"

"Both," I said. Zelda is a kosher policewoman in her own right, but over the years her excessive makeup has permeated her skin, possibly reaching her brain. Her bulb burns a little brighter than Melvin's, but not much.

"Be right over," she said and hung up.

Then I turned to the killer.

"Okay, Mr. Yetinsky, try to get a grip on yourself."

"But the colonel wasn't just my boss; he was my friend."

"Maybe you should have thought of that before you killed him."

"He didn't kill him, you idiot."

I whirled to stare at Miss Thrope. "What did you say?"

The gourmet cook shrugged like a Frenchwoman. "Okay, so maybe 'idiot' was too strong a word. But Ivan here didn't kill anyone."

I pointed to the corpse with the barrel of the gun. I was still holding it swaddled in my skirt, so I wasn't incriminating myself.

"The evidence would indicate otherwise."

"What evidence?"

"A dead man, a gun on the floor, this blubbering behemoth."

"Now who's being unkind? Tell me, Miss Yoder, did you hear a gunshot?"

"No—but there's been a lot of strange noises coming from up here. I've been trying to tune them out."

"I'm telling you, Miss Yoder, I know Ivan didn't kill him because we were together all morning. In fact, you were with us."

"Yes, until we returned to the inn. Then you two went upstairs by yourselves."

"That's correct. But we went straight to my room— *together*." She didn't even have the decency to blush.

"You're claiming each other as alibis?"

"That's exactly right. Only we weren't in my room but two minutes. Just long enough to drop off my purse and that stupid jar of preserves your so-called cook gave me."

So that's all they were doing? Well, why couldn't she say so to begin with? I get enough exercise jumping to conclusions on a normal day. I tried to review the time-line of events. I had gone straight to my bathroom and shed my clothes. I had the water going as I did so. It was possible that Miss Thrope, despite her youth, had taken that long just to get up my impossibly steep stairs. My elevator, she claimed, wasn't big enough for a dwarf sardine.

"Those preserves are scrumptious, dear," I said in Freni's defense. "Do you mean to tell me that the two of you found the colonel lying like this, in a pool of his own blood?"

Ivan stopped blubbering and nodded. "Yes, ma'am."

"If you don't believe us," Miss Thrope said, "feel him. He's as cold as the roast beef you served us for lunch. Or was that supposed to be leather?"

"Those were sandwiches! The beef was supposed to be cold." I shifted the gun to my left hand and stooped to touch the dead man's forehead. It's not the first time I've touched a corpse, mind you, but I hope it's the last.

The colonel felt even colder than my roast. The man had obviously been dead for some time. Perhaps hours. It wasn't possible for either of them to have done the dastardly deed—unless Anne had indeed made it back to the inn on her hike. Still, that was pretty unlikely. Although it would explain why she didn't have enough energy to beat me to the top of the stairs.

For the moment I decided to give her the benefit of the doubt. "Okay," I said, "so maybe you did find him like this—"

"Freeze!" Zelda shouted as she burst into the room, her own gun drawn.

9

"Let me get this straight, Yoder," Melvin Stoltzfus, the Chief of Police, said, arranging his mandibles in a sneer. "Zelda caught you red-handed, and you still deny that you killed the colonel?"

We—Melvin, Susannah, Gabe, and I—were sitting in my parlor, the body having long been moved to the morgue of Hernia's tiny hospital. Tracking down Melvin and my sister had not been an easy job, given that he has a penchant for turning off both his cell phone and beeper whenever he leaves town. If it hadn't been for Gabe the Babe, I might now be sitting in the hoosegow with an overzealous Zelda inserting bamboo slivers under my fingernails. Melvin loves to torment me, but he doesn't really think I'm capable of murder. He is, after all, married to my sister, who has been known not only to fish flies out of her soup, but to give them mouth-to-mouth resuscitation.

At any rate, the Babester didn't find them at Pat's I.G.A., which is their favorite haunt, but at their first runner-up, Madame Terri's House of Tricks. This establishment, I am ashamed to say, does not sell rabbits in hats and other sleight-of-hand novelties—although perhaps a few of their wares could be classified as that. The ugly truth is that Madame Terri's sells sex toys. I know— it's hard to believe that such a thing exists. It's even harder for me to believe that my flesh and blood sister would frequent a shop like this. If Mama were alive— well, thank the Good Lord she isn't. It's bad enough she turns over in her grave with such regularity that the town council has considered installing a generator in the cemetery. As long as Susannah didn't mend her ways, Hernia could get at least half of its electricity for free.

I glared at Melvin. It was more a ritual than an expression of emotion. "Yes, I was holding the gun. In my *left* hand. I'm right-handed, and you know it."

"But your prints are going to come up all over that piece."

"You're wasting time, dear. Doc Rosenkranz already called from the hospital and said that in his best guesstimate, the colonel had been dead five hours when his staff found him."

"So you killed him, and then took off on that sightseeing trip."

The game was getting old. "Don't be ridiculous."

"Yoder, you do have the best motive, you know. You're the only hotel in town. Yours would be the business most affected." He reached into his bulging left pocket and removed a pair of cuffs. "Sorry, Yoder, but this case looks open-and-closed to me."

The man was serious! "Why, you miserable little mantis. I ought to—"

I felt Gabe's hand on my elbow. "Easy, hon," he murmured.

"But he's accusing me—"

Gabe's fingers could double as a vise. While he gave my elbow the full treatment, his eyes were on Melvin.

"Look, Stoltzfus," he said, "you know Magdalena even better than I do. And I know for a fact she's incapable of murder. Instead of sitting here flapping our gums, at least one of us should be out looking for the real killer. By my reckoning, that person should be you."

Melvin's left eye fixed on Gabe, his right eye on the ceiling. That's as close as the mantis gets to squirming.

"But Colonel Custard was a big shot," Melvin whined. "This is going to be a high-profile case. People are going to expect results."

"So?" Gabriel Rosen is normally a softy, but when it comes to protecting me, he can be as tough as the roast beef I served for lunch.

"So, I—uh—damn it. Don't make me do this, Yoder."

"Do what?" I asked, although I knew perfectly well what was going on: business as usual. Every time a difficult case arises, my dim-witted brother-in-law insults me, then begs for my help. Two heads are definitely better than one in this partnership, because only one has a working brain.

"What my Cuddle Buns means," Susannah said, both her eyes adoringly fixed on her husband, "is that he's been under a lot of strain lately, and could use a little assistance."

What Susannah meant is that her misguided husband was running for a seat on the state legislature and had all but abandoned his job as police chief. Although why it was a man who didn't have time for work did have time to visit sex toy stores was beyond me. The bottom line was that either Zelda—who is best suited to handing out citations for littering—was going to have to solve this case, or it was up to moi, suspect numero uno.

"I'd be happy to lend *assistance,*" I hissed, "if the merry mantis over there apologizes."

"Mags," Gabe whispered, "don't push your luck."

His warning came too late. "Why should I apologize to a woman who wears her bra backwards?" Melvin demanded. This time both eyes were aimed squarely at my scrawny chest.

I leaped to my feet. "What does that mean?" I snapped.

"Mags," Susannah said, and then giggled. "Look at yourself."

I looked down. Sure, I could see every inch of my tootsies, but that was always the case. The problem was that now I could see my ankles as well. With an asbestos vest and apron to protect me, one could iron a table-cloth smooth on my front side.

"Oh my gracious!" I reached around behind me as far as I could. Sure enough, the padded brassiere I normally wear was on backwards. That's what I got for dressing in such a hurry.

"I think it's kind of attractive," Gabe said. He sounded serious, which was both alarming and endearing.

"Really?"

"You bet, hon. I think it's kind of sexy."

Of course he was just being nice, but Susannah didn't know that. She has never been a follower, or she wouldn't swaddle herself in fabric. She is, however, ex-tremely competitive. If a hunk like the Babester thought a bra on my back was sexy, then my baby sister was going to wear hers that way too.

Unfortunately, at the moment Susannah's brassiere was occupied by the mangy mite of a mongrel that she claims is really a dog, and not a rat. Although sis did her bra switching under the privacy of her mantle, it was not without a great deal of drama. Her elbows beating against the cloth gave the wicked impression that there were two people in there. To make matters worse, Shnookums was not happy with the process of reloca-tion. The pitiful pooch wailed so mournfully that even I began to feel sorry for him.

"Maybe you should just leave him where he is, dear."

"I can't," Susannah gasped. "I've got the dang thing turned halfway around already. Whoever heard of wear-ing boobs on your side?"

She had a point. Ignoring the yips and yaps of the bite-size beast, I turned to Melvin.

"I accept your apology," I said, just to show how magnanimous and mature I can be. "I'll get started on the case right away."

"But I didn't apologize, Yoder! In fact, I think I've changed my mind. I don't want—"

"Then it's all settled," Gabe said loudly, and grabbed one of Melvin's hands and proceeded to pump it like it was attached to my well. "You made a good choice, Stoltzfus. Now go off and run your campaign. There's no need to worry about this little incident anymore."

"But I didn't—"

Gabe pulled Melvin toward him and clapped an arm around my brother-in-law's bony carapace. "In fact, I was just thinking about donating a little something to the effort. How does a thousand sound?"

There was no need for him to say more.

Gabe and I were finally alone in the parlor. I was about to reward him with a peck on the cheek—it was, after all, still the middle of the afternoon—when I heard the front door open and what sounded like a herd of buffalo in the foyer, which, as it happens, also serves as my office.

"Mom! Mom!"

That word was as sweet to my ears as Gabe's "hon." No, even sweeter. From a purely practical standpoint, I was less likely to ever hear "Mom" from another's lips. I may be too old to have a baby of my own, but despite a few flaws, I am apparently capable of getting a man. Yes, I know adoption is always an option, and a wonderful one at that. But if you were on the placement board of an adoption agency, would you trust a child with me? Enough said.

"Here I am, dear," I called.

Gabe, ever patient, ever faithful, gave my shoulders a

squeeze and ducked from the room. A second later a gaggle of gangly teenage girls galloped into the room.

"Ya see," Alison said, pointing a finger at me, "what did I tell ya?"

"Awesome," a redhead said.

I didn't recognize her. In fact, I didn't recognize any of the girls except for Alison. That meant the girls weren't from Hernia, or if they were, they were relative newcomers. I pretty much know everyone in this town by first *and* middle names.

"Does it speak?" a blonde asked.

Alison nodded. "Say something, Mom."

"I'll say something all right. Who are you, and what's going on?"

All the girls except for Alison jumped back. The blonde actually shrieked.

"It does tricks too," Alison said. "Go on, Mom, jump up and down. Like you're doing jumping jacks or something."

"I beg your pardon?"

"If she doesn't do tricks," a stout brunette said, "I want my money back."

"Alison, what is going on?"

"Ah!" the redhead cried. "Bigfoot knows your name."

"Sweet," the brunette said. "Can we pet it?"

I may have a noggin that can crack coconuts, but eventually I figure things out. "I am *not* Bigfoot!" I bellowed.

The blonde shrieked again.

"Like, really sweet," the redhead said. "It sounds like the Bigfoot I saw on TV. I was like, Alison doesn't really have Bigfoot at her house, but now I'm like, wow, this is worth the five bucks."

I treated the redhead to some Bigfoot sounds. "Five dollars?" I yelled. "You charged them a measly five dollars? You should have gotten ten."

My sarcasm was lost on Alison, who hung her head in

shame. "Sorry, Mom. I shoulda come up with something like A.L.P.O., right?"

"That's my girl. Charge them extra to watch me ground you."

"Hey, Mom, you're not mad, are ya?"

"Maybe you can teach it to do your homework," the brunette said.

I stamped a big foot and roared. "Out, out, out! All of you, out! Except for Alison."

The girls climbed over each other to get through the door. Alison tried to follow but I grabbed her by the arm.

"You, young lady, are going nowhere."

"Aw, Mom!"

"Sit." I tried to steer her to a chair, but the child suddenly lost her spine. I mean that literally. One second she was standing upright like a normal human being, and the next second she slumped to the floor. The arm I was grasping felt like an octopus tentacle.

"You are so mean, ya know that?"

"That's what I've been told. Look, dear, today while you were at school something terrible happened."

The amorphous arm took shape. "Yeah? What?"

"There was a murder—"

"Where?"

"I'm afraid it was here."

Alison was back on her feet. "Cool. Who was it?"

"It was the colonel, dear."

"Where? How?"

"Why don't I tell you while we drive?"

"Drive where?"

"You see, dear, I've volunteered to help your uncle Melvin work on this case. He isn't exactly the—uh—"

"Brightest bulb in the chandelier?"

"Alison!"

"Come on, Mom, ya say that all the time."

"I do?"

"You're always saying that he wastes his time staring at orange juice containers because they say 'concentrate.'"

I slapped my own mouth—gently of course. "Well, I hope you know I was wrong to say those things. Anyway, how does staying with Freni sound?"

You wouldn't think that a girl who's from a big city and has a pierced tongue (I don't let her wear the stud, believe you me) and an elderly Amish woman would have anything in common, but they do. They absolutely adore each other. Maybe it's because opposites attract, or maybe it's because they have a bond stemming from a common goal—aggravating me. Whatever the reason, when Alison visits Freni she loves playing Amish.

"What about school?" she demanded. "Can I go to the Amish school with Sarah and Rebecca?"

"Who are Sarah and Rebecca?"

"Don't ya know anything, Mom? They're Freni's neighbors, of course. The kid neighbors, I mean."

The Amish school is a private, one-room institution, which only goes up to the eighth grade. That wouldn't be a problem, because Alison was still in seventh, but the Amish school has a heavy emphasis on the Bible and . . .

"The Amish school sounds wonderful!" I cried. "We'll see if Freni can pull a few strings and get you in. It's only for a few days."

Alison beamed. "You're the best, Mom, ya know that?"

"The best Bigfoot, you mean." Already I'd practically forgotten my irritation with the girl. My mind was on the task ahead, that of finding the colonel's crafty killer.

I don't keep my doors locked—no one in Hernia does, except for Crazy Irma, who believes aliens from outer space are out to abduct her—so gaining entry wasn't a problem. But the murderer had to have been watching my house, waiting for that moment when the colonel was alone. No, wait a minute. Since the colonel had two servants, and Freni is always in the kitchen—when she's not between jobs—the perpetrator must have made an appointment.

So that's why Colonel Custard sent me off to entertain the crabby cook and his Chevy-size chauffeur. He was planning to buy off one of his opponents, no doubt someone on the town council. And since that crooked council person wasn't me (why doesn't anyone ever try to bribe *me*?), it could only have been one of two people: my cousin Sam Yoder or Elspeth Miller.

10

Baked Vanilla Custard

Any number of delicious variations can be made by adding your choice of flavorings to this basic custard.

3 cups milk
4 large eggs
½ cup sugar

1½ teaspoons vanilla
 extract
¼ teaspoon salt

Preheat the oven to 350° F.

Slowly warm the milk in a heavy saucepan over low heat. Do not let it boil. While milk heats, mix the rest of the ingredients together with a whisk just until smooth. Slowly pour the milk into the egg mixture, whisking as you pour. Skim off any foam.

Strain the custard into six 6-ounce custard cups or a 1½-quart baking dish. Place in a bain-marie. Bake 25 to 35 minutes for cups, 50 to 60 minutes for the baking dish, or until a knife inserted near the center comes out clean. Remove from the bain-marie and let cool on a rack before covering and refrigerating.

SERVES 6

Variation:
Cinnamon Caramel Custard

Stir in ½ teaspoon ground cinnamon before pouring the custard into cups. Serve with caramel sauce.

11

I was waiting patiently on the front porch for Alison to gather her things, when Gabe strode up the driveway, carrying what looked like a huge satchel. He held it with both hands in front of him, and when he got closer I could see that it was a wire cage with a white cloth draped over it.

"What do you have there?" I asked, trying not to let the excitement show in my voice.

He grinned. "It's been a tough day, and until you find the colonel's killer, you're going to be under a lot of stress. So I thought you could use a little pick-me-up."

"I love presents," I cooed.

"This was going to be your birthday present. But don't worry. I'll get you something else for that. Something even more special."

My birthday is September twenty-first, which was still a week away. If he hurried, he might actually manage to do what he said. Call it a small character defect, but I tend to be picky about my gifts.

"Show me what you've got now," I said, my excitement mounting.

"Close your eyes, hon."

I closed them—well, not all the way. What's the use of having long pale lashes if you can't peek through them?

"They closed?" he asked.

"Yes."

Without further ado, Gabe whipped the white cloth off the wire cage. My eyes flew open and I found myself staring at the biggest cock I had ever seen.

"A rooster," I cried in dismay.

"Isn't he a beaut? Not that I know much about chickens, but both Freni and Mose said this was the finest Rhode Island Red they'd ever seen. Got him at the county fair last week over in Somerset."

He was a good-looking bird, but that wasn't the point. What woman wants a rooster for her birthday? As a general Happy Tuesday present, a big red cock is fine, but not on one's birthday. Birthday presents should be romantic, like a pair or two of nice cotton stockings, or a box of fine stationery, or—and this is what I'd really been hoping for—that elusive engagement ring.

But I am a mature woman, not given to hurting feelings intentionally—well, unless utterly provoked. "It's very nice," I said. "I'm sure the hens will love him."

Gabe's soft brown eyes fixed on my watery blue gray ones. "But you don't, do you?"

I gasped. "Love a rooster? Why, Gabe, that's against the Bible—even your version."

"You know what I mean, Mags. You're disappointed. I can tell."

"Well, I've never thought of poultry as being gift material. Now a sturdy flannel nightgown—"

"Women. I'll never figure you out."

"Would you like it if I gave you a ream of paper for your birthday?" I tried to pick something that every writer eventually needs, even in this computer age.

He smiled. "Laser or ink-jet compatible?"

"Now you're mocking me, aren't you?"

The soft eyes hardened into dark lumps, like brownies left uncovered overnight. "I know what you're getting at. You think I didn't put any thought into this gift, but I damn well did. Do you think I like visiting the livestock tents at county fairs? Stepping in sheep shit and ruining a pair of practically new Italian leather loafers?"

I clapped my hands over my ears. "I will not tolerate swearing, Gabriel M. Rosen."

"Well, I won't tolerate having my intentions misread. A normal woman, Magdalena, would have wanted roses or chocolates, or jewelry. Yeah, jewelry. Oh no, but not you. I tried my damnedest to think of what you'd like, and this is the thanks I get?"

I wrested the rooster from his hands. The stupid bird weighed as much as a small child. Yes, I needed a good cock, but I prefer to buy my own livestock. What I certainly didn't need was a lovers' (did I dare call Gabe that?) spat just as I was beginning a murder investigation.

"Thanks," I said.

"You're welcome."

But neither of us meant what we said.

I put the rooster—which I decided to call Chanticleer II—in with the hens. They took a shine to him right away, which made me even more irritable. Pertelote, my favorite hen, was the most shameless, but I gave them all a stern lecture on the impending perils of Freni's stewpot. Then, after securely latching the door, I set off to solve the mystery of the colonel's murder.

My first stop was Sam Yoder's Corner Market. If Hernia had a proper downtown, and not just a cluster of churches and a police station, Sam's little grocery would be smack-dab in the heart of things. On weekdays it *is* the heart of things, at least for those in search of a little harmless gossip.

Just for the record, Yoder's Corner Market is not a business my cousin had to build from the ground up. Sam's wife, Dorothy, comes from money, and the store was her dowry. The fact that Sam switched from being a Mennonite to being a Methodist, to make his Methodist father-in-law happy, is nothing short of shameful, if you ask me. Five hundred years of heritage down the drain, and for what? Three aisles of dusty canned goods, an aisle of sundries, and a bin of limp produce?

There were several bona fide Amish women, two conservative Mennonite women, and a possible Presbyterian on the premises, but I managed to pull Sam into the women's hygiene section for interrogation. No one but the possible Presbyterian would dare come near with someone else present, especially a man. If the possible Presby put in an appearance, I'd give her a withering glare. Sure, she might jump to the conclusion that Sam and I were engaged in a romantic assignation, but what harm could there be in that? As a former inadvertent adulteress, my reputation was already ruined. A new rumor might help displace the old, and anyway, if it got back to Gabe, it could even be beneficial. Maybe then the Babester would think I was worth more on my birthday than a Rhode Island Red.

"Sam," I whispered, "as I'm sure you've heard by now, Colonel Custard is dead."

The grocer tried unsuccessfully to tear himself away from my grasp. I am after all a penny-pincher par excellence, and over the years my bony fingers have evolved into talons. But although he tried to escape, my cousin appeared genuinely surprised.

"What did you say, Magdalena?"

"I said he was dead."

"No, I mean who?"

"Colonel Custard."

"How? When? Why? Where?" He was asking all the questions reporters should ask but seldom do anymore.

"A bullet to the head, a couple of hours ago, because he was going to ruin our town, and where else?"

"Not your inn?"

"Saaam," I wailed, like the siren on Melvin's squad car, "who's going to want to stay at a place that has seen so many deaths?"

"You could always turn that into the PennDutch's main attraction. You know, bill it as the world's most haunted full-board inn. Eat and sleep with the ghosts, that kind of thing."

"Well, I guess I could substitute C.A.S.P.E.R. for A.L.P.O."

"Casper?"

"Cavorting Among Specters Plan—" I clapped my mouth for the umpteenth time that week. What on earth was I doing discussing business with one of my prime suspects? It's just that it was so hard to think of Samuel Nevin Yoder as a cold-blooded killer. All through elementary school he'd tormented me—putting gum in my braids, making rude noises behind his hands, and sitting on my sandwiches at lunchtime. This, I later learned, was because he liked me. Anyway, the man was blood kin, and Yoders are genetically incapable of murder—or are they? A man who would trade his heritage in for tinned peas and rubbery heads of lettuce was capable of anything.

Sam knew me too well. "You actually think I might have something to do with the colonel's death, don't you?"

"Well, dear, you did have a motive."

"Not half as good as yours. Sure, my store might eventually have had to give way to one of those chains, assuming that hotel really did bring in development, but it would have happened slowly. The PennDutch, on the other hand, would have gone belly-up the first week."

"Says who?"

He had the temerity to laugh. "Let's see, what would the average person rather do, spend bundles of money for the privilege of making his or her own bed, or be coddled like a newborn?"

"Not everyone has the same tastes," I snapped. Sam didn't seem to understand the secret to my success. It isn't just the quaint surroundings that have made my place so successful, but the fact that people don't mind—even insist on—paying extra for abuse, just as long as they can view it as a cultural experience. If that's not the case, why is Paris such a popular destination?

"Face it, Magdalena. You're your own best suspect. I suggest you go home, fix yourself a cup of strong tea, and start asking yourself hard questions." He tried again to pull free of my talons, but to no avail.

"Do you have an alibi for this morning?" I demanded.

Sam has the Yoder nose, and his is every bit as big as mine, deserving of its own zip code. He pointed it at the ceiling in mock resignation.

"Let's see. This morning when I opened—at precisely eight o'clock—Thelma Kreider and Rachel Gerber were already waiting for me. Thelma bought three cans of corned beef and—"

"Just a minute." I fished in my purse and came up with an old grocery receipt—to Pat's I.G.A., my store of choice, all the way over in Bedford—and a much chewed pen. The teeth marks, by the way, belong to Freni. Little Freni, not Big. "Continue, dear," I said, pretending to write.

"Uh—yeah, facial tissues is what else she bought. Rachel picked up a bottle of chocolate syrup, a box of elbow macaroni, and a loaf of bread."

"And Rachel claims she bakes her own!"

Sam, who loves to spread gossip, grinned despite himself. "At eight fifteen Lovina Kenagy ran in and picked up a box of cream of tartar and . . ."

Cream of tartar, I wrote on the back of my receipt. I had no earthly idea what it was, but Freni said she needed some the next time I was in town.

"... and then at eight twenty-nine, Ed Fisher popped in. Said his wife needed a jar of spaghetti sauce ..."

Spaghetti sauce. Freni needed that too.

"... but Ed said her homemade sauce will turn your stomach inside out. Then at eight forty-six—no, eight forty-seven—Catherine Troyer raced into the store ..."

There was no need to hear more. It's a little-known fact, but Sam's mind was the inspiration for the computer chip. It may be small, but it holds an astonishing amount of information. By the time he started school, Sam knew not only his times tables but the periodic tables, and he was the undefeated spelling champ every year that I can recall. Sam wouldn't even have gone to school with the likes of us had there been gifted programs back in those days. Alas, the only option was to skip grades, something his strict Mennonite parents thought immodest.

That brilliant mind could have gone on to do anything. Instead, it married Dorothy the Methodist. Or perhaps it was Sam's loins that married Dorothy, because she was, admittedly, a rather attractive girl with a budding personality. Today Dorothy's middle-aged spread threatens to spread into adjoining counties, and the personality that promised to bloom has long since withered on the stalk.

But where was I? Oh yes, I had no doubts that what Sam was telling me was true. His register tape would confirm it. There was certainly no need to interview any of his alibis. I released his wrist.

"Well," I sniffed, "you might want to do a little dusting in here. And some of those veggies over in that bin have been around since Methuselah was a boy. I know, because I carved my initials in a head of iceberg lettuce last summer, and it's still there."

Although he was free, and there was somebody waiting for him at the register, Sam didn't budge. Instead he smiled.

"Magdalena, if you ever get tired of that fancy New York doctor—well, you know where to find me."

"Sam! You're married, for crying out loud."

"There is such a thing as divorce."

"I am not about to do the horizontal hootchy-kootchy with a cousin."

"Suit yourself. But like I said, if you ever get tired—"

I left Sam standing in the dust.

By then it was already three in the afternoon. I drove straight from Sam's over to Miller's Feed Store, and parked as close to the front door as I could. There was no telling how Elspeth was going to react to the sight of me, especially now that we were allies of a sort. Under normal circumstances she's been known to a take a swing at me. Why it is she hates me I can't for the life of me figure out. At any rate, in case she took to throwing pitchforks at me—and I mean that literally—I wanted to be able to make a fast getaway.

Because the majority of Elspeth's customers are Amish and she was running a sale on harnesses, all the good parking places were taken by black buggies and stomping horses. I had to watch very carefully where I stepped. Although Hernia has an ordinance requiring horses to wear nappies, it is no longer enforced. Melvin tried that, and found out just how unpopular he was with the Plain People.

I nodded and smiled my way through the throng of shoppers. I know, at least by sight, everyone in the Amish and Mennonite communities. In fact, I know just about everyone in this hamlet. There are a few Presbyterians I'm still fuzzy on, but given that some of them have been known to drink alcohol like our lone Episcopalian, they're probably fuzzy on me too.

Since her husband Roy's disappearance, Elspeth has hired three young clerks, strapping young men all, to help her. She no longer does any of the actual work herself, but flits about snapping at her employees. I know that owls can't get rabies, but if they could, I'd be tempted to say there was a dangerous bird loose in Miller's Feed Store.

I found her in her usual foul temper, berating an employee in front of embarrassed customers. While my appearance was serendipitous on his part, it filled my quota of good deeds for the day. Elspeth flew at me in a rage, the young man's incompetence all but forgotten.

"You! What are you doing here?"

"What if I said I came to buy everything in the store?"

"I would not sell to you."

"But you do. Mose buys chicken and cattle feed here all the time."

"Mose Hostetler only works for you. It is not the same."

"Elspeth, we're on the same side, remember? We're both against the huge hotel and any subsequent development."

"Yah, but the colonel stays with you. You are a Benediction Arnold."

I smiled. "As usual, dear, you're half right. About the colonel—well, I'm afraid he isn't staying with me anymore."

"You kick him out?"

"Unfortunately not. He was murdered."

Her eyes flashed behind the horn-rimmed glasses. "You did this, yah?"

"I beg your pardon?"

"You are a stronger woman than I thought." For the first time I heard respect in her voice.

"I didn't kill him!" I wailed. Yes, I know, I wail a lot. But it is one of my more charming attributes, don't you think?

"He was an evil man, Magdalena."

"He was ambitious. That's hardly the same."

"But he did not care that he would destroy our way of life."

Our way? Yes, Elspeth's native tongue was German, and she used it to communicate with the Amish, who spoke an Americanized dialect of that language, but our way was hardly hers. She didn't even go to church, for Pete's sake, and I have it on good authority that she has been seen around neighboring Bedford knocking back beers with her bratwurst.

"There is no justification for taking a human life." If Elspeth had really been one of us, she would have known we Mennonites and our Amish cousins are pacifists. During colonial days, when my family was Amish, they refused to defend themselves against a Delaware Indian attack. As a result two of my ancestors were taken captive, and another, my great-great-great-great-great-great grandmother, was scalped.

"There are always exceptions, yah? Magdalena, you do not need to be shy with me. I understand these things."

"For the last time, I didn't kill the colonel." Our conversation was generating a lot more interest than discounted harnesses, but I didn't care. "As a matter of fact, I came here to question you."

"Me? You think I killed the colonel?

There were gasps and muttering in Pennsylvania Dutch, but the crowd edged closer. Agnes Bontrager, a buxom woman with a nose for news, actually nudged me with her bosoms. I have no doubt her intent was to push me forward into Elspeth's space, in hopes of escalating the confrontation. Agnes may be a pacifist by conviction, but her hobby is spectator sports. This is a pastime the Amish don't normally make time for, and I think the big-breasted woman was hungry for some action.

I smiled pleasantly at my friends and neighbors, at least those I could see. "I haven't made any allegations, Elspeth. I'm merely here to ask a few questions."

"There will be no questions, Magdalena. You will leave now."

"Of course we don't have to have this conversation in the open. How about we retire to your storeroom?"

"Out! Out! Out!" With each word she flapped her arms, but was unable to achieve liftoff. "Get out of my store, you pigamist!"

"What did you say?"

"You heard me—*pigamist*."

"Ah, you mean bigamist. I hate to tell you this, dear, but that is such old news it's not worth wrapping the garbage in."

A number of the Amish present murmured their agreement. There wasn't a soul in Hernia, with the exception of our five hearing-impaired citizens, who hadn't heard the story of Aaron and me, and if once, at least a dozen times. The Amish, more than anyone, know the futility of beating a dead horse. One by one they turned away to pursue their business. It was all I could do to keep from neighing gratefully.

"So," I said, "are we going to have our little chat in the back room, or out here?"

"You!" Elspeth cried, as if it was the worst insult she could think of.

Then, as preposterous as it sounds, she did achieve liftoff. I'm quite sure of that. Although Elspeth comes only to my sternum, she managed to butt me on the chin. It's true what they say; the bigger they are, the harder they fall. I teetered on my narrow heels for a second or two before landing on my back like a ton of Freni's pound cakes.

"She's dead," I heard someone say, just before it all went black.

12

I didn't die, of course, but I have no doubt that I was knocked cold. When I came to, I could hear birds chirping. Bavarian cuckoo clock birds. I tried to raise my head, and nearly fell forward on my face. It would seem that someone had propped me in a chair.

A smart Magdalena would have opened her eyes before moving. A *really* smart Magdalena would have closed them the second she opened them. I did neither, and found myself staring across a small desk at Elspeth Miller.

We were in a room the size of a broom closet—proof it wasn't Hell. And like I said there was Elspeth—proof it wasn't Heaven. I know that's an unchristian thing for me to say, and I'm not supposed to judge, but sometimes I can't help it. At any rate, the scrawny woman was perched on a chair of her own across the desk. Between us was a mound of paperwork, and on the wall behind Elspeth was a walnut cuckoo clock.

"Ah, you are awake," she said.

"Am I?"

"How many fingers do you see?" She held up two digits, both of which I could see quite clearly.

"Three."

The look of alarm on her face was worth the pain in my head. "Don't play games, Magdalena!"

"One," I said. Since I was merely counting in a random order, it wasn't exactly a lie.

"You are *sure*?" The owl had turned white behind the horn-rimmed glasses.

I glanced at the cuckoo clock. "Now I don't see any fingers."

"Now how many?" She had folded her index finger, leaving only the middle one. Like I told you, Elspeth Miller was not one of us.

I sat bolt upright. "I could sue, you know. Or get you arrested on assault and battery. Maybe I should do both. After all, there were tons of witnesses."

"But you will not do either, yah?"

"Says who?"

Elspeth smiled. As you might expect with a bird, she had no teeth. Well, at least they weren't visible.

"Your witnesses were all Amish, Magdalena. You know how much they hate to go to court. So, I suggest that we make a deal."

She was right about the Amish. They are, perhaps, our least litigious segment of society. They take care of their own, and prefer to handle all but the most pressing problems "in house," so to speak. Finding an Amish witness to testify against Elspeth would be as hard as pulling a hen's—make that Elspeth's—teeth.

"What sort of deal?" I asked warily. I am a woman of principle and cannot be bought. Besides, I have enough money of my own.

Elspeth pushed up her glasses just enough to massage the bridge of her beak. "If you promise to stop harassing me, I will give you some information that you might find very helpful in this little investigation of yours."

The word "little" grated on me like sixty-grit sandpaper. She was making it sound like a hobby. The truth is

I *am* the law in Hernia, just not officially. Between the two of them, Melvin and Zelda don't have enough mental amps to power a flashlight. But since Mama always said that honey catches more flies than vinegar, and Elspeth was definitely capable of flight, I gave the storm trooper's daughter the thirty-two-teeth salute. Besides, it takes fewer muscles to smile than it does to frown.

"I haven't exactly been harassing you, Elspeth, but I'd be happy to hear your little bit of information."

She leaned forward just as the door in the clock above her popped open and the little wooden bird stuck its head out. Cuckoo. Cuckoo. Cuckoo. Cuckoo.

"Oh my gracious, Elspeth, it's four o'clock. I've been out even longer than I thought. Please make this fast."

"The clock is not accurate, Magdalena. Now where was I?" Please understand that is only an approximation of Elspeth's words, since her *w*'s were *v*'s, and the other way around—which leads me to think the Germans may have intended to name their arthropodan automobile "Wolksvagon."

"You were about to enlighten me in regards to the very complicated case I'm working on."

"Yah. I was about to tell you that you are shouting up the wrong tree."

"That would be 'barking,' dear."

She glared behind the flaring frames. "Anyway, the person you need to talk to is Lodema Schrock."

"Lodema?" I was genuinely surprised. Sure the two women knew each other—in a town this small a merchant and a pastor's wife are both part of the upper crust—but I never, in a million years, would have expected Lodema's name to just roll from Elspeth's lips. Although a Lutheran by birth, Elspeth does not belong to any church, and Lodema would have no use for farm supplies.

Elspeth clearly enjoyed my shock. "I keep my eyes and nose open, Magdalena. There is much I know."

"You mean your ears," I cried.

"That is what I said."

"Tell me more," I begged, my conk on the head all but forgotten.

She gave me another toothless smile. "I think I have told you enough. So, now you talk to Lodema, yah?"

"Yah—I mean, yes. But can't you at least . . ."

Cuckoo. Cuckoo. Cuckoo. The confused bird popped back into its cubbyhole. Of the three of us, it was perhaps the sanest.

I had intended to swing by the high school after the feed store and visit Herman Middledorf, the principal, who had been quite vocal in his opposition to the colonel's hotel. But the Lodema Schrock thing intrigued me— and, I must admit, a valid excuse to egg her on was just too good of an opportunity to miss.

To reach Lodema's, I had to backtrack to the center of town. Beechy Grove Mennonite Church, which sits back from a country road, is nowhere near the parsonage. The latter is right around the corner from Sam's store in the Victorian part of town. The pastor and his wife live in a white gingerbread house on a corner lot shaded by towering maples. One would expect a kind, rosy-cheeked couple to live there, and if one did, one would be half right.

I rang the bell with a mixture of excitement and trepidation, fully expecting Lodema to fling open the door in her customary rage. Silly me, I certainly did not expect the reverend to open the door.

"Good afternoon, Magdalena," he said with a smile that was quite genuine. Reverend Schrock and I truly get along, and even if we didn't, I contribute more money to the cause than any other member of his congregation.

"Is your lovely wife in?" Compliments do not fall under the category of lies, if you ask me. They are merely good deeds, unsupported by facts. Besides, the woman in question might well have a comely visage. I wouldn't know, because the second I met her, we got off on the wrong foot. In my mind she has always looked like Medusa.

"Lodema?"

"No, your other wife."

The good man was taken aback. "I—uh—Magdalena, are you joshing with me?"

"Certainly, Reverend. Is she home?"

"Ah, yes. She's in the kitchen—"

"No, I'm not." Lodema shoved her long-suffering husband aside and planted her feet firmly in the doorway. "What is it you want, Magdalena?"

Her poor husband sighed. "If you ladies need me—"

"Stir the pasta," she snapped.

While my spiritual shepherd trotted off to do his wife's bidding, I prayed for patience. If the Good Lord chose not to answer that prayer on the steps of a parsonage, then He just plain didn't mean for me to have that virtue.

"So," Lodema said, interrupting my petition, "what brings you here? You finally decided to join the Cookie Brigade? Well, if you have, first you need to apologize."

Lodema has been after me for months to join a group of devout women who have taken upon themselves to bake cookies to send to the state prison. She views this as a ministry. I loathe baking. I have also tasted many of the Brigade's efforts. It was with that knowledge in mind that I proposed, at the organizational meeting, that we purchase our cookies from the Girl Scouts—repackage them if need be—and send them along to the lockup. We'd be doing both the Scouts and the cons a huge favor *and* save ourselves a whole lot of bother. Much to my surprise, my suggestion was met with stony stares.

"This isn't about cookies," I said, still waiting for my dose of divine patience. "It's about Colonel Custard."

"What about him? No, let me guess. You and your cronies aren't having any luck in railroading the poor man out of town, so you've come for my help. Well, I told you before, Magdalena, I think the hotel is a good thing. It's a golden opportunity to save souls."

"Let's hope the colonel's was saved," I mumbled.

"What was that?"

"Lodema, dear, the colonel was murdered this morning."

She stared mutely while her skin went through several color changes. "Where?" she finally asked.

"My inn. He was shot in the head."

"Magdalena, you"—she shook her head—"no, even you aren't that cold-blooded."

"Why, thank you. And I don't suspect you either— although a little birdie did send me this way."

"Who?" She looked more sad than startled.

"I can't reveal my sources, dear." Although I had not promised Elspeth that I'd protect her, there is power to be wielded by withholding information. Keep them guessing, Mama always said, and the fact that she was referring to her age does not change the wisdom inherent in her statement.

Lodema's face underwent several more color changes, and then it appeared to dissolve. She put her hands over it, presumably to hold what remained of it in place—well, that's how it looked to me. And no, I most certainly did not experiment with hallucinogenic drugs in the sixties.

"I was so young," she sobbed.

"There, there," I said, relieved that the strange transformation was only apparent, and due to tears— something I never in a million years would have associated with Lodema—and not related to the knock to my noggin earlier that day.

" 'Be sure that your sin will find you out,' " she blubbered, quoting from the Book of Numbers. "And my sin has found me out, hasn't it?"

"Well—"

"You won't tell the reverend, will you, Magdalena?"

I laid a bony arm around her well-padded, but sloped, shoulders. "Tell me everything you don't want me to tell him, dear. And please be specific. Sometimes it's hard for me to keep my stories straight."

She turned her tearstained face to the door. "Can't we please talk somewhere else?"

From inside came the smell of something burning—the pasta, no doubt—and the sound of clanging pots. I doubted if Reverend Schrock was paying any attention to our conversation, but I was not about to let this golden opportunity slip through my mitts.

"Any suggestions, dear?"

"There's a gazebo over there." She pointed to the side yard, where a flimsy white structure struggled to stand in the spreading shade of a sugar maple.

"You got it."

Just because the Good Lord was a carpenter is no reason one of His pious servants should fancy himself one. What was supposed to be a garden ornament looked more like an outhouse that had seen hurricane-force winds. I know we don't pay our pastor as much as we should (it's for his own spiritual good, mind you) but it looked like he had scavenged for the materials at the town dump. Every kind of board imaginable had been incorporated, and even a few pieces of plastic. At least he'd had the sense to paint the mess white.

There were supposed to be benches inside the gazebo, but the plywood shelves wouldn't have been able to support the mere thought of sitting, much less the actual thing. We both stood.

"Now tell all, dear," I reminded her.

First she needed to blow her nose in the worst way. Unfortunately, she hadn't come to the door prepared to cry, and the only tissues I had were in my bra. If I were to remove them I would become a carpenter's dream, and thereby risk being utilized in a possible expansion of the so-called gazebo. Therefore I suggested Lodema use the hem of her skirt to clear her sinus passages, and to her credit, she gamely complied.

"I was only a college freshman," she said, sniffing. "A very impressionable one at that. You see, Mama and Daddy were very protective—and I didn't, uh, have any experience with the world, if you know what I mean."

"I do indeed. I thought babies grew under cabbages until I—"

"Magdalena, this isn't about you."

I slapped my mouth lightly. "Indeed it's not."

"So anyway, when I met Colonel Custard—"

"You met him in *college*?"

"Yes, but he wasn't a colonel yet; he was my biology professor. Now, where was I? Magdalena, it is so hard to talk when you're constantly interrupting."

"You'd just met," I said, and then mimed locking my lips and throwing away the key.

"Yes, well, he was the most handsome man I'd ever laid eyes on. Magdalena, he just exuded charm and like I said, I was only eighteen and—uh—I don't know how to put this delicately—"

"Horny?" I hate that crude word, but it is a succinct description of a crude human condition.

"Magdalena!"

I pretended to lock my lips with a second key. In addition to patience, I should have prayed for a case of lockjaw.

"I wasn't that word you said," she growled. "I have never experienced those base carnal urges that seem to be driving the young folks of today."

"Not even with the reverend?" I slapped my mouth so hard I tasted blood, and she didn't bother to chide me.

"But I did experience a certain lack of judgment."

13

It is hard to communicate with only one's eyes, especially when shouting is called for. I rolled my eyes with such vigor the left one nearly popped out. Since it is by far the better-looking of the two, I did my best to hold it in place, and just roll the right.

"I'm getting there, Magdalena," she said, reading my eye. "Well, I don't know any other way to say it, except that I eventually agreed to know him. In the biblical sense, I mean."

My right eye came dangerously close to leaving its cozy socket, but Lodema got the message.

"It happened only once, and I didn't experience a moment of pleasure. But once I did it—well, a card played is a card laid, as they say. Not that I play card games either. You understand."

Despite the impression I sometimes give, I am only human. "Try substituting the word 'woman' for 'card.' That man used you, and you were barely more than a babe in arms."

"You're right; I was just a child. So I really can't be held responsible for that, can I?"

"I certainly don't," I said. Well, I mostly didn't hold

her responsible. I'd like to think that I would have remained virtuous, but to tell the truth, if either Aaron or the Babester had come along when I was that age—I shuddered to think what might have happened. Then I shuddered again to re-create the feeling. And to think I'd settled for my Maytag all those years.

"In retrospect," Lodema said, "I should have had my head examined. Sure he was handsome and all, but his hands always smelled of formaldehyde, and he had this thing about snakes."

"Snakes?"

"There was this huge terrarium in the biology lab, and Professor Custard—that's what we called him then—had a pet snake he kept in it. An African rock python. I remember, because before we got a passing grade, we each had to feed it a mouse."

"Gross. Wasn't that dangerous?"

"Not really; we just had to drop the mouse in the tank. Of course legally he couldn't make us do it, but it was a tradition in the department. Kind of like a rite of passage."

"We all had to take turns clapping erasers," I said. I was talking about fifth grade, but she didn't need to know that.

"Magdalena, you're not going to tell the reverend, are you?"

I started to shake my head, but it throbbed. "*I'm* not a busybody."

"And you think I am?"

"If the shoe fits, dear. What I can't figure out is why you of all people would welcome the colonel to town— no—wait a minute! He was blackmailing you, wasn't he?"

She shook her head like the paint mixer at the Home Depot over in Bedford. No sign of concussion there.

"Actually he wasn't blackmailing me. But you see, there was always the possibility that he might. That's why when he first wrote last year and asked about development potential—"

"He wrote last *year*?"

"Yes, but—"

"So you're the one who got him interested in Hernia in the first place?"

"What was I supposed to do? I didn't want to appear unfriendly."

"You knew his plans all along?"

"I still think that hotel would have presented a good opportunity for us to share our witness."

"And I think the bridge mix is missing a nut," I said, not without charity. "Do you know the meaning of playing with fire?"

"Magdalena, you said you wouldn't tell my husband."

I happened to glance past her to the house. Silhouetted in the window was the forlorn figure of my friend and pastor, Reverend Schrock. He looked like a burned gingerbread man. I couldn't even tell if he was looking at us or away.

"I won't tell him. You have my word."

Lodema extended her arms, as if she meant to hug me. Just as I started to respond in a likewise if highly uncharacteristic manner, she hugged herself.

"I hope you don't climb up on your high horse now, Magdalena. If so, let me remind you that you are a former bigamist who plans to marry a man of a different faith."

I was out of there faster than a greased pig shot from a cannon—not that I've seen a whole lot of those, mind you. But I had yet to lose my patience. For the first time, the Good Lord had seen it fit to answer that prayer. I wasn't about to mess that up.

Where does one go to celebrate an answered prayer, especially if one is ravenous, and not inclined to cook? Why, the Sausage Barn, of course!

This satisfying restaurant is part of the backlash against the low-fat trend of the nineties. Wanda Hemphopple, Mennonite owner of the joint, subscribes to that time-honored Anabaptist tradition that fat is where it's at. Although Wanda was the second worst cook in our home economics class (I was the worst), she managed to find a pair of Mennonite cooks who know a thousand and one tasty ways to serve lard. Everything at the Sausage Barn comes swimming in grease of some kind. But to her credit Wanda makes up for this, in part, by banning smoking altogether. At the Sausage Barn nonsmokers get to eat their grease in peace.

Please understand that by praising the Sausage Barn, I am not espousing high cholesterol or advocating heart attacks. I am merely stating a fact: Fat tastes good. Animal fat tastes the best. What can compare to a greasy strip of bacon, fried crisp on the ends but with just a little play in the middle? Didn't the Good Lord forbid His Chosen People to eat pork so that the rest of us could have more? Frankly, as a good Christian I consider it my religious duty to eat as much bacon as possible, thereby sparing Jews temptation. In short, I do it for Gabe.

But just because I frequent the Sausage doesn't mean I'm a welcome guest. Wanda Hemphopple and I have never gotten along. It all started back in high school when I inadvertently stuck a pencil through Wanda's beehive hairdo, thinking it was the pencil sharpener. It was not, as Wanda claims, a malicious act intended to focus attention on me.

I have long since forgiven Wanda for this accusation. She, on the other hand, has not forgiven me. If you look closely you can still see a faint indentation where my writing implement penetrated her lacquered coiffure. Perhaps this is why she refuses to wash her hair. At any rate, my advice is to eat Wanda's grease, but stay away from her if you can help it.

Taking my own advice, I tried to sneak past the hostess station and seat myself in a booth at the back. This is my favorite booth because it is so well screened by plastic ferns in hanging baskets and plastic philodendrons in cheap divider walls, it's almost like entering a canopy bed—one with plastic green curtains. *Dusty* curtains.

Because it's near the rest rooms, which are not the most hygienic in the world, most customers elect not to take this booth. What they don't realize is that it is also close to the kitchen, so that your hotcakes arrive hot, and with any luck, your bacon still sizzles.

"Whew!" I said and plunked myself down on the green Naugahyde seat. It had been touch and go there for a second. Wanda had been on the phone, her back to the door when I entered, and turned just as I dived into my sanctuary.

"Well, it's about time."

I jumped so high my bun bumped a basket of ferns. "Gabe!"

"That would be me."

"What are you doing here?"

"Waiting for my dinner to be served. Mind if I ask you the same?"

I waved away a cloud of settling dust. "I came to eat, but I didn't expect to find you."

He grinned. "You're the one who showed me this secret spot."

"So I did."

"Look, Mags, I realize that we didn't part on the best of terms—"

"Maybe you didn't, but I did." Okay, so *that* was an out-and-out lie. But when I got down on my knees to say my prayers that night, I would confess it. In the meantime, what did I have to gain by letting him know that I carried a grudge over a silly thing like a rooster?

"Yeah, you're right, I was a little pissed—pardon my French. But then I got to thinking; it really was my fault.

I gave you something I thought you needed, not something I thought you might like."

I picked up the plastic-coated menu, which was covered with enough grease to lubricate the axles of an eighteen-wheeler. I knew everything on it by heart, but in order to come across as nonchalant, I had to look busy.

"Like, schmike, I really don't care. What counted was the thought, right?" Not that a chicken took a whole lot of thought.

"But maybe you will care about this," he said. Gabe fumbled in his pants for a moment. Given that we were in such a secluded booth, I began to worry. "Here," he said at last, and placed a black velvet box on the table between us.

My heart pounded like a madman on a xylophone. "What's that?"

"Open it and see."

I'm not as dumb as I look. I knew darn well what was in that box—at least what I hoped was in it. And it wasn't a rooster. Even the smallest bantam wouldn't fit in that box. My fingers shook as I opened it, and I kept one eye closed for psychological protection; if I didn't like what I saw, then only half of me saw it.

"Oh my stars!"

"You like it?"

"Uh—uh—" For the first time since I could talk, I was speechless. What was not to like? It was a sapphire and diamond engagement ring, just like the one Prince Charles gave to Diana, only a wee bit smaller. I know whereof I speak, because I saw that ring once.

Gabe was on a mind-reading roll. "It's a replica of Princess Diana's, only a bit smaller. I'm a retired doctor, not the Prince of Wales. But that sapphire is just over five carats and the diamonds are all VVS grade."

The woman who had dished out a thousand scoldings couldn't find her tongue.

"I could have gotten you a diamond solitaire, but sapphire is your birthstone, and anyway, solitaires are too common. But you're not, hon. Poor Diana never became queen, but you're already queen of my heart."

I found my tongue, just where I'd left it. "Stop it."

"I was going to save it for your actual birthday—the chicken was more of a gag—but when you got so upset . . . Mags, hon, believe me. I wouldn't hurt you for the world. You mean everything to me."

"Stop it," I begged. "Pleeease."

Gabe sighed. "You don't like it. I knew I was taking a chance. Damn it—"

My arms when fully extended can reach from Hernia to Cleveland. I barely had to stretch to clamp one of my mitts over the Babester's mug.

"I love it, Gabe! And I love you. But you're making me cry. And Magdalena Portulacca Yoder does not like to cry in public." I blinked back the tears, some of which had already escaped and fallen on the plastic menu.

"What's going on?" a high-pitched voice demanded.

I turned my head. "Wanda!"

"Magdalena, are you trying to smother this man?"

I let my hand drop. "This is a private conversation, dear."

"It didn't look like no conversation to me. It looked like you were trying to smother him. And I won't have that, because Doc here is one of my regulars."

"Doc—I mean Gabe—gave me a ring." I grabbed the velvet box and shoved it under her nose. "Isn't it beautiful?"

Wanda sniffed, as if the ring were supposed to emit a scent of some kind. "Got me one just like that for Mother's Day from Janet. That's my oldest."

"I don't think so, dear. This is almost as large as the one Princess Diana had—just not quite."

"Looks the same as mine. Janet got it at a Service Merchandise over in Pittsburgh that went out of business. Paid two hundred dollars for it. Thinks a lot of her old mama, don't she?"

I shook the box. "*This* cost more than two hundred dollars."

"If you say so."

"Gabe, tell her."

"Tell her what, hon?"

"How much you paid for this."

"Mags, you know that's not right."

"Ha," Wanda said, as if Gabriel's good manners were a victory for her.

"Where is your ring?" I asked.

"Too flashy for me, that's what I told Janet. Made her take it back."

"She returned it to a store that was going out of business?"

Wanda nodded, her beehive wobbling precariously. "Yup."

"Let me guess, you had her donate the money to charity instead."

Gabe grabbed the box from my right hand, and then he grabbed my left hand. That was a clever ploy, because it shut me right up. Without further ado, in front of Wanda Hemphopple, he slid his ring on the finger that had once worn Aaron Miller's.

The new ring was much heavier than I expected. By comparison, Aaron Miller's—now, *that* was a diamond that cost two hundred dollars—had felt like a Cracker Jack toy. I waved my hand so that the five-carat sapphire and eye-clean diamonds flashed in the restaurant's poor light.

"Harrumph," Hemphopple said. Wanda doesn't usually wait on customers herself, but she pulled an order pad and a stubby pencil from the pocket of her apron. "Youse ready to order?"

"I am," Gabe said, with more enthusiasm than was called for.

"Me too," I said. "And then, Wanda, you and I need to chat."

She grimaced. "Okay, so maybe my ring wasn't as nice as yours, but you don't need to brag."

"I don't want to talk to you about the ring, dear. I want to talk to you about Colonel Custard."

"What about him?"

"He's dead."

Wanda looked like she'd eaten some of her own cooking. "Did you say dead?"

"As dead as the bacon I hope is on my plate in the next twenty minutes." I didn't mean to sound callous, but stress makes me ravenous, and at that moment I was more stressed than I'd been since my wedding night to Aaron. Who knew the Good Lord had such a bizarre sense of humor? Tab A into slot B, indeed!

Wanda patted her bun. It may have been just nervousness on her part, or it may have been a veiled threat of germ warfare.

"You saying I did it, Magdalena?"

"No. I'm just saying we need to talk."

Her hand dropped to her side, the threat of annihilation over. "Let's talk in the kitchen," she said.

That, I soon learned, was a huge mistake.

14

────

While a word to the wise is usually sufficient, folks like me need reams of it. Allow me to try and save you some trouble: Never enter the kitchen of a commercial restaurant unless you are prepared to never eat in that establishment again.

The Sausage Barn's kitchen looked like a herd of swine had exploded in it. Perhaps some weeks ago. Fortunately I wear sturdy Christian brogans with thick sensible soles. And since I am no slouch, I'm not in the habit of leaning against things.

Wanda read my mind. Frankly, it doesn't take a whole lot of doing.

"Sometimes we get backed up. But I've hired a dishwasher for the evening shift. She should be in any minute."

"Was the old one shanghaied by roaches?"

Wanda ignored my jibe. She has the irritating ability to shift gears faster than a NASCAR racer. "Tell me everything," she demanded, as if she were in charge of the investigation.

"Well, he was shot in the head this morning—hey, I'm the one who's supposed to be asking you the questions."

"Says who? That worthless brother-in-law of yours?"

"Pretty strong words for a Mennonite, Wanda."

"Yeah, well, there is nothing wrong with telling the truth."

"Agreed. Now, dear, what were you doing today—say, between the hours of nine and two?"

"So you really think I am a suspect!"

"Everyone is a suspect, until proven innocent." So maybe that is not the American way, but I didn't have a hand in writing the Constitution.

"I was here of course."

"Witnesses?"

"Your fiancé out there for one. Came in at eight forty-five for a pecan waffle and, uh, a large OJ, coffee black—yeah, that's all. Let's see, then there were the Hershbergers—like to eat late, you know. Amanda ordered the Happy Farmer Platter, which I'm sure comes as no surprise, and Herbert just had poached eggs and toast—on Amanda's orders, of course. I tell you, Magdalena, she keeps getting bigger while he keeps getting smaller. One of these nights she's going to roll over on him and then you'll have yourself another homicide to solve. Because believe you me, it won't have been by accident."

As fascinating as this information was, I had to put a stop to it. Wanda, I should have remembered, had a world-class memory when it came to gossip, and what better venue for collecting it than a small-town hangout? I decided to skip alibi and go straight to motive. A good segue was needed.

"You know I would never speak ill of the dead, Wanda, but you have to admit it was arrogant of an outsider to come here and want to virtually take over like he did."

Perhaps Wanda had an auxiliary brain hidden in her bun. She was certainly quicker on her rubber-soled shoes than I gave her credit for.

"Your point, Magdalena, is to get me to agree that I wanted to see the colonel gone, right? Well, you know I did. I made that clear at the town meeting. In fact, I wanted him gone so bad that I tried to bribe him."

"You what?"

Wanda fixed her eyes on mine, but she was clearly nervous. The beehive bobbled, but now that I knew it contained a miniature cerebellum and not the plague, I didn't feel threatened.

"I tried to grease his palm."

I glanced around me. "That shouldn't have been hard."

"Must you always make jokes, Magdalena?"

"Not always," I said. "Not during church. But please, tell me about this bribe."

"Well, the colonel came in one day a few months ago—"

"Et tu, Brutus?"

The brain in the bun seemed to have run out of battery power. "Magdalena, you know my name is Wanda, not Brutus."

I smiled. "Sorry, I was having a senior moment. Wanda, what you're saying is that you knew the colonel had been in town scouting around, and that his plans would ultimately destroy our way of life?"

"Why, yes—"

"And you didn't give me a heads up?"

"But I did try to stop him with my bribe."

"Ah yes, the bribe. How much was it for?"

"I didn't offer him money," she said hotly. "That would be wrong."

I gasped. "Not your—I mean, Wanda, I know you belong to the First Mennonite Church, which is more liberal than mine, but even your bunch—" I gasped again. "It wasn't the home run you offered him, was it?"

Wanda's right eyebrow shot up so high the bun tilted rakishly. "Magdalena, you're even nuttier than they say."

"I beg your pardon!" I gasped again. "Than *who* says?"

"Why, everyone. Mad as a hatter, they all say. What on earth is a hatter, Magdalena?"

A quick change of subject is the best way to preserve the appearance of wisdom. "Are you going to tell me what it is you offered him?"

"Food. All he could eat every time he was in town—which, between you and me, I hoped wasn't very often. He never travels anywhere without that prissy cook of his and Goliath, his chauffeur. That chauffeur eats more than even Amanda Hershberger. Of course that prissy cook won't touch a thing, except for black coffee. Too much fat, she says. Ha! If you ask me, she was in a snit about something, and it didn't involve food."

I stole another glance around me. The good news was that if the Board of Health didn't shut down the Sausage Barn, the PennDutch need never worry. William Penn was a boy the last time Wanda had her skillets washed or her floor mopped. The bad news was that I was never going to be able to stomach eating here again. Not without a lobotomy.

"So," I said, "the colonel turned your offer of food down, and that's the end of it? Weren't you seething with rage at the insult?"

"What insult would that be?" The auxiliary brain kicked in. "For your information, he loved my food. If I was going to kill anyone—which of course I never would—I'd have gone after that cook of his. Said my poached eggs were hard enough to break windows."

I sighed. I am not a betting woman, but if I were, I'd agree to lick one of Wanda's pots clean if she was guilty of the colonel's murder.

"There's nothing wrong with hard eggs, dear. That's how to avoid salmonella."

"That's what I told her. So, Magdalena, are we all done here? Is the inquisition over?"

"Why, I never!"

"Except with the bigamist Aaron Miller."

"That's unfair, and you know it."

Wanda's smile was one of pure satisfaction. In the war of the wits, she's been taken prisoner many times. This was her first victory that I can recall.

"If you're serious about finding the colonel's killer," she said, now that she could afford to be helpful, "you'll find him less than a mile down the road."

"Excuse me?"

"Magdalena, Magdalena, and I thought you were always the bright one. Always raising those huge hands of yours at school whenever the teacher asked for volunteers."

I hadn't known all the answers back then, but I wasn't about to admit it now. As a schoolgirl, I'd been acutely aware of image. I learned that by waving my arm whenever a question was asked, even the teacher became convinced I knew the material. Of course half the time I didn't.

"Wanda, dear, just cut to the chase. If you know the killer's name, spit it out."

Now that she had some power, she was every bit as reluctant to give it up as Strom Thurmond. "Remember when the county was talking about burying the power lines along Route 96, on account of in the wintertime a lot of folks were sliding into the poles?"

"Yes, but they didn't bury the lines. Too many people objected to the assessment fees."

"Correct. But who objected the loudest?"

"Wanda, the most handsome man on earth is waiting out there"—I pointed to the dining room—"in a plastic jungle. Or have you forgotten?"

"How could I forget, Magdalena? Your ring is blinding me—although I still say the one my daughter gave me was every bit as good. Anyway, the guy you're after, the one who objected the loudest to burying the power lines, was that reverend friend of yours."

"You mean Reverend Richard Nixon? Spiritual leader of the church with the thirty-two names? Looks a little bit like Abe Lincoln, only ganglier?"

"Haven't wasted my time counting them names, Magdalena, but he's the one I mean. And do you know why he objected, and why he killed the colonel?"

I shook my head. "Do tell."

"Because that church is built illegally right on the easement," she said. "If this so-called progress comes to Hernia and the road gets widened, that little fact is sure to be discovered. Then it's curtains for the church with all them names, because they won't be able to afford to relocate."

"You sure about the easement? How do you know?"

There are few things worse than triumphant grins on other people's faces. "Because business is so good here, I want to expand." She paused long enough to see the effect that would have on me. When all she got was a face suitable for Mount Rushmore, she scowled. "Well, anyway, the zoning board turned me down. Said I was already as close to the highway as I could legally get. Which got me to thinking—I'm not nearly as close to the road as that little church. In fact, I went down to the courthouse and researched their plat. Sure enough, the church is over the line."

"You didn't turn them in, did you?" Reverend Nixon's theology was not my cup of thee, but he and his bunch meant well.

"Of course I didn't turn them in. What kind of woman do you think I am?"

"A bitch."

I whirled. Gabe was standing in the door, trying to restrain a very large dog that was determined to push its way into the kitchen.

"She's obviously pregnant," he said. "Followed this couple in and headed straight back here."

Wanda didn't seem the least bit surprised. "Daisy, go home!"

"Is that your new dishwasher?" I asked innocently.

Gabe had the good sense to grab me by the arm and whisk me back to the safety of our plastic bower.

The Babester ate a full, saturated supper, while I opted for a liquid repast. Orange juice—bottled orange juice.

"The human stomach was designed to take a lot of punishment," he said, and shoveled a forkful of hash browns into his mouth.

"There are limits to everything," I said, "and that kitchen is beyond the pale."

"You obviously didn't share a bachelor's pad in medical school. Hon, do you think she might be on to something? About the reverend, I mean. I've only met him a few times, but he seems like a stand-up guy to me."

"Anything is possible, dear. But I agree. If Richard Nixon is guilty of the colonel's murder I'll eat my—"

"Birthday dinner here?"

I was going to say "hat," but since I don't own one, I was willing to eat my prayer cap. It's made of organza and is light and airy, if somewhat chewy. Besides, a good ranch dressing makes anything palatable—why else do the English insist on their daily quota of leaves? Leafy greens, they prefer to call them, but a leaf is a leaf, and without ranch dressing, they are best left up to giraffes.

"Okay, I'll eat here—but only if I'm wrong. If it's somebody else, I get to pick."

"Deal. Hon, I was thinking, it's going to be little spooky for you tonight at the inn, right? I mean, Alison's over at Freni's, and it's going to be just you and those two characters from a Mel Brooks movie."

I knew where this was going. Gabriel is a complete gentleman, but as straight as an airport runway. I take it as a compliment that from time to time he asks me to spend the night, even when he knows the answer is a standing, and resounding, "No."

"I'm flattered, dear," I said, "but I'll be just fine. Besides, I've got Grandma Yoder's ghost to watch over me."

Gabe grunted. Most Mennonites don't subscribe to the idea of ghosts, and neither does my Jewish beau. But I know from personal experience that Papa's mama, who died in an upstairs bedroom, is still around, trying to run the house with a spectral fist. I have seen her on three occasions, and each time she looked just as imposing as she had in life. If the colonel's weird staff tried to harm me, I had no doubt that Granny Yoder would send them packing. Why she didn't stop whoever it was from killing the colonel in the first place, thereby saving me a peck of trouble, is beyond me. When I die—if I have the nerve—perhaps I'll ask her.

"You need me," Gabe said as he stood to leave, "just call. And by all means, hon, don't take any chances."

"Chances?"

"Mags, there's no predicting what you will do. That's one of the things I love about you. But this time I mean it. And promise me you're going directly home from here."

"I promise."

"Tell you what, you drive first and I'll follow."

I am not a child, and though he meant well, my bun bristled. "I'll follow you. I might get lost otherwise."

"Yeah, right. Like you haven't been up and down that road just about every day of your life."

In the end he conceded, and led the way out of the parking lot. I followed faithfully for a few yards, but then opportunity knocked. I would have been an idiot not to answer the door.

15

Blood Orange Custard

This is an adaptation of a little-known Catalan dessert called Millasons.

1½ teaspoons unsalted
    butter
2 large eggs
2 egg yolks
½ cup sugar
⅓ cup all-purpose flour

1 cup freshly squeezed
    blood orange or
    tangerine juice
2 tablespoons lemon juice
1 cup milk, scalded and
    slightly cooled

Preheat the oven to 350° F. Butter six 6-ounce custard cups.

With a whisk or electric mixer, beat the eggs, yolks, and sugar until ribbony and pale yellow, then slowly beat in the flour and juices. Add the milk and combine well. Pour into the cups.

Bake in a bain-marie for about 40 minutes, or until a knife inserted near the center comes out clean. Let cool to room temperature, then refrigerate. Unmold and serve cold.

SERVES 6

16

Opportunity is often a gift from God, and what kind of a Christian would I be if I denied my Maker the pleasure of bestowing a gift on me? Faithful believer that I am, I stomped on the brakes when I saw the light on in the little church with the thirty-two names. Gabe must have been listening to a favorite CD, because he sailed off into the night.

I screeched to a halt in the gravel parking lot, grateful that I had recently sold my sinfully red BMW and bought a car more fitting for a woman of my persuasion. The Reverend Richard Nixon lives in a trailer adjacent to the church, and his was the only other car in the lot. The minuscule congregation often has weeknight meetings, but this obviously was not the case tonight. Therefore I felt no compunction about imposing myself on the scene. The last time I barged into the church, I found the good reverend on his knees, cleaning the floor with Murphy Oil Soap.

The door was again unlocked. I opened it wide enough to insert my horsey head and peered around. Sure enough, the good man was on his knees again, but there was no aroma of cleaning solution.

"I beseech thee, Lord," I heard him say. "Have mercy on me, a sinner."

"Reverend," I called softly, wishing not to intrude, but to make my presence known. "Reverend."

He looked up, scanning the low soundboard ceiling. In moments of religious fervor, he's been known to bump it with his head. Still, the reverend, who takes things even more literally than I do, must have assumed that God was always above.

"Lord," he called, "is that you?"

"Not unless the Lord is a woman," I said.

"You're a woman, Lord?" At some point the reverend had gotten too much Murphy Oil Soap in his ears.

"Would that be so bad?" I know—it's a sin to impersonate the Lord, but as long as I repented before the moment of truth, what did it really matter?

"I knew it," the reverend cried. "I knew you were a woman. All that attention to detail in creation, the way you're able to multitask—I just knew it!"

I gasped. I'd only been joking, and it was wrong of me to do so. Everyone knows that God is a man—well, not a man, exactly, but definitely male. The Bible quite clearly calls the Lord a "He." Says so right there in the King James Version. And anyway, if God was a she, She would have given men menstrual periods.

"Shame on you, Reverend. I am not the Lord—although Gabe has been known to call me a goddess. Of course I discourage that kind of talk."

"Magdalena, it's only you." The poor man's disappointment was palpable. Imagine, if you will, the disappointment some Baptists feel when they get to Heaven and discover that they're not the only ones there.

"Reverend, since I happened to find you on the job, I'd like to have a moment of your time, if I may."

Reverend Nixon sighed and struggled to his feet. It was like watching a foal take its first steps.

"Magdalena, there is no denying you this request, is there?"

"Not if you want a peaceful night's sleep." He was free to interpret that anyway he wished.

"Then, please, sit. I will stand, if you don't mind."

"By all means." With limbs that long, I'd be loath to reposition them too.

He waited until I'd settled my bony butt, as best I could, on the hard oak bench. "So, what is troubling you now?"

"Now? It's not like I come running to you every little whipstitch."

"You come enough times," he said.

"Maybe, but this time I haven't come to ask your advice; I've come to question you."

"Me?" He seemed genuinely surprised, which meant he was either a very good liar—not uncommon among men of the cloth, I'm afraid—or as innocent as that newborn foal.

"Reverend, did you know Colonel Custard had been murdered?"

Again, there was the distressed look of innocence brought up short. "You mean he's dead?"

"Deader than that skunk near my house."

"How?"

"A bullet to the head."

"Self-inflicted?"

"Definitely not. The entry hole was small and uniformly round, meaning the gun had to be fired from more than an arm's length away—unless, of course, one had arms as long as yours. Which the colonel didn't."

He nodded. "Did this happen at the PennDutch?"

"You guessed it."

He looked me straight in the eyes. "And you think maybe I did it?"

I prefer shifty and canny to mournful and sincere. "Well, uh—it *is* possible you have a motive."

"Because I am against the big hotel? Magdalena, that will only bring sin to Hernia."

"And perhaps a wider road."

I hate feeling sympathy for a suspect, but the poor man looked so disconsolate, I wanted to hug him. Fortunately I'm genetically disinclined to hug anyone, even a close relative.

"Yes," I said, "I know all about the easement violation."

He looked down at his feet. His shoes were in need of a good polishing, so I looked away.

"It was an honest mistake," he said. "This church was built by members, you see. We got a building permit and everything, and of course we had to have the county inspector come out—but he only came out once, just when we were getting started. Then we made a slight adjustment to our plans—I know we shouldn't have— but it put us over the line, something we didn't realize until we were done.

"Magdalena, this has caused many a sleepless night, and not just for me. We have prayed about it many times, and many times we have come close to telling the authorities, but . . ." He sounded like he was walking away from me in the Allegheny Tunnel.

"But you thought you would take your chances?"

He hung his head, his long chin resting on the Windsor knot in his polyester tie. Clergy in Hernia do not wear Roman collars.

"They said the road would never be widened—not in our lifetime. Who wants to go to Hernia, except for those people already living there?"

I nodded. It's been said that Hernia, because of its remoteness, will be the last place to experience the Second Coming.

"I understand your predicament, Reverend, but surely the zoning board would have made an exception."

"Not at the time. The commissioner wasn't happy about giving us a permit to begin with. Thought we were a bunch of weirdos, I guess, on account of our name."

"Which you must admit is a little long."

He said nothing.

"But catchy," I added.

"Magdalena, as time passed we found ourselves in a situation we couldn't easily explain. It got to the point where it seemed wiser to do nothing. But that wasn't the right thing, of course."

"Of course."

"I'm guilty of lying by omission, but I am not"—he dragged each word out, as if they would be his last three—"guilty of murder. That's one of the big ten, you know."

"Indeed, it is." There was no point in reminding him that some folks would consider him guilty of breaking the ninth commandment. Besides, those folks would be wrong. That one commands us not to bear false testimony against our neighbors—as in lying about them in a court case. It has nothing whatsoever to do with everyday fibs, and the Pennsylvania Department of Transportation was certainly not the good reverend's neighbor.

"What are you going to do?" he finally asked.

"Go home and go to bed."

"I mean, what are you going to do about this—uh—situation?"

"I'm not."

"I beg your pardon?"

"But you will. Tomorrow you will go to the zoning board—it's in the Bedford County Courthouse—and explain your situation. Speak to a woman named Claire, if you can. It was an honest mistake, and if you present it as such, you may just get a slap on the wrist. In my opinion—for what it's worth—the worst they will do is levy a small fine."

"They won't make us move the church?"

I shrugged. "I can't imagine that they would, but I'm not in any position to make promises. Still, the sooner you fess up, the better off you'll be."

He grabbed my hand and squeezed. It felt like I was being mauled by artichokes.

"Thank you, Magdalena. Thank you. If you weren't engaged to that doctor fellow, I'd—well, he's a lucky man."

I allowed myself the pleasure of a brief fantasy. There is nothing wrong with that, as long as you don't take it too far. Mrs. Richard Nixon had a certain ring to it—or would that be the Reverend Mrs. Richard Nixon? That was even better. Fortunately my fantasy ran out of steam on its own just when I got to the point of imagining us doing the horizontal hootchy-kootchy. It would be like wrestling with a pile of telephone poles, and a gal could get seriously hurt.

The reverend was oblivious to my thoughts, thanks to the beauty of the human mind. Or perhaps he may have been having similar thoughts. After all, many clergymen I've met—Reverend Schrock excluded—have a randy side. At any rate, when I left, Richard Nixon was relaxed and smiling. He had his snug little trailer to retire to, maybe even dreams of me. I, on the other hand, faced the prospect of sleeping in an inn that was empty, except for two of the strangest people I'd encountered in almost a decade of innkeeping.

"Pray for me," were my parting words.

17

I said my prayers before going to bed. As usual, I started off with the Lord's Prayer. Then I took the liberty of asking the Good Lord to hold off giving my sister Susannah any babies until He was sure Melvin Stoltzfus was the one and only man for her—hopefully sometime after the twelfth of never—and until she stopped carrying a pooch around in her bra. Even then, unless my nephew or niece was very tiny, he or she was not going to get a comfy ride. I prayed that Gabe the Babe would see the light, but not be blinded like Saul of Tarsus. I requested blessings for Freni and family, imploring the Lord to compel Freni to return to work as soon as possible, and to help Alison deal with her adjustment to a new school.

Finally I prayed for myself. "I know I've caused you a lot of trouble," I whispered, "but if you help me solve the colonel's murder, I promise not to bother—"

The ringing of my bedside phone made me jump. On the outside chance AT&T had a satellite link with Heaven, I answered immediately. One of these days I was going to pay someone to pry my parsimonious fist open wide enough to spring for Caller ID.

"Hello?"

"Yoder, it's about time."

"Good evening, Melvin." Frankly, I was relieved it was merely the mantis, and not his Maker. "What can I do for you?"

"What's with all this false cheer, Yoder? Never mind. Where were you all night?"

"The night has just begun, dear. And I'm home in bed, snug as a bug—"

"Yoder, I don't care if you're hanging by your toes from the chandelier. I've been calling every five minutes for the last three hours—"

"No, you haven't. I've been home for half an hour, and the phone hasn't rung once."

"Don't interrupt me, Yoder. This is police business."

"Yah wohl, mein kommandant."

"You swearing at me in Dutch?"

"I don't swear, Melvin. That line is from an old TV show your wife watches. *Brogan's Heroes,* or something like that. Now tell me, what is so important that it can't wait until morning?"

"Got me a preliminary autopsy report, that's what."

I ordered both ears to listen, and propped a pillow behind my back. "And?"

"The colonel was shot all right, but he'd been squeezed too."

"Squeezed?"

"Yeah, that's what I said. Squeezed, like a tube of toothpaste. The coroner said it was as though he'd been hugged or something—by somebody really strong. One rib was actually cracked. A few showed hairline fractures. Did you know he had a hairy chest, Yoder?"

There is no point in trying to blow out a trick birthday cake candle. "I never saw his chest, Melvin. But I must say, this sounds a little—are you sure that's what the coroner said?"

"Yoder, I'm not stupid. I know English when I hear it.

Anyway, we got ourselves a very interesting problem on our hands."

"I'll say. Was he shot before, or after, he was squeezed?"

"Uh—that's not why I'm calling, Yoder. We got to get ourselves a posse together and hunt down this thing."

"Thing?"

"Bigfoot, you idiot."

I sighed. "You're not telling me that you think it was an ape man who killed the colonel, are you? Please, Melvin, tell me you're not."

"Of course, Yoder. It's as obvious as that nose on your face."

"You don't need to be rude, dear. Ridiculous should be enough."

"It's all around town, Yoder, or haven't you heard?"

"I've heard. I've also heard about the tooth fairy."

"Yoder, I don't have time for this crap. Bigfoot is fact. You can read all about him on the Internet if you don't believe me. Anyway, you're wasting my time. We're supposed to be putting a posse together. I was thinking that Jewish fellow of yours—"

"His name is Gabriel. Dr. Gabriel Rosen, and he's about to become your brother-in-law."

"Yeah, whatever. You think he knows how to handle a gun?"

"I certainly hope not!"

"Israelis know how to handle guns. He one of them by any chance?"

"He's from Manhattan. Before that, Connecticut."

"Is that a yes or a no, Yoder?"

I'm sure there are doctors who hunt. Old Doc Shafor in Hernia used to hunt—before he mistook a gray SUV for an elephant. What he thought a pachyderm was doing in a Pennsylvania woods is beyond me. At any rate, I couldn't imagine the Babester killing anything but time, or some character in the frankly tepid murder mysteries he tries to get published.

"He knows how to handle a staple gun," I said. "Oh, and a hot glue gun."

There was enough silence to allow me to adjust my pillow, which has a bad habit of slipping sideways. What I heard next was either static or Melvin thinking.

"A staple gun is not going to penetrate all that fur," he said finally, "but if he uses Krazy Glue in that gun, maybe your boyfriend can get enough on that thing, so that it gets stuck to a tree when we're chasing him through the woods."

"And maybe tonight while you're sleeping, Susannah will roll the rock off your brain, so that it has a chance to grow." Okay, I admit it. That was not a Christian thing to say, but I'd asked to be delivered from temptation, not Melvin. That sin requires its own amendment.

There was a blessed moment of peace while Melvin processed my remark. "Yoder, you just insulted me, didn't you?"

I prayed for patience. To my astonishment, the Lord must have answered that prayer.

"Melvin," I heard myself say, "there is no such thing as Bigfoot. You need to find out whether the colonel was shot first and crushed later, or the other way around. It may have a bearing on this case."

"Yoder, you're wasting my time. I've got to get this posse together tonight, so we can start our search first thing in the morning. You think the Mishler brothers are up to joining?"

"They're both blind, dear. Look, Melvin, if you persist with this posse idea, you're going to shoot yourself in the foot—both literally and figuratively. When you don't find your monster, you're going to be the laughingstock of Bedford County, maybe even the Commonwealth of Pennsylvania. Then what will your chances be of winning a seat on the legislature? Because, Melvin dearest, if you don't stop this nonsense at once, I'm going to remove myself from the case.

Wash my hands like Pilate. Is that what you really want?"

If silence was truly golden—and it is not, I assure you—I could have become an even richer woman. Finally, the miserable mantis moved his mandibles enough to mutter something almost intelligible.

"What was that? I didn't quite hear you."

"Maybe you're right."

"What was that, dear?"

"Look, Yoder, keep doing what you're doing."

"Does that mean you won't be chasing hairy things in the woods?"

"Yeah."

"And that applies to the Stucky sisters," I said. Agnes and Polenta Stucky are Veronica's younger sisters—you know, the hairy gal who went off to Maine to be a logger.

"You don't think—" Melvin started to say, which proved that he obviously didn't.

"Don't even go there, dear. I've known them since they were babies. Besides, they'll shed again come spring. I'm going to hang up now and get some shut-eye. I suggest you do the same."

Melvin must have done what he was told, because he didn't call back. Sleep, however, was not forthcoming. No sooner did I settle my bun into my pillow than the entire inn shook. For a second I thought I was experiencing my first earthquake.

"And if I die before I wake," I cried, "I pray the Lord my soul to take." Of course it was silly of me to add that partial prayer, because I had yet to fall asleep. And if it was an earthquake, lying in bed was not the right thing to do.

The house shook again, and I realized that what I was hearing were thuds coming from upstairs. I sat up, my blood pressure having already reached a dangerous level.

"Take it easy, up there," I hollered. "This is a genuine restoration of a Pennsylvania Dutch farmhouse."

The noise continued. I threw on my modest terry robe, crammed my size elevens into pink bunny slippers, and thundered up my impossibly steep stairs. I do have an elevator, but it is for timid or incapacitated guests. It is certainly not for the impatient.

At the top of the stairs I had to wait until my breathing slowed before I could hear the next thump. It was not forthcoming, but there was the sound of voices coming from room 5. It is my best room, and the one where the colonel was killed. There had been official police tape across the door the last time I saw it, and no one but Melvin and his sidekick Zelda, or I, had the right to be in there.

I flew to the door and flung it open. Mr. Ivan Yetinsky and Miss Anne Thrope stood facing me, looking not the least bit surprised. In fact, they looked like the girl caught with her hand in the cookie jar, who knew her mama was coming but refused to drop the goodie and pretend she was innocent. She deserved that cookie, after all. If her mama hadn't been so busy doting on the new baby, and fixed the little girl a proper supper—well, I digress. My point is that the guilty couple didn't look that way.

"This room is off-limits," I roared.

"We're sorry; we didn't know." Ivan Yetinsky hung his massive head so low it was going to take a winch to get it into an upright position again.

"How could you not know? There's yellow tape on the door with black letters that quite clearly state this a crime scene, and you are not allowed to enter."

"Ha," Miss Anne Thrope barked. "There isn't any tape now."

"Of course there is." I turned to double-check. Imagine my consternation when I discovered she was right. "Well, there was! What did you do with it?"

"Me?"

"Yes, you. Or him. One of you took it down."

She produced a smirk worthy of a twelve-year-old girl. "For your information, Miss Yoder, it was your police chief who took it down."

"Melvin Stoltzfus?"

"He's the one."

"Are you sure?"

"Of course I'm sure. What do you take me for, an idiot?"

For the second time that day my prayer for patience was answered. "Describe him, please," I heard myself say.

"Well, let's see . . . looks like some kind of an insect. A giant cockroach, I'd say. Has these—"

"That's him," I cried, "but he looks like a mantis, not a roach. Never mind that, though. He's not working the case—I am."

She shrugged and muttered something that I couldn't hear, but that I am sure was derogatory. Only a minute ago, I would have felt my blood pressure soar. However, now that she'd confirmed my belief that Melvin was indeed an arthropod, I was inclined to feel kindly toward her.

"This matter of the tape aside, what were you two doing in this room?"

Ivan, without the benefit of a mechanical device, raised his head to speak. "Miss Yoder, we have a confession to make. We came in here to—"

"Make love," Miss Thrope practically shouted.

I reeled. "What did you say?"

She grabbed the big galoot's arm. "We're married, Ivan and I. It was us that you heard. If we disturbed you, I'm sorry. We'll try to keep the noise down."

I gave them the once-, twice-, and thrice-over. They were both fully clothed, and while Ivan was sweating profusely, neither of them appeared particularly rumpled. Although I would never share details of my personal life—i.e., my ill-fated marriage to the bigamist Aaron—I will say that our marital encounters at least produced a modicum of mess. Why, once even my bun came undone.

"You—you don't look like that's what you've been doing," I stammered. One would think that with feet as big as mine, thinking fast on them would be a breeze.

"That's because we like to jump around first. We pretend we're bonobos."

"I beg your pardon!"

"It's like a chimpanzee, only slightly smaller. I saw it on the Nature Channel. It's the most highly sexed primate there is. Members of the group settle all their conflicts that way."

Either Miss Thrope was telling the truth, or her brain and her tootsies had a far better connection than did mine. In any case, I didn't like what I'd heard.

"Nobody does the mattress mambo in this house unless they're married." The sentiment was mine, but the words came straight from my Presbyterian sister's mouth. She's a fallen Presbyterian, I might add, for whom the mambo—vertical or horizontal—is not a sin.

Miss Thrope resurrected her smirk. "We're not only lovers, but we're married."

"Since when? The colonel said nothing about that."

"We've been keeping it a secret, haven't we, Ivan?"

The shaggy head swayed from side to side. I took that as a yes.

"Why a secret, Miss Thrope? Or is your name per chance Yetinsky?"

"It's still Thrope," the cunning cook claimed. "I have to keep it for professional reasons. Anyway, George—the colonel, I mean—had this thing for me. If Ivan and I wanted to keep our jobs, well—we didn't dare tell him."

"Abraham pretended he wasn't married to Sarah,

dear. It caused a great deal of trouble for all concerned."

"Sorry about these friends of yours, Miss Yoder, but I can assure you that my marriage to Ivan has nothing to do with the colonel's murder."

"*Friends* of mine? I was talking about Sarah and Abraham in the Bible, for pity's sake!"

A smirk can get only so wide before it bisects the head, threatening decapitation. Miss Thrope's noggin was only millimeters away from falling on my hardwood floor.

"I don't read much," she said, "except for cookbooks. I'm afraid I don't have the time."

I took a deep breath. I'd really pushed the Good Lord on the patience bit.

"Speaking of time, dear, it's time you vamoosed. This is still a crime scene. As for what you claimed you were doing in here"—I shook a bony finger at each in turn—"even if you are married, I don't want to hear a thing."

Perhaps I was being hypocritical. When Aaron called me a hoot that time, he didn't mean I was funny; the Good Lord knows I don't have a funny bone in my body. At any rate, Ivan seemed to regard my admonishment as a dismissal, and he virtually bolted from the room. The snippety Miss Thrope, on the other hand, sashayed past me like she had all the time in the world. Had I not been a good Christian, one with five hundred years of pacifist blood in my veins, I'd have planted one of my black brogans on her beckoning backside.

Sleep, if it came that night, was fleeting, but I stayed in bed on principle. I got up with the first light and padded into the kitchen for a much-needed cup of tea, only to find the duplicitous duo in the kitchen eating. One might expect servants to be in the habit of rising before their masters, but this was ridiculous. If I was going to have a hot breakfast, I would have to drive the twelve miles into Bedford. Either that or have another go-around with Wanda Hemphopple at the Sausage Barn. I chose the drive.

But first I had to feed the chickens. I was up with them, after all. Later on in the morning, Mose, Freni's husband, would stop by to milk my two cows, Matilda and Betsey. I never keep the milk from these two because it is "raw," but Mose takes it home with him, adds it to his daily output, and ships the shebang off to get pasteurized. Although it has been suggested that I get rid of my cows, which will soon be too old to milk, I hang on to them for sentimental reasons. Papa was a dairy farmer, and I have grown to love the smell of sun-dried manure. Besides, these buxom bovines provide extra cash from time to time. Some of my more adventurous guests—not the likes of the colonel and his crew—are happy to pay a premium for the privilege of tapping teats, or even mucking out the barn.

As fond as I am of Betsey and Matilda, I enjoy my chickens even more. However, with the exception of Pertelote, my alpha hen, I wouldn't say I love them. These fowls have personalities just like people, but when they irritate me too much and put me in a foul mood, they're likely to end up in a stewpot.

It pleased me that morning to see that the giant cockerel Gabriel had given me appeared to be getting along well with his harem. In fact, when I entered the pen he was doing the mattress mambo with Mabel, one of my more promiscuous hens. While I do not permit such wanton behavior between my paying guests, I actually encourage it in my livestock. They're *real* animals, after all, and the Good Lord has given them blanket compensation.

After I'd fed the birds and given them fresh water—but not collected the eggs—I climbed into my Toyota Camry and buried the accelerator in the floor. I have been accused of having a lead foot, and I will not deny this, but I never drive so fast that I can't enjoy the scenery.

Ours is a beautiful part of the country that has always been, and I hope will always be, underappreciated. Our mountains may not qualify as such to folks hailing from the Rockies, but they are enough to impress visitors from Louisiana and Florida. To get to Bedford one must drive alongside Buffalo Mountain, which is a high, wooded ridge by any account. The road crosses Slave Creek just outside Hernia, and then follows it halfway to town. On the side opposite the creek and ridge are some of the tidiest farms you'll ever set eyes on, most of them Amish.

This is not a very wide valley and the farms back up to smaller mountains, the names of which do not appear on the map, but are known to the locals as Scotch Breath, Old Woman, Blue Ball, and my personal favorite, Cuckold's Knob. It has been suggested that the names for these four landmarks were all drawn from a single historical incident, but I fail to see the connection. At any rate, just after Cuckold's Knob one passes the church with thirty-two names, the Sausage Barn, and then bingo, one is on the turnpike, where the world is one's oyster—if one is inclined to eat slimy things. Which I'm not. My destination was the new Waffle House. I'd eaten there before, and must confess a fondness for their scrambled eggs with cheese and buttered raisin toast. Throw in some bacon—not too crisp—and coffee strong enough to revive the dead, and the grub there is every bit as good as Wanda's.

But the Waffle House is small, and being a party of one, I was bound to find myself sitting at the counter, perhaps even jammed between two burly truck drivers. This called for a little planning. While a man dining alone is just that, a woman alone in a restaurant is to be either pitied or scorned. Although I prefer scorn to pity, I have discovered that a book or newspaper can help to insulate me from either reaction. In fact a very good book, say one by JoAnna Carl, Nancy Martin, or Edie Claire, is even better than the company of a man. One can't blame a book for not holding up its half of the conversation, and I've never known one to belch.

Alas, I'd forgotten to bring any reading material with me, so I had no choice but to duck into the Bedford Newsstand. I was hoping to find a copy of the Sunday edition of the *New York Times* still available; we in the smaller burgs are quite content to get our news a day or so late. But my search for the *Times* was aborted the moment I walked in the door. For a second or two I couldn't believe my peepers.

18

There before me, like a nightmare in black and white, were at least a half dozen pictures of my mug. And I'm not talking about still lifes of my favorite coffee cup. These were photos of my face—which was understandably distorted in rage—and they were on the covers of the most insidious gossip rags. Some of the headlines read: BIGFOOT PREGNANT WITH FUTURE CONGRESSMAN'S BABY, MENNONITE MONSTER TERRORIZES HERNIA, SASQUATCH—THE FACE THAT COULD SINK A THOUSAND SHIPS.

But the worst of the lot was one simply titled A YETI NAMED YODER. "This fearsome creature," it began, "has been hiding out in a dump called the PennDutch Inn . . ."

"A dump!" I bellowed. "How dare they call it that!"

Unfortunately my ejaculation drew the attention of everyone in the store. Immediately to my left were a pair of teenage girls. What they were doing up at that hour is beyond me. At any rate, they looked at me, then at the row of my likeness, screamed like banshees on steroids, and ran out of the store. Meanwhile, a middle-aged man in an overcoat popped out of the stacks like a jack-in-the-box, took a gander at me, and popped back in again. I could hear him dial his cell phone behind the muscle magazines.

"You won't believe what just walked into this store," he whispered into the device. "And she's even uglier in person."

That did it. That hiked my hackles so high that I gave myself what Susannah would call a wedgie. For a moment I teetered on the threshold of yielding to temptation, that of pushing the entire rack over on the deserving man. But in the end I did the sensible thing and bought every single copy of the gossip rags containing my name or displaying my face. I had to make two trips to the checkout counter, behind which cowered a woman old enough to know better. When I paid for the pile of bile with a check, she had the temerity to ask me for an ID.

I kept several copies of each rag, figuring they might come handy should I decide to sue, but the rest I hurled into the nearest Dumpster. Any sensible person would have headed straight home from there and pulled the covers over her head, remaining in that quilted cocoon for the rest of her natural life. But I had still to eat breakfast, and the Waffle House beckoned. Besides, I'd been made a laughingstock before, and it's really not all that bad—once one has a chance to calm down a bit. It's the surprise element that is so distressing. As for my business suffering, the truth is, there is no such thing as bad publicity.

Holding my much publicized head high, I proceeded to the Waffle House and had a lovely and very peaceful breakfast. I even got a booth. The family that fled left a perfectly good side order of bacon behind, so I got extra with my meal. All I had to do was glare to get the waitress to treat me like royalty. And the cook—now, there was a picture of servitude. Although her knees were knocking the whole time, she came over and asked for an autograph when she was through frying up my order, which, by the way, she delivered. So good was the service that I made a mental note to revive the Bigfoot legend on at least a semiannual basis.

"If life hands you a lemon, make lemonade," Granny Yoder used to say. She had apparently had a lot of practice, because she looked like she'd spent her life sucking sour citrus. Nonetheless, hers was a point well-taken.

Too bad the kids at Hernia High/Middle School didn't see how noble I was behaving. School had not quite started, and a pair of hooligans hung from the windows like apes and hooted the minute I pulled in front of the school.

"Hoo, hoo, hoo! There she is! There's Bigfoot."

"She's Alison's mother."

"Alison who?"

"You know, that dorky new kid from Chicago."

"Yeah. Hoo, hoo. Hoo!"

I stomped one of my trademark feet. "She isn't from Chicago; she's from Minnesota."

"Minisoda, minisoda," they mocked. "Don't you know that here we say pop?"

Clearly, they'd never heard of the state. I said a quiet word of thanks that Freni had promised to try to get the child into the Amish school for a few days. Then I forged ahead like I own the place, which in a way, I do, as I pay more taxes than anyone else in the district. Out of the corner of my eye I could see the boys leap back through the classroom windows; no doubt they were running for their lives. A gal could get used to the power inherent in a good rumor.

There was no need to ask where the principal's office was. Its location hasn't changed in fifty years, and I spent my fair share of time in that miserable, dark, paneled room. Before you jump to conclusions, let me assure you that I was *not* a discipline problem. It is not my fault that others perceived me as such. Miss Quiring, in particular, could not stand the fact that I am prone to speak my mind. Many was the time she pulled me out of my seat by an ear and dragged me down the long halls to Mr. Reiger's office. Mr. Reiger had no compunctions about paddling girls, and when I got home Mama paddled me as well. It's no wonder I grew up to have a bony butt; my pleasing feminine fat was spanked off as fast as it could accumulate.

Thank heavens corporal punishment has long since been outlawed at Hernia High/Middle School. But there are still young people who misbehave, and they still wait their turn outside the principal's office. Just what their punishment will be, I haven't the slightest idea. Whatever it is, they wear the same looks of dread we did. One student in particular looked dreadful.

"Oh gawd!" she said when she saw me, and buried her face in her hands.

"Alison?"

My newly acquired daughter peeked through her fingers. "I'm busted, ain't I?"

I beckoned to her with a crooked finger. It was a gesture she didn't resist, especially since I am capable of pulling a loaded semitruck with said finger when properly motivated. Thank heavens the school secretary was out of the room at the moment. I'd rather face down a panzer division than Miss Odelphia Pringle.

Alison, who was second in the line for the "door of death," as we called it in our day, slid off the well-worn chair and sauntered over to me. The other five students in the antechamber watched in wide-eyed fascination, but their eyes were on me, not Alison.

"She doesn't smell so bad," a boy said. I didn't know his name, but his narrow-set eyes gave him away as a Swartzendruber.

"You must constantly be shaving," Roberta Kauffman said. This was a girl I'd known since birth, mind you.

"The paper said it takes her three hours." Mary Livingston didn't have room to talk; she was the only teenage girl I knew with a five-o'clock shadow.

"I most certainly do not shave," I shouted, for all the world to hear. And that, if you must know, is the truth. I have been blessed with a paucity of epidermal extensions in all but the cranial zone. I say "blessed" because Mama forbade me to shave what little I had. If the Good Lord wanted it removed, she said, He wouldn't have put it there in the first place.

"Of course she shaves," Alison cried. "She does it all the time. I seen her do it."

I would have clamped a hand over the child's mouth, but experience has taught me that she has no qualms about biting the hand that feeds her. Instead I pulled her out of the room and down the hallway to the teachers' lounge. Much to my surprise, Alison was a willing follower. She smiled and waved with her free arm to her openmouthed classmates.

This was the first time I'd set toe in the lounge, which I'd always regarded as a holy of holies. I'd imagined gossiping faculty lounging about on velvet fainting couches, nibbling on seedless grapes, or maybe bonbons, but definitely drinking tea from real china cups. It was both a shock and a relief to see that my tax dollars went to a pair of ripped brown Naugahyde sofas that were held together with gray duct tape, and a purple-and-green plaid armchair, the bottom of which scraped the floor. The only comestible to be seen was a half-eaten slice of cake stuffed in a cup next to an empty coffeepot. The cup, by the way, was Styrofoam.

There were teachers in the lounge, of course, but I gave them a glare guaranteed to make raisins out of grapes, and steered my charge to the least populated corner. It smelled strangely of gym socks—which might explain its unpopularity—but a lecturing mother can't afford to be picky.

"What are you doing here today, Alison? I thought Freni was going to get you into the Amish school."

"They have to be there at seven thirty. This don't start 'til eight thirty."

"But I thought you were looking forward to attending that school for a few days. Didn't you say Freni's neighbor kids go there?"

"Yeah, but I got to thinking that it was kind of a dumb idea, on account I ain't really Amish, and even Sarah and Rebecca get freaked by my holes, and they seen them a million times."

"Holes?" Surely the child was past that stage. I was four when I played doctor with the Stutzman twins. Thank heavens it was their mama who caught us, not mine.

"Ya know, like in my tongue and stuff, 'cause you won't let me wear my stud."

My sigh of relief stirred up a fresh wave of sock stench. "As well I shouldn't, dear. When you grow up to be a doctor or an astronaut, you'll thank me." I would have said "President," but the girl is without guile.

"I ain't gonna be no astronaut."

"Doctor, then. 'My daughter, the doctor.' Has a certain ring to it, don't you think?"

"Ain't gonna be no doctor neither."

"What, then? A nurse? A teacher?"

"Jimmy's wife."

I couldn't believe my ears. I jiggled a pinkie in each, just to make sure they were working.

"That seventeen-year-old? The one whose car can't start?"

"He'll have him a new car by then," she said, and stuck her lower lip a full inch in front of her face.

Arguing with a teenager, even one just barely on the cusp like Alison, is like running blindfolded through a maze. No doubt about it, she was blindfolded as well, but she had still managed to lead me far away from my original agenda.

"Alison, why were you in the principal's office?"

"I wasn't. I was outside."

"Whatever," I said, and rolled my eyes. This is a trick I learned from Susannah, and it annoys her to no end. However, it didn't seem to have the same effect on Alison. "So what were you doing *outside* the principal's office? And don't you dare say 'waiting.' "

"All right, all right, ya don't have to get so huffy. He wanted to yell at me for making a little money, that's all. And I'm like, I only made one hundred and sixty dollars, so what's the big deal?"

I gasped, which was a huge mistake. You can be sure the next time I set foot in the teachers' lounge, I would take an assortment of air fresheners with me. Even a hunk of Limburger cheese would be a vast improvement.

"This doesn't have to do with Bigfoot, does it?"

She nodded.

"Alison," I said, trying to keep the pride out of my voice, "how could you?"

"It was your idea, Mom. You said five dollars was too little, so I drew up these tickets on the back of some papers—Freni don't own a copy machine, ya know—and was selling them for ten bucks when I got busted."

"Sixteen kids paid to see me?"

She nodded again. "You're hot stuff, Mom. Of course last night when I made up them tickets, I didn't know you'd be on the cover of all them magazines. Could have sold a lot more if I had. Why didn't ya tell me?"

"I didn't know myself. Usually it takes a few days for those rags to come out. Someone must have been standing by the presses, with one foot in the door of a jet plane. Anyway, those girls yesterday—the ones you brought to the house—they go to this school?"

"Nah. They're from Bedford."

"Then how do you know them?"

"They're Jimmy's cousins. I seen them over at Jimmy's house."

"You what?" At that point, every faculty member's head in the room swiveled in our direction. What were they doing loafing about at that hour, even if they weren't nibbling on grapes or bonbons?

"Is everything all right over there?" someone asked.

"Go pull some ears," I hissed.

They returned to their tasks, which, come to think of it, looked a lot like grading papers. I turned to my problem child.

"When were you at Jimmy's house?"

"When the youth group met at his house for the barbecue Sunday before last."

I slapped my forehead, almost knocking myself over. Too bad I didn't. Maybe a fall would have knocked some sense into me.

"You mean Jimmy Mast?" Much like the public high school, Beechy Grove Mennonite Church combines its junior and senior groups.

"Yeah. Ya know him?"

"I know his mama."

"Ya ain't gonna call her, are ya?"

"Well, I have to talk to someone in that family. I will not have you dating a seventeen-year-old. Or *anyone* for that matter."

I expected an outburst. But instead Alison seemed to implode. "Oh Mom, please don't talk to no one."

"I'm sorry, dear, but I have to."

"No, you don't, 'cause I don't hardly know Jimmy Mast."

"But you said—"

"I was just hoping, that's all."

"Hoping for what?"

"Don't ya get it? I was hoping Jimmy would ask me out on account of he's real cute. 'Course he didn't—and never mind. Ain't nobody gonna pay me no attention in this stupid shoot-hole of a school." She actually used a term much worse than that.

"Alison!"

"Sorry, Mom, but it just slipped out. Anyway, that's why I asked them girls over. And that's why I made up that story about you being Bigfoot. Don't ya see?"

"Well, uh—I'm afraid I don't, dear." Perhaps if the Good Lord had given me the opportunity to raise a child from birth, I'd understand the machinations of the newly pubescent mind.

"Because I'm lonely," she cried. "That's why!"

Defying five hundred years of inbred standoffishness, I flung my bony arms around the child. "There, there," I said.

To my astonishment, Alison hugged me back. Her arms encircled me for a good three seconds before she pulled away with a jerk.

"So," she said, rubbing her sleeve across her eyes, "you're cool with this, right? I mean, you ain't gonna say nothing to Jimmy or his mom, right?"

"Right."

"And you ain't mad about the Bigfoot thing."

"I'm not angry, but you have to stop selling tickets, *and* you have to give the money back."

She stamped a foot. It was a pitiful gesture; Susannah and I can both do a lot better. Either we were going to have to give her lessons, or she was going to have to grow a whole lot more foot.

"Dang," she said, but didn't sound all that upset.

I walked her back to the "door of death." She was now in first place, and suddenly seemed very small.

"Don't worry, dear," I said. "I'm not going to get you off, but I will make sure Mr. Middledorf keeps an open mind."

Although the intransigent children waiting in Principal Middledorf's outer office had been unattended when I'd snagged Alison, the school secretary was now back on duty. The prune-faced Odelphia Pringle had been school secretary when I was a girl. In fact rumor had it—and this one I did start—she'd dated George Washington. In the story it was George who broke off the relationship, unable to stand the woman's acerbic personality. Another, more credible source than I claims quinine was invented when Odelphia stooped to donate blood in the war to end all wars.

But it is undeniable that the secretary is ancient. Her hair has been dyed so many times over the centuries that the follicles have been fooled into producing pigment again. Her skin has not been so lucky, and a wag named Mags once quipped that Odelphia had a face only a shar-pei could love. In a more perfect world the bitter woman would have long since been forced to retire, and might even now be pushing up daisies—wilted ones to be sure. But since everyone in the district has at one time or another been under her glare, no one has the nerve to make her step down.

It has only been since my ill-fated marriage to Aaron that I have become bold enough to maintain full bladder control while looking the woman in the granite pebbles she uses for eyes.

"Well, well, if it isn't Magdalena Yoder," she snarled. With each word her wrinkled cheeks expanded and contracted, like a beige paper fan.

"It is indeed me," I said. I didn't pause, however, but strode boldly to the principal's door.

"You can't go in there," Odelphia croaked. "You don't have an appointment."

"Sure I do." I rapped on the door with the knuckles that are the envy of woodpeckers.

"You do not have an appointment. I forbid you to go in there."

Thanks to all the trouble I'd seen in the intervening years, the voice that had once caused me to wet myself sounded about as threatening now as the droning of a bee. "Try and stop me, dear," I said sweetly.

The collective gasp from the captive students stirred

decades of dust. Hernia High has never had a janitor worthy of his broom.

I waited until it was safe to breathe and rapped again. "Herman, it's Magdalena. I need to see you at once."

"Just a minute." The reply was so muffled I began to worry that maybe the previous delinquent had bound and gagged the principal. Or perhaps the current troublemaker was holding him hostage. One would think that Odelphia would be wise to a situation such as this, if one was the sort to believe that pigs could fly, and politicians told the truth.

At any rate, if indeed the principal's mouth was taped shut, it was nothing short of a life-threatening situation. Especially if he caught a whiff of what was cooking in the cafeteria kitchen. I had no choice, therefore, but to barge in on an errand of mercy.

Imagine my surprise when I saw the principal alone and unfettered. Imagine my shock when I saw that he was staring at a computer screen, upon which cavorted naked and nubile young women.

19

He jerked his attention away from the ladies, and when he saw me, his jaw dropped so low I thought it had become unhinged.

"W-what are you doing here?"

"Observing how my tax dollars are spent."

"This isn't what you think."

"Oh really? For your information, Herman, I've looked at myself a couple of times in a mirror. I know what a naked woman looks like."

To be honest, these naked ladies looked nothing like me. Their limbs were just as skinny, to be sure, but these beauties had silicone supplements. A few of the frolicking females were, in fact, so well endowed they looked in need of pushcarts, or perhaps brassieres equipped with wheels, should they ever contemplate serious locomotion. In a word, every one of them was deformed.

"Looks painful," I said, "not that I would know."

He fumbled with a button, but managed to shut the machine off. "I was doing research, Magdalena."

"On what? How to get fired?"

"But you can't do that."

"Not by myself, I can't. But as a member of the school

board—the one with the biggest mouth—well, we'll just see about that."

Quicker than double-geared lightning, Herman knocked over his chair and lunged in my direction. For a second I thought he meant to grab me. In a million years—or even just Odelphia Pringle's lifetime—I wouldn't have expected him to literally throw himself at my feet.

"Please, Magdalena. You have to believe me. I really was doing research."

Although the Good Lord admonishes us not to judge, I'm sure He means we shouldn't do so without all the facts. Therefore, by gathering such facts, we become obedient disciples, and that is, of course, a good thing.

I closed the door behind me. "Herman, you have one minute. Starting now." I looked at the second hand on my watch.

"Uh—yeah—uh—one of the students, Harlan Blough, says he acts up all the time because he gets his instructions from the Devil. Off the Web. He gave me the Web site name, you see, and when I typed it in—well, there was this porno. I had just gotten the site up when you barged in."

I am the first to admit that I get my exercise from jumping to conclusions, but at least I'm fit. There was, perhaps, a minuscule chance that Herman Middledorf was telling the truth. I say that because the one time I got on the 'net, at Susannah's, I accidentally stumbled on a site that made it undeniably clear that all men are *not* created equal.

Herman must have heard the wheels of justice turning slowly in my cranium. An empty space that large does create quite an echo.

"Harlan Blough, you say?"

He nodded. "And I don't know if you had a chance to see, Magdalena, but those were not young girls on the screen. They were mature women."

I had seen that much. It was good to know. If one day I woke up without any morals, and the name of a good plastic surgeon, I too could get a job cavorting in cyberspace.

"I'll talk to Harlan," I said. "You can count on that. And if he doesn't corroborate your story, not only will I tell the school board, but I'll have a chat with Odelphia Pringle as well."

Herman smiled, which all but confirmed his innocence. "If you do that, call the paramedics first."

"In case she has a heart attack?"

"No, to put together what's left of me. So, Magdalena, what's really on your mind?"

"The late Colonel Custard."

He nodded. "Heard about that. Heard too about you calling yourself Bigfoot. You think that was wise?"

"They were asking for it," I wailed.

"Perhaps. But what about the effect it has on Alison? The rumors keep growing, you know. First I heard that you slept with her uncle Melvin—"

"Not technically an uncle, and definitely not true."

He smiled patiently until I was quite done interrupting. "Now I understand there are several eligible bachelors in town who are dying to meet you."

I frowned. "Herman, not you?"

If he'd recoiled any faster his head would have spun off his neck and done irreparable damage to the framed portrait of his predecessor, Delbert Dick.

"No offense, Magdalena, but I don't go in for the gangly type."

We were past due for a change of subject. "You inquired about Alison. Well, I think she's actually proud of it. My notoriety, I mean—my status as someone worthy of being quoted. In her eyes that's like being a celebrity. Besides, I'm not really the hairy honey of Hernia some make me out to be."

"It's her self-esteem I'm worried about, Magdalena. She hasn't been adjusting all that well."

"Sure she has. The child's as happy as a lark."

"She's crying out for attention. And those rings of hers aren't the right kind of attention, I assure you."

"Rings?" It was one of those questions one asked when one unequivocally knew the answer, like "Oh, is that your toe I stepped on?"

"Those body piercing rings. You know she wears them, right?"

I gulped. "Certainly. But I make her take them out whenever she does, and she never goes to school with them in."

"Is that so?" Herman Middledorf yanked a metal desk drawer open and retrieved a spaghetti sauce jar. He shook it and then spread the contents out beside his computer like they were jacks and a ball. For a second I half expected him to challenge me to a game.

But alas, I recognized the pile of metal—at least some of it. These were the bits of stainless steel that seemed to pin my foster daughter together. There were even a few chains that I hadn't seen before, but which in context made perfect sense. Connect tab A to tab B and then . . .

"Magdalena, are you denying that these are Alison's?"

"No, although I've never seen that neon ball that looks like it would glow in the dark. Where do you suppose that will go—" I slapped my hand to my mouth. "I'll try harder."

"See that you do. Every morning I send her straight in to see the school nurse. The next day it happens all over again. The child must have brought a trunk load of the stuff with her from Minnesota."

"I'm so sorry, I'll put a stop to this. You can count on that."

"I'm sure I can, because if I can't, I'm afraid I will have to expel the girl."

"I see," I said through lips taut enough to slice boiled eggs.

"And don't think you can make me change my mind because of what you just saw on my computer. I already explained that."

"So you did. Perhaps you'd care to explain a little more."

He stared at me like Freni would gape at a head of fresh broccoli. "Huh?"

"Why were you so vocal at the council meeting? I should think that from your point of view, growth would be good for Hernia. A larger tax base means more and better qualified teachers. I know the biology teacher will be happy—sewing up those pig fetuses for reuse every year has got to be a drag."

He grimaced. "I help him do it every summer. It's really not so bad."

"But more funds would mean a new copy machine. From what I hear Odelphia still can't get all the marks off it, thanks to Donald Sidewaller trying to take a picture of his derriere."

"Magdalena, you don't get it. Like I said at the meeting, new kids mean new ways. Some of those new ways are just superficial, like the body jewelry your Alison wears. But believe me, next we'll be dealing with pregnancy, drugs, maybe even AIDS. Is this what you want for our community?"

I'd been looking him in the eyes, but had to suddenly look away. The man was crying, for Pete's sake. Tears the size of olives were forcing their way through stretched ducts. The once middle-American face of Herman Middledorf was red and contorted beyond recognition.

I let him blubber for a minute or two. Trying to get coherent words from him at this stage was a waste of both of our times. I even lent him a wad of semiclean tissues from my left bra cup, the side of me least in need.

Herman used the tissues well. When he was quite through blowing and honking, a small flock of Canada geese had gathered in the school yard—but I digress.

"Herman, dear, what on earth has gotten you so worked up? Oh—you really were using that computer for naughty purposes, weren't you?"

He shook his head vigorously. "Honestly, I wasn't! Magdalena, it's just that I'm afraid."

"Afraid of what?"

Before he could respond he required some of the tissues from my right cup. I was happy to comply. One hates to be unbalanced.

"Magdalena, I'm Herman Middledorf."

"What's your point?"

"I'm a nobody—just a principal of a small southern Pennsylvania secondary school. We have grades seven through twelve under one roof, for crying out loud."

"Again, dear, what's your point?"

"If that hotel had been built, if that led to a population explosion like everyone has been predicting, then we'd need a new high school, right?"

"Quite possibly—oh, I see. You were afraid you'd have no place in this city of the future. Am I right?"

"I wasn't made for big cities, Magdalena. I wasn't made for high-stress jobs. I'm Herman Middledorf, remember?"

"Indeed, I do." My better nature felt an impulse to reach out and hug him, to tell him that I thought he was capable of any challenge the Good Lord threw his way. It is not my fault that five hundred years of Swiss inbreeding left me incapable of physically touching him, and barely capable of uttering words of comfort. Still, I did my best.

"There, there," I said. "We don't even have to think about such a thing now that the colonel is dead."

He sniffed back a glob of something that could have buried Pittsburgh. "Yeah, you're right. Thanks for coming by, Magdalena. I feel better just talking to you."

I said good-bye and stepped back into the antechamber, where Alison's eyes screamed a question at me. I gave her a thumbs-up before sauntering over to Odelphia Pringle's desk.

Any fear I'd had of the woman, I'd left behind with the facial tissues. In fact, she looked afraid of me.

I leaned over her desk so I wouldn't have to shout into the ears that had heard baby Moses gurgle among the bulrushes.

"Check in on Herman now and then, dear. Take a special peek at his computer screen. If you see anything that looks in the least bit naughty, call me."

She gave me a quizzical look, but said nothing. Then I turned on my narrow, but hairless, heels and literally skipped from the office.

Thanks to my persistence, and Herman's outburst, there was one less suspect on my list. But two steps out into the hallway, I tripped by snagging my right heel on my left big toe and fell flat on my face. Fortunately, I wasn't hurt. However, a superstitious Magdalena might have taken this unexpected spill as a portent of things to come.

20

Lemon-Scented Flan

Whether it's flan in Spain and Mexico, crème caramel renversée in France, or caramel custard in America, it's all the same soothing egg custard cloaked with an amber caramel sauce. This recipe can easily be halved.

1½ cups sugar
¼ cup water
4 cups milk
1 2-inch piece of vanilla bean, split and cut in half

1 2-inch strip of lemon zest
4 large eggs
6 large egg yolks

Preheat oven to 350° F.

Combine 1 cup sugar and the water in a heavy saucepan. Caramelize the sugar over medium-high heat until light golden. Immediately pour into an ungreased 1½-quart mold, quickly tilting the mold to completely cover the bottom and sides. Set aside to cool.

In another pan, combine the milk, remaining sugar, vanilla bean, and lemon zest. Bring to a boil over medium-high heat; lower the heat and simmer for about 15 minutes, or until the milk reduces to about 3½ cups.

Set aside to cool. Remove the vanilla bean and lemon zest.

Gently beat together the eggs and yolks. With a wooden spoon, stir in the cooled milk just until blended. Strain into the mold and bake in a bain-marie for 50 to 60 minutes, or until a sharp knife inserted near the center comes out clean.

Let cool on a rack for 1 hour. Cover and refrigerate until well chilled, at least 4 hours. To unmold, quickly dip the mold in hot water, then invert onto a large serving dish. Slice, and spoon some sauce over each portion.

SERVES 10 TO 12

21

A hunch from a woman is worth two facts from a man. Trust me on this. While I don't go in for fortune-telling and crystal balls, I believe we should each listen to our inner voice—just as long as what it's telling us is not a sin.

When I left the high school my inner voice was shouting at me. "Go back to the inn, Magdalena! Go back now!"

But I had no reason to return home. I'd fed the chickens, Alison was safely in school, and I certainly had not left the stove on. Lollygagging about the inn would be a waste of time, especially since I wasn't expecting any new guests to fill my coffers. Now *that* is a sin. Nevertheless, I pointed my car in the direction of home, and even though it didn't make a lick of sense, it felt right.

With no particular reason for being there, I ambled into the kitchen, poured myself a tall glass of fresh milk, and sat at the scarred wooden table to drink it. I eat very little meat, and my cholesterol is as low as Melvin's IQ, so I am one of the lucky few who can indulge in the full-fat version without a twinge of guilt. Milk with a blue ring is not for me.

Mama used to scold me if I blew bubbles in my milk. For that very reason I sipped my milk through a straw, stopping every now and then to fill the glass with froth. It was during one of my bubble breaks that I heard the strange sound.

At first I thought it was a cat meowing. A Siamese cat, to be exact. That breed has a loud, distinctive voice, and there is no mistaking it for another. As jumping to conclusions is my best sport, I immediately pinned this one on Mama. Believe me, Yoder women are quite capable of interfering from beyond the grave.

"Okay," I wailed, "I won't blow any more bubbles, but no fair making cat noises. You know how much it hurt to give up Little Freni when I took in Alison."

Mama showed no mercy and the meowing continued. To spite her, I blew even harder—until the most fantastic thought permeated my pumpkin head. Perhaps that really wasn't Mama I heard, but an actual cat. Could it possibly even be Little Freni? After all, I read stories of felines with amazing homing instincts. One, I think, had traveled a thousand miles to rejoin its human family. In contrast, Little Freni's new home was only a few miles away.

My mood shifted abruptly from self-pity to utter joy. "Little Freni," I cried, "I'm on my way!" I knocked over the chair in my haste and thundered up my impossibly steep stairs in record time.

At the top landing I had to pause for a few seconds, because my breathing was so loud I couldn't hear my baby's meows. When I heard them again, I had no doubt they were coming from Miss Anne Thrope's room.

By now I fully expected to scoop a furry bundle of joy into my arms and smother it with kisses. Therefore I was stunned when the following scene greeted my eager eyes.

The room looked like I'd rented it to a fraternity party for the night. Everything was topsy-turvy. My genuine imitation mahogany veneer bedside table was on the floor, the Pottery Barn Chinese vase lamp smashed to smithereens. Even the sheets and quilt had been pulled off the bed.

Sitting cross-legged on the floor was the gentle giant Ivan Yetinsky. In his massive arms he cradled the limp body of Miss Anne Thrope. The man was beside himself with grief and was sobbing so hard I feared he might be holding back Lake Meade with his bulging eyes. Should one of them pop, I'd be swept back down the stairs like a piece of driftwood.

"What happened?" I demanded.

He burbled something unintelligible; it was barely more than a meow.

I approached and searched for a pulse. As I suspected, there was none.

I decided to give Ivan a moment of privacy and called my idiot brother-in-law from the downstairs phone. I realize that is an uncharitable way to refer to him, but someday when I'm retired and have nothing else to do, I'll repent of that sin. Melvin actually made me spell the word "dead" over the phone. Then he had the audacity to tell me there was no *a* in it.

After hanging up on the doofus, I hoofed it back upstairs to comfort Ivan. I should have remembered that praying mantises have wings and are capable of flight, because I barely had time to trot out the "there, there's," when I heard the squeal of tires on Hertzler Road, followed by the ping of gravel in my driveway. Seconds later Melvin and his sidekick squeezed through the door together like children called for dessert.

There is no limit to the duo's ineptness. They both had their pistols drawn, and from Zelda's free hand dangled a pair of cuffs.

"Freeze!" Melvin shouted.

"Don't be ridiculous, Melvin," I said quietly.

"Stand back, Yoder."

"But Melvin—"

"You have the right to remain silent. You have the right to—"

"At least a modicum of common sense?" I asked.

Because Melvin's eyes operate independently of each other, he is incapable of a full-strength glare. Still, he gave me the fifty percent job with his left orb.

"Do you want that I should arrest you too, Yoder?"

"On what grounds?"

"Obstruction of justice."

"How am I obstructing justice?"

"By yapping, Yoder." He waved his gun at Ivan like it was a laser pointer. "The man is as guilty as Cain. Look, he's still holding the victim."

"Melvin—dear," I said, struggling with my tongue, "if Mr. Yetinsky had wanted, he could have bolted when he saw me. In fact, he could have killed me too. That way there wouldn't have been any witnesses."

Zelda teetered forward. "This kind of thing happens all the time, Magdalena. Why just this morning I was reading in the paper about a woman in Philadelphia who killed her husband, called the police, and then sat with the body until they arrived."

"Yes, but *I* called the police, not Mr. Yetinsky."

She frowned, sending flakes of her makeup floating to the floor. "You can be so particular, Magdalena."

"I think the correct word is 'responsible.' "

"Whatever."

"Yoder," Melvin said through clenched mandibles, "either shut up or leave the room."

There was no sense in trying to reason with them. In general two heads may be better than one, but even a cabbage could outwit Chief Stoltzfus and his sidekick. Not having a cabbage with me, I decided to appeal to Melvin's higher authority. But first I addressed my higher authority and said a silent prayer on the deceased's behalf.

Susannah and Melvin live in a modest aluminum house on the south side of Hernia, as far away from me as one can get and still reside within the town limits. This is a new neighborhood of blue-collar folks, and bears the lofty but nonsensical name of Foxcroft. In my dictionary a croft is either a small, enclosed field adjoining a house, or a small farm worked by tenants. It has nothing to do with rows of identical homes on postage-stamp lots.

As usual, it took me forever to find the right house. All the streets have foxy names and her number, 66, is so small one needs a pair of good binoculars to spot it from the street. Alas, I'd neglected to bring my pair with me. I made two complete circuits each of Foxhaven, Foxmoor, and Foxmoss before spotting a telltale strip of red at one of the windows. Susannah's living room drapes are the color of fresh blood, and the neighborhood association made her line them with white. But Susannah, being who she is, keeps one edge turned outward so that a sliver of red shows—*if* you are approaching from the right direction. This is not just an act of defiance, but helps Melvin and Susannah find their home as well.

I found Susannah at home, wrestling with a bolt of cloth (at least that's what it looked like to me), but it took only a second for my sister's thoughts to turn from fabric to jewelry. Not the most subtle of folks, she feigned blindness.

"Get that away from me, Mags. I'll tell the truth—just don't shine that light in my eyes."

"Very funny, Susannah." I wiggled my ring finger, sending rainbows dancing across the small room. "Isn't it beautiful?"

"If you like that gaudy sort of thing."

That from a woman who wears lime green plastic sandals with her fuchsia chiffon. I should have known she'd be jealous, and broken news of the engagement ring to her gently. The microscopic diamond Melvin gave her has so many inclusions it looks more like an old dental filling than a gem.

"It's a little large," I conceded.

"A little? Sarah Hughes couldn't even skate across that thing without getting tired. Mags, you know you're going to get flak from the church ladies."

That was for sure. Mama hadn't even been allowed a ring with a stone in her day.

"What can I say, Susannah, Gabe is a very generous man."

"I'll say. Once I saw a ring just like that in a jewelry store in Pittsburgh. It cost over twenty thousand dollars."

"Get out of town!" I was shocked, but pleased as well. I had the feeling Gabe could afford a ring like that, but he could have gotten away with much less.

"Susannah, do you think Mama would disapprove— if she were here today, I mean?"

"She's probably turning over in her grave right now."

I found myself smiling. "Now, tell me about these bolts of cloth. What did you do, rob a fabric store?" There were at least a dozen unrolled bolts of cloth draped over the couch, living room chairs, and dining room suite. If I hadn't known any better, I would have thought I was staring at the contents of an exploded fabric store.

"I got these from the Material Girl up in Bedford."

"You bought all these?"

"Don't be silly, Mags. They're on loan until I make up mind."

"About what?"

"A new outfit to wear to Melvin's inaugural dinner."

"He's running for President now?"

"No, silly. But when he's elected to the legislature,

we're going to have a special dinner. We're even going to invite you and Gabe."

"How very generous of you."

Sarcasm is wasted on Susannah. "Of course, you're going to get a new outfit too, right?"

"I am?"

"No offense, Mags, but you still dress like Mama. And those shoes—they're like major clodhoppers."

"They're comfy," I sniffed. Until Gabe complained, I wasn't about to trade comfort for fashion.

"Well, I'm wearing black, velvet-covered stilettos. Got them for only $12.99 at Payless. But I can't decide which of these bolts is prettier, this hot pink silk or that royal blue over there on the chair."

"Definitely the royal."

"But it's polyester."

"There's nothing wrong with that—especially if you have a little cotton mixed in with it to help it breathe." Although frankly, Susannah's outfits don't need any help breathing. The diaphanous material she generally uses has less substance than gauze, and the pulsating pooch in her bosom offers ample proof that life can exist within her ensembles.

"You don't get it, Mags. If I'm going to be a congressman's wife, I need to set a good example."

"Your point, dear?"

"I was reading this article about the endangered polyester bush. They grow only on Madagascar, you know, and polyester seedpods—that's where they get polyester from—can only be harvested from wild bushes. The article said there has been a bad drought for the last three years, and unless—"

"Susannah, dear, there is no such thing as a polyester bush. Polyester is made from esters, which—"

"Mags, I was yanking your chain. Just like you were doing to those reporters."

•

I swallowed. It was not a mouthful of guilt, but surprise. Who knew she'd even heard of Madagascar?

"Ah, the Bigfoot articles," I said. "Has Melvin seen them?"

"No. But when he does, you know he'll go ballistic."

"You're right. When I saw him a few minutes ago he was merely his usual incompetent, irritating self."

Susannah has thrown a few tantrums in my presence over the years. The standard procedure is for her eyes to roll back while she stamps her feet and waves her arms like a symphony conductor. Often there's a good deal of cursing involved—thanks to that Presbyterian first husband of hers. Now, however, she was standing with both feet on the ground, her arms to her sides, and her irises fully exposed. When she spoke it was in hushed tones that sent chills up my bony spine.

"That bit about him being the father of your—I mean, Bigfoot's—child was going too far."

"It was a joke, dear. No one really believes those rags."

"Like I said, Mags, you still don't get it. This could lose Melvin the election if people don't take him seriously."

It was touching to see my baby sister stand by her man, but what she didn't get was the fact that no one with a lick of sense took Melvin Stoltzfus seriously. If something strange got in the district's water and caused the people to vote my brother-in-law into office, I would have to leave the country. Perhaps Alec Baldwin or Kim Basinger would take me in.

With a sinking heart, I realized there was no point in trying to dissuade Susannah of the notion that Melvin was truly a viable candidate. The only thing I could do was to respect the fact that she loved and believed in my nemesis. What really mattered was that we maintained our close bond as sisters.

"I'll apologize to Melvin next time I see him, dear.

And if you really insist, I'll issue a statement to a reputable paper retracting that love child bit, although frankly, it could backfire. Folks tend to remember key words, rather than the truth." I reached into my purse, which is a plain brown leather bag, like the Good Lord intended us to have, and pulled out my checkbook. "I'd say five thousand dollars' worth of positive ads will go a long way to taking folks' minds off that silly little prank of mine, wouldn't you?"

"Oh, Mags—"

"Okay, you drive a hard bargain. I'll make it ten, but not a penny more."

Susannah squealed like a pig that had been hugged too hard—not that I've done a whole lot of that, mind you—and threw herself into my arms. The woman is every bit as skinny as me, so it wasn't her weight that knocked me over, but the shock of such intimate contact. She lost her balance as well, and whereas I landed on my back, she landed on my front. Shnookums, the pitiful pooch she carries in her bra, was squished between us like the filling between two halves of an Oreo. Unlike Mama and Papa, who had the decency to die when squished between the milk tanker and the semi-trailer filled with state-of-the-art running shoes, the mangy mutt was merely enraged.

The minuscule monster weighs all of two pounds—one of which is sphincter muscle; the other, teeth. Both ends got right down to work, and I felt like I was under attack from a sulfur-belching piranha. Were it not for my sturdy Christian underwear, my meager bosom would have been as endangered as the polyester bushes of Madagascar.

"Help! Help!"

Fortunately Susannah has quick reflexes, especially if the situation involves her little precious. She rolled off to one side and, after ascertaining that the hound from Hades was essentially unharmed, burst into laughter.

"I fail to see what's so funny," I sniffed.

"You, Mags. If someone even gets close to touching you, you go bonkers. I pity Gabe on your wedding night."

I leaped to my feet. "That will not be a problem."

"Are you sure? Because if there's anything you need to know—"

"There isn't." I couldn't believe I was having this conversation with anyone, much less a flesh and blood relative. Mama had not been alive when I'd married Aaron, which, come to think of it, was just as well. When I reached puberty and thought I was bleeding to death, she muttered something about a monthly seed that needed to be fertilized, or else the body rejected it. That was it, no mention of either birds or bees. Just seeds—none of which I ever found. No telling what she would have had to say about the deed itself.

Susannah struggled to her feet. Fifteen feet of filmy fabric is hard to navigate. "Sis, you're not mad, are you?"

"I still plan to donate the ten grand to his campaign, if that's what you mean. But I do want something a little extra in return." The truth is, I was only now getting around to the purpose of my visit.

"What do you want, Mags?"

"I want you to talk some sense into that husband of yours. He's arrested an innocent man. You talk about bad publicity—if Mr. Yetinsky sues for false arrest, Melvin's going to have a hard time getting a job cleaning public rest rooms."

"They can do that? Sue for false arrest, I mean?"

"If he had no grounds, and he knew it. Susannah, your dear sweet hubby just wants to make an arrest. He's not even thinking. Last night he called and said he was organizing a posse to track down Bigfoot."

"But he didn't, did he?"

"That's because I talked him out of it. Susannah, you

have got to talk him into releasing Mr. Yetinsky. The man is grieving, for crying out loud."

"Mags, you know how Melvin can be."

"Indeed, I do. The man's a—" I put a cork in it. My baby sister looked like she was about to cry. As hard as this may be to believe, I have never, in all her thirty-six years, seen her shed tears. Even as a baby, she screamed for her bottle, but she never cried. "Susannah, is something wrong?"

She nodded as a single tear etched a channel through her makeup.

22

"Susannah, what is it?" I would have taken her into my arms, despite my inbred inhibitions, but I remembered the mutt in her Maidenform.

"He doesn't love me anymore." It came out as a wail, which was unfortunate, because the cur took up her cry of anguish. I don't know what key they were aiming for, but they both missed. Within seconds dogs around the neighborhood were howling, and even one car alarm responded.

I waited patiently until the din had abated enough that I could hear myself speak. "What do you mean he doesn't love you? That arthropod—I mean, man—worships the ground you walk on."

"Not anymore. All he thinks about now is this stupid campaign. It's gotten to the point where sometimes I find myself hoping he loses."

"Nonsense. You want to be a congressman's wife. You were even making plans to redecorate the White House someday, right?"

"I was, but not anymore. I just want my dear sweet hubby to be the man I married."

"Have you shared that with him?"

"Mags, you know I can't do that. Melvin is so sensitive."

"Like a stone," I muttered. It wasn't meant to be heard.

"He really is, Mags. He suffers from low self-esteem."

I prayed that the Good Lord would send an angel to keep my mouth shut, just like He did for Daniel in the lions' den. The danger here wasn't from big cats, but from big feet. Mine.

"Would you mind explaining?" I said, choosing each word carefully.

"It's all Elvina's fault."

"His mother?"

"His whole life she's never done anything but criticize him. He was never smart enough, never good enough—she even criticized the way he looked, which is totally unfair. My cutesy-wutesy pudding pie can't help it that he looks just like his daddy."

I had to think about that. I guess there was a vague resemblance, although I barely remember Orlando Stoltzfus. The man died the year Melvin was born. The official story is that he suffered a heart attack at the dinner table, but I've heard from more than one source that he drowned, facedown, in a bowl of vegetable soup, having fallen asleep during one of Elvina's interminable lectures. In fact, I heard this story from Freni, who just happens to be best friends with the woman.

"Elvina would be hard to live with," I conceded.

"You know that story about my Melkins being kicked in the head by a bull?"

"The one he tried to milk?"

"She started that."

"His own mother?"

"The ice cream story too."

"Yes, in which he sent a gallon of ice cream by UPS to his favorite aunt."

"It wasn't UPS; it was Priority Mail. Besides it was

wintertime, not summer like she says. Not all of it melted."

I shoved several bolts of cloth off the nearest chair and threw my lanky frame into it. Feeling sorry for the mantis was going to take some getting used to. Kind of like feeling sorry for the flu virus.

"What can I do to help, Susannah? Besides lay off him—not that I pick on him first, mind you."

"Make him lose."

"I beg your pardon?"

"The election. Instead of donating the money to his campaign, donate it to his opponent—Mrs. What's-Her-Name from Bedford."

At one point the Reverend Richard Nixon had planned to run for the vacant seat, but was talked out of it by his congregation. I'd planned to vote for the Lincoln look-alike and was initially disappointed. The woman from Bedford, however, really seemed to have her act together.

"Hornsby," I said. "Gloria Hornsby. Surely you know her name."

"Yeah, but I promised never to say it in this house. Give the money to her."

"But just a minute ago you threw yourself into my arms when I offered you ten grand. And I have the scars to prove it." Although Shnookums's teeth had failed to penetrate my sturdy Christian underwear, there were undoubtedly emotional scars inflicted.

"That was an act, Mags. That's what you expected me to do, not what I really felt."

"So you really want me to sabotage your pudding pie's election?"

She nodded vigorously. "Would you?"

"But what would *that* do to his self-esteem?"

My poor sister looked like she'd been asked to choose between a poor-grade chocolate cone and a premium vanilla. "Mags, I don't ever want to say anything bad about my sweetiekins, but I—well, I . . . it's possible he wouldn't make such a good congressman. On account of his low self-esteem and all."

"Gotcha. In that case, Susannah, I'd be happy to bring your hubby down—in a manner of speaking. But I suppose you meant it when you said you didn't have the power to convince Melvin to take it easy on Mr. Yetinsky."

"Sorry, Mags."

"That's okay. So far I haven't been banned from the jailhouse, so I think I'll pop over there and see what I can learn."

Susannah was no longer listening. She hummed to herself as she gathered the bolts to return to Material Girl. At least her life was going to soon be back on track.

I am intimately familiar with Hernia's jail, having once spent a night there myself. I had done nothing to break the law, I assure you. The only crime I'd committed was to open my big mouth one time too many. Perhaps it was because I'd been unjustly incarcerated by the mantis that I felt so strongly about Ivan Yetinsky's arrest. And the man was innocent—I just knew it. I knew it from the top of my bun to the tips of my stocking-clad toes.

Zelda, of course, was convinced otherwise. When not helping Melvin issue citations (mostly to folks who park their cars an inch too far from the curb), Zelda answers the phone, shuffles papers, and tends to the jail—which is almost always empty. The only other thing of note the woman does is worship my sister's husband. I mean that literally.

Don't ask me how I know, but she has a shrine to him in a closet in her home, complete with altar and candles. Melvin's sidekick believes that if she is faithful in her devotion, someday he will leave my sister and find his way into the policewoman's stubby arms. This is about as likely to happen as a woman becoming President, but one can always hope. Not that I wish my baby sister any heartbreak, mind you, but there has got to be somebody better out there. At any rate, Zelda adores Melvin to the point she no longer thinks for herself.

"Good morning, Zelda," I said cheerfully, as if greeting her for the first time that day. False cheer, by the way, is not forbidden by the Bible.

"It's you," she said, and went back to her task, which at the moment was a crossword puzzle.

I waved my new rock collection between her and the newspaper. The light from the monstrous sapphire and its diamond attendants sent rainbows dancing across the page. She swatted at the prisms a couple of times before realizing their source.

"That's very nice, Magdalena."

"That's all you've got to say about the biggest, most knockout ring you've ever laid your eyes on?"

"Garish comes to mind."

"I beg your pardon!"

"Well, that is the answer to number eleven across."

"Do you really think it is—garish, I mean?" I can't believe I was asking this question of a woman who applied her makeup with a trowel and cut her hair with pinking shears.

"Duh. Magdalena, what do you think people are going to say when they look at your prayer cap and then down at your ring? No one's going to take you seriously, that's what."

"You're calling the kettle black," I wailed.

Apparently pots don't have ears. "What's a six-letter word for a musical instrument?"

"Henway."

"What's a henway?"

"About three pounds—four if it's really plump."

Zelda was not amused. "Anyway it starts with the letter *v*."

"Try violin."

"Yeah, that's it. Thanks. Now what's an eight-letter—"

I can shift gears faster than a cross-country cyclist. "How's the prisoner doing?"

Zelda put puzzle and pencil down. "Magdalena, I hope you're not planning to give me a hard time."

"Moi?"

"Melvin's gone into Bedford on official business, and I'm in charge. He left me strict orders not to let you see the suspect."

"But did he say I couldn't talk to him?"

"That's the kind of trouble I mean."

"But you see, dear, talking and seeing are not the same thing. I'll even let you put a hood over my head, if you like—just as long as it doesn't come to a white point on top. Then when I'm through speaking with Mr. Yetinsky, I thought you and I could have ourselves a nice little chat. I just came from Susannah's, you see, and I learned the most interesting thing."

Zelda blinked. With an ounce of eye shadow on each lid, it is not a quick process.

"What sort of interesting thing?"

"I'm afraid the details will have to wait until after my chat with the prisoner."

"Does it have to do with Melvin?"

"Doesn't everything involving Susannah have to do with Melvin?"

"Hmm." I might have been able to hear the wheels turn in Zelda's head, had it not been for all that muffling makeup. "I don't have a hood, Magdalena, but I can blindfold you, if that's all right."

"Blindfold away!"

Zelda began looking in her desk, presumably for a blindfold, but stopped midway through the second drawer. "What if you just promise not to tell Melvin you were here *and* I lead you into the cell area backwards. You have to also promise not to turn around in there."

"Consider it done."

The top-heavy woman sighed as she stood. She wasn't happy, but she'd get over it. In the meantime, justice once again stood a chance of being served and, in a weird way, thanks to my bothersome brother-in-law.

There is no point in talking to a silent man if you have to keep your back turned. Yes, I'd made a bargain with Zelda, but that's just it—a bargain has two sides, doesn't it? If I didn't get a peep out of Ivan, then Zelda wasn't going to hear what I had to say about Melvin. She surely wasn't going to like that. And anyway, she'd used the word "promise," not me. So you see, I had no choice but to turn around.

Ivan Yetinsky's body language may as well have been Greek. He was sitting with his legs open, his arms crossed, and his head down. I tried not to look past the pillars of decency that were his knees.

"You look good in stripes, dear." For the record, Melvin insists that his prisoners wear black-and-white-striped uniforms.

"You think so?"

I was shocked, but of course pleased, that I had gotten a response. "Definitely. Because they're horizontal, those stripes make your shoulders look so broad." They make my shoulders look broad as well, which is one of the reasons I've resolved not to end up in the pokey again.

"And my waist?"

Who knew the man had a vain streak? He wasn't exactly hanging his head; he was studying his middle.

"I could put my thumb and index finger around it, dear."

He looked at me and smiled. "It's a terrible thing to lose a friend—two friends. But to look bad too, well—that was more than I could bear."

It is possible to gasp with one's lips only slightly

parted. I learned this trick at church. In fact, I learned it from Lodema and her friends. They emit ventriloquist-style gasps every time someone shows up at church wearing inappropriate attire (in their opinion) or, the Good Lord forbid, a truly serious sinner darkens the door. The sanctuary was sucked empty of oxygen the first Sunday after word got out that I was an inadvertent bigamist.

"I don't see how a man like you could ever look bad," I said, remembering to move my lips.

"Believe it or not, it's happened. I had a particularly bad day in 1982."

I was more than a bit taken aback. I'd pegged Ivan Yetinsky for the strong, silent type. But garrulous and vain? Who knew? Perhaps I'd been wrong about him altogether.

"Mr. Yetinsky—"

"Please, Ivan."

"Ivan, then. This morning you looked so sad holding Miss Thrope. I mean—your wife."

"She wasn't my wife."

"You lied?"

"Yes, but she was my best friend."

I prayed for guidance. I had a lot better chance of having that one answered than a prayer for a silent tongue. Even if my lingua was to be severed surgically, it would continue to babble.

"Well, I'm glad she wasn't your wife, because it was my understanding that Miss Thrope and the colonel were—uh—intimately involved."

"There is no need to mince words, Miss Yoder. They were lovers."

"And you were okay with that?"

"Why wouldn't I be?" He laughed then. It came out as a loud bark, and fearing that it would get Zelda's attention, I quickly turned my back on the man.

"What's so funny?" If I learned that my boyfriend

was doing the mattress mambo with some bimbo, I'd be livid.

"Miss Yoder, like I just said. Anne and I were friends. Best friends, yes, but that's all."

"That's what they all say."

"Are they all gay?"

I whirled. Let Zelda walk in; I'd deal with those consequences later.

"Gay as in happy, or the Rosie O'Donnell way?"

"Rosie's way—although of course I'm not a lesbian. But I loved Anne like a sister."

I'm a God-fearing woman, one who reads her Bible on a daily basis. I will not, however, poke my proboscis into other folks' sex lives. Who am I to judge, after all? And no, I am not referring to my ill-fated marriage to Aaron, but my three-legged Maytag washer. I innocently thought I could hold the renegade machine in place during spin cycle by sitting on it. I was right, of course—it's just that—well, like I said, I'm not one to judge.

"Ivan, please tell me the circumstances of you finding her. Where she was, where you were, what happened, etcetera."

"I was in my room reading."

"Oh?"

"Miss Yoder, just because I'm a big guy, and a chauffeur, doesn't mean I don't like to read."

"All I said was 'oh.' "

"But you meant something else."

"What were you reading?" I asked pleasantly.

"Plato."

"A comic book?" Yes, it was hard to keep the sarcasm from my voice.

"The philosopher."

"Oh."

"I was brushing up on the *Apology*."

"No need to apologize, dear; I'm the one who jumped to conclusions. So, Ivan, you were reading. Then what?"

"I heard a thump coming from the room next door— the colonel's room—and since there wasn't supposed to be anyone in there, I went to investigate. That's when I found Anne. She was lying on the floor."

"In what position?"

"Huh?"

"Facedown, on her back, what?"

"On her back. Mostly. Her head and shoulders were propped up against the side of the bed. Sort of like she'd slid off."

"And she was dead at this point?"

"Yes, ma'am. Near as I could tell—I checked her pulse."

"Then what did you do?"

"I called 911, of course. Then I scooped her up. Held her in my arms. That's what I was doing when you came in."

"There was, of course, no one else in the room when you came in."

He blinked. "That's right. No one."

"But she'd obviously struggled with someone—"

"Miss Yoder, how do you feel about snakes?"

I shuddered. Satan was a serpent, wasn't he? I know—it's unreasonable of me, but I practically jump out of my brogans every time I see a harmless garter snake.

"I despise them, dear."

"Then I'm afraid you have a big problem, Miss Yoder."

I did an involuntary triple lutz. "Where? Is there a snake in this jail?"

"No, ma'am, but there's a very large one in your house."

23

Aaron Miller had been a snake—in more ways than one—but he was long gone. Ivan Yetinsky had to be talking about a real snake, one with scales and a flickering tongue.

"What kind of snake? Where?"

"It's a twenty-five-foot African rock python named Charlie. I wish I knew where he was at the moment."

I chuckled, obliging at his little joke.

"Why are you laughing, Miss Yoder?"

"Because I thought you said there was a python loose at the inn."

"I did."

Although I was looking at the muscular man, I felt like he had sneaked around me and punched me on the soft spots behind my knees. I had to struggle to remain standing, and given that I am a bit on the lofty side, I swayed like a white pine during an Arctic Express. A lumberjack observing the scene might have been tempted to shout "timber."

"But that's impossible," I heard myself say.

I thought my voice sounded far away, like it was coming from another room. Apparently it *was* coming from another room, but as an echo. While I was still reeling from shock, Zelda burst into the hallway that fronted the cells, her gun drawn from its holster.

"What the hell is going on here? Magdalena, why are you dancing?"

"I'm not dancing," I wailed. "I'm in shock."

"She needs to sit," Ivan said.

Zelda's Swiss-German bloodlines have made her so rigid that when she buys the proverbial farm, the onset of rigor mortis will be useless in pinpointing the time of death. "She needs to go home, that's what."

"And not tell you about Melvin?" I squeaked.

Zelda was torn between duty and desire. "Does this have anything to do with Miss Thrope's murder?"

"It wasn't a murder," Ivan said.

Just the thought of what he implied made me woozy. I swayed even harder, which was clearly a threat to Zelda, over whom I towered. Should I topple, a direct blow could shatter her makeup, perhaps finally revealing Jimmy Hoffa.

"Let me get a chair," she growled. She was back in a jiffy with her desk chair. "Sit. But you better make this good."

I plunked my patooty in the plastic seat. "He says there's a giant boa constrictor loose at the PennDutch. Apparently it's what killed Miss Thrope."

Ivan stood and approached the bars. "It's an African rock python, not a boa. They both kill by constriction, but boa constrictors are from the Americas. Incidentally, neither of them are poisonous."

Zelda appeared to take him seriously. "Then how did this African snake get into Magdalena's inn?"

"It was the colonel's pet."

"But I don't allow pets! Certainly not snakes." I did bend the rules for Jacko, but guanacos are such cuddly-looking creatures. Besides, he promised to teach me how to moonwalk. Of course that was a huge mistake. I can barely move my clodhoppers forward in a straight line, much less backwards, and despite Jacko's assurances, guanaco guano was not that easy to get out of the carpet.

Ivan spread his ham-size mitts in a gesture of appeasement. "He had that snake as long as I worked for him. Said he got it as a baby. Never went anywhere without it."

"What did it eat?" Zelda asked. "People?"

The chauffeur started to laugh, but caught himself just in time. "No, ma'am. Not people. Although a snake the size of Charlie could swallow a child, or a very small adult. In Africa they've been known to swallow antelope and goats. The colonel used to feed Charlie live rats, but in recent years it's been rabbits."

I shuddered. "How on earth did you get that monster past me without me noticing?"

"That wasn't easy, ma'am. The colonel made us wait until after you were in bed the first night. But Charlie—he's heavy. Took all three of us to get him upstairs. Charlie's cold-blooded, as are all reptiles, and likes to sleep next to the colonel on cool nights, but then sometimes he gets too warm, see, so he drops to the floor. Can make quite a noise. The colonel was worried you might have heard that."

"Which I did," I cried. "So that was a *snake*? A twenty-five-foot snake?"

"Magdalena, calm down."

"That's easy for you to say, Zelda. You don't have Satan's older brother slithering around in your house."

The policewoman didn't dare scowl lest she cause an avalanche of loose makeup. But the glitter in her eyes intensified, and I knew she was put out.

"You think you've got problems, Magdalena? What about poor Melvin when he discovers he was wrong?"

"Don't worry. He's used to that." I turned back to the

grieving hulk. "I heard thumps *after* the colonel's death. What was up with that?"

"That was because of Harry."

"Who?"

"Harry was a rabbit—supposed to be Charlie's next meal. Don't know why the colonel insisted on naming Charlie's meals—always found that part a little strange. Anyway, I'm afraid your register vents aren't in the best condition. Harry was able to push his way under one and escape. Anne and I took it off altogether so we could catch that damn rabbit, but then Charlie got it into his mind he wanted to eat immediately and . . . Well, there's really no stopping a snake that big when he's determined. We tried to wrestle him out of the vent, but it didn't work. Miss Yoder, you should really put in new screws."

"So now it's my fault?"

"If the shoe fits," Zelda said.

"Is that a jibe?" I can't help it that the old woman who lives in a shoe used one of my castoffs as her starter home.

"Ladies, please," Ivan said, "arguing is not going to get Charlie back. Not unharmed. And the colonel said I could have him when the time came."

"Time for what?" Zelda asked.

"The colonel was dying," I said.

Ivan smiled. "So you knew."

"Of course."

"Why am I not surprised? I sensed the chemistry between you two. So did Anne. She was furious."

"Well, she needn't have been. I have a perfectly good man of my own."

Zelda risked a frown. "What is going on? Magdalena, what are you withholding?"

"Why, nothing, dear. You know all about Gabe."

The petite, but buxom, officer of the law stamped a foot so tiny a butterfly wouldn't get drunk imbibing champagne from her shoe. Still, the jolt was enough to send a shower of loose face powder southward.

"One of you get back to that part about the colonel dying."

"Certainly. The colonel had melanoma. It had gone undiagnosed too long."

"Hmm." She was thinking aloud again. With less makeup to muffle the sound, I was going to have plug my ears. "So Magdalena, now we've got three possibilities, right?"

"No, dear, just two. It was either the gun or the snake."

"How do you know?"

"Because one doesn't just topple over from cancer. Besides, he was well enough to plan a drive into Pittsburgh that day to see some doctors. What you guys need to do is figure what came first, the chicken or the egg."

"Magdalena, this is no time to talk about your livestock."

I don't wear a shed of makeup, so I have no compunctions about frowning. "Zelda, dear, the gun or the snake—which came first? That's something the coroner can figure out. In fact, you should have heard by now."

"Well, we did get in a couple of faxes, but I always leave them for Melvin. He is the Chief, you know."

"Of a tribe of two—three, if you count Susannah."

"Ladies," Ivan said with unnecessary sharpness, "it was the gun."

We gave him our full attention. "How do you know?" I asked pleasantly.

"Because the colonel knew how to defend himself. He had to. Snakes aren't like dogs—they don't form the same kind of attachments—and African rock pythons are among the most aggressive snakes in the world. But the colonel had cared for him since he was a baby, and knew how to handle him."

"Imagine that," Zelda said, "a pet that will attack its master."

Ivan nodded. "Yeah, but if it had attacked, the colonel

would have put up a good fight. Charlie would have too. Pythons don't chew their food, but they do have re-curved teeth for holding their prey. Trust me, there would have been blood everywhere, and not just from the bullet wound. Anyway—"

"Like there was with Anne?" I gave myself a mental slap for having been so insensitive.

"Yeah, like with her. He was getting ready to swallow her—well, try, at any rate. The tail muscles are weakest, so I started there. I basically unwrapped him. Thought for a while he was going to go for me, but when I got him half unwrapped he just let go of Anne and headed back to the vent."

"Which was tightly in place when you arrived, I assure you," I said.

"Is he in the vent now?" Zelda asked. It was perhaps her most sensible question all day.

Ivan shrugged. "Or maybe just loose in the inn. Anyway, I was about to say earlier that what probably happened was that the colonel was shot by whoever—and it wasn't me—and *then* Charlie crawled out of the vent when he smelled the opportunity."

"Smelled?" It was Zelda again. Oh well, a latent curiosity was better than none.

"That's how snakes find their prey. Scent, as well as temperature. They have heat-sensing organs in their jaws, you see. Won't eat something that's stone-cold. You can give them a rabbit that's been frozen, but you have to dip it in boiling water first. My guess is that Charlie smelled the blood from the still warm body, and didn't give it a thought that it was the colonel. But I'm also guessing—and I'm not an expert here, just know about Charlie—that the colonel was starting to cool down, and that's why Charlie changed his mind."

I'd already learned enough about snakes to last me a lifetime. A little more knowledge wasn't going to kill me.

"The coroner said—"

"You can't tell him what the coroner said," Zelda snapped.

I glared at her. I am a humble and peace-loving woman. In fact, I'm proud of my humility and will, if pushed, defend my pacifism tooth and nail. Zelda, however, is what some behaviorists would call an alpha female. Sometimes the only way to deal effectively with an alpha female is to act like one.

"I can and I will," I said.

"If you do, Melvin will—"

"Let him. Whatever it is, let him. Ivan, dear, the coroner said that the colonel showed signs of being squeezed. I know that pythons constrict their prey, but would they do that even if the prey were dead?"

"Yeah, I've seen it happen with the rabbits. The frozen ones we heat up. I guess it's instinct—going through the motions."

I gasped as a new thought penetrated my thick skull. "You didn't heat up any rabbits in my kitchen, did you?" Freni is normally an excellent cook, but sometimes she has her off days. It seems that I had been smelling the remnants of a few of her off days recently, or that could have been Miss Thrope's supposedly gourmet fare.

"Nah. Like I said, Harry escaped down the vent. He was very much alive."

"Bet he's not alive now," Zelda said.

Practice makes perfect, even when it comes to glaring. "What we can extrapolate from all this," I said, "is that the person who shot the colonel did so just after we left the house. Then several hours later that horrible serpent crawled out of the vent and thought about eating his master. Fortunately he changed his mind."

With her face already in shreds, Zelda had nothing to lose. She returned my glare.

"And how do we know all this?"

"Because, dear, the human body stays warm to the touch for approximately three hours after death. After four hours it feels cool. We were gone for five."

This basic information I would have thought any policewoman would know off the top of her spiked and bleached head. Apparently Zelda didn't. She looked so flustered I felt sorry for her.

"Well, uh—Magdalena, would you mind telling all this to . . . What I mean is—"

"You want me to set your nincompoop boss straight?"

She nodded, precipitating another shower of cheap cosmetics.

"I'd be happy to, dear." I gave her a warm smile, intended as a dismissal, but she didn't take the hint. "Zelda, is that your phone I hear ringing?"

"I don't hear anything."

I leaned over and whispered behind the back of my bony hand, "Your face looks like a thousand-year-old fresco, dear. You might want to respackle it before Melvin gets back."

That did the trick.

"Now," I said to Ivan when we were alone again, "is there anyone you can think of that might have had it in for the colonel?"

"Besides that mob of loonies at the town council meeting the other night?"

I didn't know why, but that remark really irritated me. Yes, Hernia has its warts, but it is my town, and those are my loonies. Wanda Hemphopple is like a mosquito bite on the backside, and you can double that for Elspeth Miller. Lodema Schrock makes me so mad I've considered switching religions (maybe become a Baptist or a Methodist—but certainly not a beer-bathing Presbyterian). I am allowed to criticize them, because they are my neighbors, and I have to live with them. But for an out-

sider to bad-mouth them—well, that was just uncalled-
for. I gave Ivan a piece of my mind. Fortunately for him,
I've given away a lot of those in recent years, so the
piece he got was very small.

"Sorry," he said, in just the right tone.

"Apology accepted. Now, dear, perhaps you'll answer
my question."

Ivan scratched his head. "The colonel was a business-
man, and not all his deals worked out—"

"He told me. This was supposed to be his last stand."

"Yeah, but even though not everyone he'd done business with was happy, he didn't have any real enemies either. It was hard not to like Colonel Custard—and I
don't mean it that way, just because I'm gay. You know
what I mean."

"Indeed I do. He was a charmer." I stood. "Well, I
guess I'll have to go back and reinterview some of those
loonies you mentioned."

He smiled. "Sorry again. Hey, I don't know if this will
help at all—it may not even be connected, but you know
there's that dip in the road by your place?"

"Yes, what about it?" I knew the dip well, only not as
well as Susannah. When she was coming home from her
dates, back when our parents were alive, she'd have her
boyfriends park there. I knew this, because I could see
the car disappear into the dip a good twenty minutes
before her curfew and not emerge until the very last
second. My sister never told me what went on in those
intervening minutes, but I wouldn't be surprised if what
she and her beaux did rivaled dancing on the scale of
sins. Maybe even ranked a ten.

Ivan drew an imaginary road in the air, and dropped
his hand dramatically for the dip. "I could see that from
my window. It was kinda neat—especially when a horse
and buggy went by. Clop. Clop, clop, then they disappeared for a few seconds. Then clop, clop, clop, and I
could see just the horse's head, and then all the rest.

"Anyway, on the morning the colonel was killed, I was in my room getting ready to go on your little tour of the town, and this blue car comes along. It goes down into the dip, of course, but then it never comes back out."

"At all?"

"Not 'til after we left, at any rate. I kept trying to see behind me, if the car was maybe following us, but you stopped me."

I frowned. "I remember, dear. You were about to drill a hole in my roof with that oversize head of yours."

My tone was not unkind, and anyway, Ivan laughed. "It is kind of big. My mama says I owe her one. But like I was going to say, Miss Yoder, I'd check out that blue car if I were you."

"What was the model?"

"Beats me."

"But you're a chauffeur, for crying out loud."

"Yeah, but I wasn't paying attention to what kind of car, only that it disappeared. The blue part I couldn't help noticing, but I'm not so good at my colors, so I could be wrong."

"You're color-blind?"

"To a degree. I can't distinguish blue from some shades of purple, and I can't tell aquamarine. But it had blue in it—that much I can tell."

I nodded. Mama had been color-blind. Most folks think it's only a man's disorder, and indeed, there are twenty color-blind men for every color-blind woman, but there are plenty of the latter—over a million in this country alone. At any rate, I knew that the most common form of the condition is not the inability to see color at all, but the inability to see red and green in certain combinations.

"Great," I said. "Now all I have to do is find a bluish car that stopped in the dip just after eight in the morning. Should be a piece of cake."

"If you let me out, I could help."

"I wish I could, but I don't have the authority. I'm not a real policewoman."

"That's a shame, if you ask me, because you'd make a damn good one."

So he was gay and behind bars, and I was happily engaged. I still blushed.

"Thanks. And thanks for your help. Well—sorry to have to leave you here, but I have to go."

"Off to slay the dragon?"

"Not this one. This one I'm going to visit in her lair."

24

A fuming Freni can be a fearsome thing. She practically flew at me, like a bantam hen, flapping her stubby arms and squawking something unintelligible.

"English, please, dear."

"Yah, I give you the English all right. This Alison, she drives me pecans."

"You mean nuts."

"Yah, that is what I said. Lipstick, Magdalena! Now my neighbor will never speak to you."

"She put lipstick on your neighbor?"

"Not the mother, the girls. Sarah and Rebecca."

I sucked in my breath sharply. "Sorry, I didn't know."

Freni continued to flap her arms. She's much more stout than Elspeth, but one of these days, if my kinswoman is wearing her black travel bonnet with the big ruffles, and the wind is just right, she's going to achieve liftoff. I just hope it doesn't happen during turkey season.

"Bright red lipstick, Magdalena. The little ones look like harlots, yah?"

"So that's the real reason she didn't go to the Amish school this morning. Well, don't you worry, Freni. I may spare the rod, but I won't spoil the child. As soon as things return to normal I'll ground her. And dock her allowance if you want. When I get through with her, Alison will rue the day she rouged those little girls' lips."

"Ach! She is a good girl, Magdalena."

"But you just said—"

"I was vending, yah?"

"You mean venting?"

"That's what I said. Now I feel better. So, you will not be too hard on her, yah?"

"I reserve the right to play it by ear—an unpierced ear, I might add."

Half the things I say to Freni go right over her head, and it's not just because I'm so much taller. She stared at me through bottle-thick glasses dusted with flour.

"Magdalena, must you always speak in riddles?"

"Was Jacob Amman Amish?" The answer is yes, by the way. He was, in fact, the very first of that faith.

Freni stared at me, a mixture of horror and fascination on her pudgy face. "Magdalena, this you do not know?"

"Of course I know it. I was just joking. Look, can we go inside, maybe have a cup of tea or something?"

"Yah, yah, come in. Barbara," she said, referring to the daughter-in-law who is the bane of her existence, "has taken the triplets over to visit Esther Gingerich. And Mose and Jonathan are taking the last of the apples to the press."

That settled it. I followed the stout woman into her immaculate kitchen, give or take a little flour on the floor, and had a cup of milky tea with plenty of sugar, and the best molasses cookies I've ever eaten. The secret of any good cookie, as Freni will tell you, is whether or not it can bend at a forty-five-degree angle without breaking. Some of her best efforts can be folded in half and still not snap.

It took Freni until I was halfway through my second

cookie to notice. She grabbed my left hand. "Magdalena, what is this?"

I jerked away. "It's nothing."

Freni shook her head. "Ach, so bawdy."

"I think you mean gaudy, and it's my engagement ring."

"To Dr. Rosen?"

"No, to the man in the moon. Of *course* it's to Gabe."

Freni feigned interest in the wood grain pattern of her kitchen table. This lasted all of five seconds.

"You think he will convert?"

"You know he won't—not in the foreseeable future."

"So, Magdalena, you do not think it is wrong, this unequal joking?"

"I can't help it if I have a better sense of humor than you, dear."

"No, not joke like funny, ha-ha, but joke like in egg, only not the same."

"Now I'm afraid I'm totally in the dark."

"The ox and the ass," she cried in frustration.

"Ah, you mean 'yoke.' " The image of a believer and a nonbeliever being unequally yoked, like an ox and ass together to a plowshare, is popular among some preachers. It is based on 2 Corinthians 6:14. Just which one the Christian is supposed to be, the ass or the ox, is never specified, since this Scripture passage mentions yokes but no farm animals.

"Magdalena, what would your mama say?"

"Leave her out of it. She's been dead almost twelve years."

"She would roll over in her grave, that is what."

Mama gets more exercise dead than she ever did alive. No doubt she is the fittest soul in Heaven, no small thanks to me. Susannah was always Mama's favorite. The fact that my sister drinks upon occasion, smoked in the past (and more than just cigarettes, I might add), never goes to church, has not only been divorced, but remarried, pales in comparison to my sin of inadvertent adultery, and now my desire to marry a man of the Jewish faith.

"Freni, we've been over this a million times. Jesus was Jewish; so were his parents; so were all twelve of his disciples."

"Yah, maybe. But they didn't have rings like that."

I looked down at the ring, which should have filled me with nothing but pride. Maybe that was it—pride. This sin is the perennial biggie among folks of my religious persuasion, many of whom, like me, are proud of their humility. Freni was afraid that I would be caught up in the race for material possessions. And since I would be unequally yoked with a Jewish mate—I'd be the ass, and he the ox—there would be no one of my background to put a stop to this. Except, of course, for her.

"Do you honestly think I should ask Gabe if he wouldn't mind if I traded this in for a less ostentatious model?" After all, I had traded in my sinfully red BMW for the more Christian Toyota Camry, so I was quite capable of downsizing.

"Magdalena, how much do you think a ring like that costs?"

"I honestly don't know. Maybe twenty thousand."

Freni gasped so hard it sucked the flour off her lenses. "Dollars?"

"Well, that's what Susannah thinks."

"And how much food can twenty thousand dollars buy?"

"Like for the starving children in India? Or is it Africa now?" I grew up on stories of children starving in Third World countries. The sometimes morbid accounts were intended to make me eat my lima beans, not my favorite vegetable. The one time I suggested Mama package up my stone-cold beans and send them to some more deserving child, she made me eat soap for dessert. *After* I finished the beans.

My elderly kinswoman nodded. "Or even in America, yah?"

I grabbed another cookie just to be contrary. Why is it that whenever something spectacular happens in my life, somebody always has to object? If I gave away everything that I had, broke my engagement to Gabe, and did nothing but charitable works for the rest of my life, someone, somewhere, would still find reason to criticize me. "There goes Magdalena Yoder, who thinks she's a saint." The intonation I heard in my head was Lodema Schrock's, but it could have been anybody's.

Still, Freni had a point. A smaller ring, with a carat or less of diamonds, would still be lovely, and it wouldn't be sending anyone the wrong message. Not to mention, I wouldn't have to worry so much about it becoming a soap catcher or snagging my good stockings. Besides, a sapphire the size of the one I now sported made it impossible to wear gloves, which are a necessity during our cold Hernia winters. A knockout ring would only draw attention to my chapped hands.

That settled it. I would ask the Babester if he wouldn't mind if I traded down. For now, I wouldn't mention it to Freni, lest she think she deserved the credit for my enlightenment, and get a big head herself. What kind of friend and cousin would I be if I handed her the sin of pride on a pewter platter (silver is pride-inducing in and of itself)?

"Freni, dear, I need to change the subject. I'm afraid there's been another death at the inn."

"Ach, so many!"

"Yes, I know. I feel like I should post a sign that reads STAY HERE AT YOUR OWN PERIL."

"So, who dies this time?"

"That young cook, Miss Anne Thrope."

Now that her lenses were clean, I could see Freni's beady eyes gleam. "Now I get my job back, yah?"

"Freni, for shame! You could at least say something about being sorry."

"Yah, I'm sorry." She sounded about as sorry as Susannah did when she borrowed my best sweater and squirted ketchup down the front.

"Not that you seem to care, dear, but she wasn't murdered."

"A heart attack," Freni said, proud of her knowledge. "It kills more women than cancer. I read this in *Reader's Digest*." The aforementioned journal is very popular among the Amish. Because they do not watch television or listen to the radio, in many cases it is their primary source of information about the outside world.

"It wasn't a heart attack, Freni. It was a snake."

It is possible for a stout woman with a stubby neck to recoil as fast as any serpent. "Snake?"

"A twenty-five-foot, two-hundred-and-fifty-pound python—that's a kind of snake. Anyway, it squeezed all the air out of her."

"Magdalena, have you been drinking again?"

"That was only once," I wailed. "How was I to know what a mimosa was?"

"There is not such a snake in Hernia. Little garter snakes, yah, and sometimes in the woods, rattlesnakes."

"It was the colonel's pet. He brought it with him."

"Into the house?"

"Apparently it took all three of them to carry it in."

"Where is this snake now?"

"I wish I knew. Somewhere loose in the inn. Ivan and Miss Thrope even pretended to be married once when I caught them alone in a room. Turns out they were wrestling with the snake—trying to subdue it. But it got away."

She shuddered. "So now I quit again."

"Freni, dear, there isn't going to be anyone to cook

for until someone finds that snake—I'm sure not going to do it myself—and removes it."

"Who docs such a thing?"

"I wish I knew. A pest extermination company, I guess. I came straight over here from the jail, where I learned about this from the chauffeur."

The precursor to a smile tugged at the right corner of her mouth. "So you come to me because I am like your mama, yah?"

The truth is Freni was more like a mother to me than my own had ever been. But not having been raised by the ideal mother, I didn't have the graciousness to tell my surrogate mother that yes, I had come seeking comfort and succor. And especially warm molasses cookies.

"My mother was as skinny as a clothesline, and her nose was bigger than mine."

"Yah," Freni said. It was, after all, pointless to argue with the truth. "And she had a temper like Elspeth Miller."

"Now that's going too far!"

"This morning," Freni said, "I go to the feed store to get some mash for my pullets. I must get there early so Mose and Jonathan can use the wagon for the apples later, yah? There is a man from the water company who says there is maybe a water leak someplace outside, and can he take look. Elspeth she turns white, and then she grabs a broom and chases him all the way to his car."

"At least she didn't use a pitchfork, like she did once on me."

Freni nodded. "Yah, your mama, she would have used the pitchfork."

That was enough time spent going down memory lane. "Well, dear, I should be going." I snatched one last cookie and stood. "I don't suppose you'd be willing to let me spend the night—if that horrible creature isn't caught by then?"

"You do not want to spend it with the doctor?" she asked slyly.

"Freni!"

"Yah, sure you can spend the night."

That was the answer I'd counted on. Freni's womb had only yielded up one child, Jonathan. But even with the triplets plus Alison, there was room, thanks to the Amish custom of building large houses. On a rotational basis Freni and Mose were expected to host the entire congregation for Sunday services in the downstairs public rooms. Upstairs there were plenty of bedrooms, most of which got used only when daughter-in-law Barbara's family visited from Iowa. Eventually the elder Hostetlers planned to retire to a smaller, adjoining residence called the Grossdawdy house, but for now there was no need to do that.

"Thanks, Freni, you're a peach." To show my gratitude—and yes, partly to annoy her—I defied tradition and gave her a peck on the cheek.

"Ach!" she squawked and waved her stubby arms to fend off any more unseemly behavior.

"There is where I came in," I cried, and then I skedaddled.

There is a public phone just outside Sam Yoder's Corner Market. It is used primarily by local Amish, who call long-distance relatives at other public phone booths. Due to the fact that the parties called are generally out of town, there is little need for a directory. This is fortunate, because the phone books always disappear the weekend of high school graduation and are not replaced until after Labor Day. This year, although it was already mid-September, the black protective cover was empty. That's only one of the reasons I ducked into Sam's.

He smiled when he saw me. "So you decided the horizontal hootchy-kootchy with a cousin wasn't such a bad idea."

"Not if you were the second last man in the world."

"And who would have the honor of being the last—ah, your nemesis, good old Melvin. Well, at least I'm not on the bottom. And if I'm not what brings you here, what does?"

"Sam, dear, what color is your car?"

"Excuse me?"

"Your automobile. Vroom, vroom. What color is it?"

"Tan, in my opinion, but the official name is something like Wheat Dust, or Wheat Sheaves. Why?"

"Just taking a poll, dear. What color is Dorothy's?"

"Red. But a purple red, not a sinful red like your BMW."

"*Was.* I sold it, remember?"

"Yeah. What's with the poll?"

"You know what color Wanda Hemphopple drives?"

"Haven't the slightest. Magdalena, what are you up to now?"

"Oh, just some more of my foolish shenanigans. You know how I am."

"A hell of a lot more interesting than my Dorothy."

"Sam, please don't say that word around me."

"The *D* word?"

"No, the *h* word. You know how I feel about swearing."

"Always a prude, but that's part of your charm too."

"I'll take that as a compliment. I need to use your phone book. I have to call an exterminator."

"Bats in the belfry?"

"Snakes in the cellar," I said, just for the joy of alliteration. "Although actually it's a twenty-five-foot python and it could be anywhere."

"Magdalena, you flatter me."

I felt my face turn the color of Freni's pickled beets. "Sam!"

He handed me the Bedford phone book, which contains both white and yellow pages. "You're kidding about the snake, right?"

"I wish I was. You wouldn't have any recommendations on who to call, would you?"

"Come on, Magdalena, a twenty-five-foot snake?"

"It was Colonel Custard's pet." I flipped through pages. "How about Dandy Dan's? Says here he'll exterminate anything."

Sam shrugged. "Never heard of him, but I wonder if he'd be willing to exterminate Dorothy's mom. All it would take is a wooden stake through the heart—or maybe a silver bullet."

It was a sin for me to derive any pleasure from hearing Sam bad-mouth his mother-in-law, but as the Bible says, I am sinful by nature. Therefore, I was just doing what came naturally. Besides, Sam knew better than to marry for money, and a Methodist at that.

"She driving you crazy again?"

"Speaking of the number twenty-five, you know that Dorothy and I have been planning to go to Europe for our twenty-fifth wedding anniversary, right?"

"I believe you've mentioned that."

"Adele thinks she and Larry have the right to come along."

"Because they're paying for it?"

"Details, details. They offered, and they didn't say anything about coming along until after we accepted. Three weeks, Magdalena. Three weeks of traipsing through ruins with a woman who makes them all look young by comparison."

"Sam, you're not going to get any sympathy from me. A free trip to Europe—well, just zip your lip and have fun. That's my advice."

"And what would you do if Gabriel's mother insinuated herself into your life?"

"Why, I'd welcome her with open arms." I smiled. "Fortunately the woman in question is afraid to leave Manhattan for the wilds of the Hamptons, much less Hernia, Pennsylvania. I'll only have to deal with her on trips to the Big Apple, and since I've never been farther east than Harrisburg, and Gabe is so content here, I really don't foresee a problem. Sure, we'll go visit her—but only once or twice a year—and then only for a few days at a time. I can handle that."

"We'll see about that when the time comes," Sam said. "Roy Miller thought he was getting off the hook because his mother-in-law lived in Germany."

"Oh, I'd forgotten about that. Elspeth's mother came and stayed for six months, didn't she?"

"Roy was over here every day during that visit, just to escape for a few minutes. It was bad enough him living with Elspeth, but Frau Schmidt made her daughter look like Mother Teresa."

"You and Roy were close friends, weren't you? Tell me honestly, Sam, have you ever heard from him? I promise I won't tell Elspeth."

I could tell by his eyes I shouldn't have asked the question. It was clear that Roy's sudden disappearance had wounded his friend deeply.

"We had a fishing trip planned, Magdalena. I still can't believe he just bailed on me like that. I wouldn't have done that to him."

"No, you wouldn't have."

Not knowing what else to say, I grabbed Sam's phone and started calling exterminators. I began with Dandy Dan, who informed me in no uncertain terms that he couldn't even bring himself to set foot in the reptile house at the Pittsburgh Zoo. I went back to the top of the list, but not a soul I reached was interested in tackling a twenty-five-foot python. One person even hung up on me, after chiding me for making a prank call.

I was on the verge of tears—more so from frustration than from despair—when my knight in shining armor walked through the door.

25

Stirred Custard

Stirred or soft custard is the basis for various sauces and desserts. It is often erroneously referred to as boiled custard. Serve alone as a cold dessert or use as a custard sauce.

2½ cups milk
4 large eggs or 7 egg yolks, lightly beaten
⅓ to ½ cup (or to taste) sugar
⅛ teaspoon salt
1½ teaspoons vanilla extract

Warm the milk in a heavy saucepan to just remove the chill. Take off heat. Beat together the eggs, sugar, and salt in a bowl until well combined. Strain into milk. Stirring constantly, cook over low heat until the mixture has thickened and coats the back of a metal spoon, about 15 minutes. Do not let the custard boil or it will curdle. Immediately remove from the heat and plunge the pan into a bowl of ice water. Add the vanilla, and stir until the custard is cool, to prevent further cooking. Pour into cups or a bowl and serve at once, or cover with plastic wrap placed directly on the surface and refrigerate until ready to use.

SERVES 4 OR 5

26

"Gabe!"

Oblivious to Sam's presence, and that of the two Amish women who floated in on his heels, my fiancé grabbed me and planted a brief kiss on my meager mug. I, who was not oblivious, pushed him away.

"Gabe," I cried again, "*please*. Everyone's watching."

"Well, I missed you."

"I missed you too, but—"

The hunky doctor grabbed me again and maneuvered me next to the cooler that held Sam's supposedly fresh produce. My fiancé knew that no sane person would buy that stuff, and he was right. The Amish women, who were of sound mind, gave us wide berth. Gabe shamelessly kissed me again, and again I pushed him away, lest what we were doing lead to dancing. After all, I was feeling pretty light on my feet.

"I need an exterminator," I gasped.

"A what?"

"There's a twenty-five-foot python loose in my inn."

Gabe shook his head. He has dark curly hair and an olive complexion, both of which were accented by his dazzling white grin.

"Magdalena, you never cease to amaze me. Why is it that I believe you?"

"Because I don't lie—well, not on a regular basis."

"Please, start at the beginning."

I did. I told him everything that had happened that day, except for Freni's insinuation that I would consider spending the night at his place. When I was through he took out his cell phone and, without even consulting a phone book, dialed. Within minutes he had made arrangements to have the snake captured.

"How did you do that?"

"It's the pet shop where I got Little Freni. Harold, the owner, is big on snakes. He can't do it today, Mags, but first thing in the morning he'll be there with his crew. That's if you'll let him keep the thing."

"I don't care if he keeps it—but it isn't mine. Legally, it belongs to the colonel's heirs. But then again, they say possession is nine-tenths of the law, right?"

"Atta girl, and in any case we won't say anything to Harold until after he catches and removes it. Then it will be in his possession."

I felt better already. "Gabe, maybe here in front of the wilted veggies is not the right place to ask, but—"

"You had lunch yet?"

"Just some of Freni's cookies."

"They're the best, but that's not lunch. I need to talk to you about something as well. Let's talk over lunch."

"You mean at your house?" The Babester is, after all, a pretty good cook.

"No," he said quickly. "My place is a mess. Let's drive into Bedford."

I didn't have the time to drive all the way into town. Not unless it meant I could kill two birds with one scone—so to speak.

"The Sausage Barn," I said. "But we have to take two cars, because I have errands to run."

"But, hon, we were just there yesterday. Besides, you sure you want to run into Wanda again? You two don't hit it off very well."

Not to mention the fact that I'd promised myself never to set foot on those greasy premises again. However, I take my sleuthing duties seriously, even if I'm not paid, and I had a new question for Wanda. Anyway, there was always a chance that a miracle had occurred overnight and the woman with the bobbling beehive had been infected by a cleaning virus.

"I need a pancake fix," I said firmly. "And don't you worry about Wanda and me; we go way back. We're as close as Cain and Abel." The Genesis reference was for Gabe's benefit, since he knows virtually nothing about the New Testament.

He grinned appropriately. "But as I recall from Hebrew school, Cain killed Abel."

"Okay, so that was a bad example. We're as close as David and Jonathan, although if you ask me, they were a little too close. Trust me, Wanda and I don't go that far back—not that I personally think there's anything wrong with it, mind you."

"It's all right, hon. The Sausage Barn it is. Just promise me one thing."

"Even up to half my kingdom," I said, continuing the biblical theme.

But Gabe was no longer smiling. "I know you've got something up your sleeve—some police business, I'm sure. I also know there's no way I'm going to stop you, but please, *please,* be careful."

It would be wrong to say that Gabe's pleas fell on deaf ears. I heard them, I just chose to ignore them.

The news that I was a seven-foot ape woman had reached every soul in the county by then, and even a few tourists. The minute we stepped into Wanda's establishment I was besieged by autograph requests and more photo opportunities. One couple, visitors from Ohio (it was obvious by their strange clothes), dragged their young son with them to meet me.

"She won't bite," the father told his whimpering heir.

"Ya sure?"

"Yeah, she's harmless," the mother said. "Besides, you can tell it's a costume."

"She ain't so hairy," the impertinent child said, emboldened. He pulled loose from his father's grip and took a step closer. "But, man, is she ever ugly."

"I beg your pardon!" I stamped a size eleven.

The crowd gasped and stepped back.

"Hey Bigfoot lady, ya do any tricks, or do ya just stand there like a big idiot?"

The crowd stepped forward.

"Do I do what?"

The urchin's confidence grew along with the crowd's expectations. "Ya heard me, tricks."

"Oh, I do tricks all right." I growled, and then snapped my jaws like the mangy mutt my sister carries in her bra.

The crowd gasped and stepped back again. With all this backward and forward movement, they may as well have been dancing. Or having sex.

The bigmouthed brat had met his match. He burst into tears and ran to hide behind his mother's generous derriere.

"Hon," Gabe whispered, "easy on the kid."

"You heard him call me an idiot," I cried.

There is no denying that Wanda Hemphopple is an outstanding businesswoman. "Folks, folks," she yelled, clapping her hands, "let's give Bigfoot a round of applause."

There was the faint sound of two hands coming together. They may not even have belonged to the same person.

"And now," Wanda said, quite undcterred, "for just a dollar Bigfoot will be happy to sign your place mats." The mats were paper, by the way, and probably cost Wanda less than a penny each.

"That's two bucks a signature," I hissed. "Bigfoot has to live too."

"Ah, she's fake," someone besides the kid said. The crowd drifted back to their congealing meals.

Wanda was fit to be tied. "Thanks a lot, Magdalena."

"Hey, at least I provided your patrons with some free entertainment."

"She did do that," Gabe said. He winked at Wanda, which made her blush. "Mrs. Hemphopple, we've come to do some serious eating. Any chance we can have that booth with all the vines?"

Wanda mumbled something, probably directed at me, but she grabbed a pair of menus and led us to my favorite booth at the rear.

"I can send Dorothy to wait on youse," she said, "or I can get your usuals myself."

I smiled pleasantly. "I don't have a usual, dear."

"Oh, yes, you do."

"Is that so?"

"You're darn tooting." Wanda can get away with that kind of language because she belongs to a more liberal branch of Mennonites.

"And just what would that be?"

"Two eggs poached hard, bacon not too crisp, wheat toast with marmalade, and buttermilk pancakes—don't make the pancakes too dark. Oh, and coffee with enough half-and-half to start an ice cream factory."

"Lucky guess, dear."

"Ha." Wanda started to walk away.

"But you don't know Gabe's!"

She wheeled. "Three eggs over easy—"

"Yeah, yeah, whatever. Look, Wanda, I need to talk to you."

"I'm innocent," she hissed. "I thought I made that clear."

"Oh, well, this is something different altogether." Surely there is special dispensation for lying during the course of performing one's civic duty.

"So, talk."

"Here?"

"Isn't my kitchen too greasy for you?"

"Well, that's no reason to be nasty and put me on the spot." I turned to Gabe. "Would you mind terribly running out to my car to see if I left my purse in it?"

"It's on the seat beside you, hon."

I've been accused of having a glare that can turn fresh plums into prunes in a matter of seconds. I'm really not that fierce. Gabe knew, however, not to get between me and my work, which at the moment was Wanda. He slid out of the booth and slipped quietly away.

"Sit down, dear," I said to the woman with the Tower of Babel bun.

"I don't think so, Magdalena. This is my restaurant, in case you've forgotten."

"Suit yourself, dear. Now, where was I? Oh yes, what color car do you drive?"

"Blue. Do I win a prize?"

She was being sarcastic, but I was too shocked by her answer to pick up on it at first. I hadn't expected to strike gold on my second spadeful of earth.

"What did you say?"

"Magdalena, do you have a hearing problem?"

"You said 'blue,' right?"

"That's what I said. So now what? Is that hunk you tricked into marrying you going to come back with the grand prize?"

"Huh?"

"Or is he the prize?"

"Hey, just one minute! He's a prize all right, but he's mine. Although he is a hunk, isn't he?"

"Oh, I get it! You sent him away because you want to have that little talk with me—you know, the sex talk. Frankly, Magdalena, I should think you would have learned all the answers to those questions during that so-called marriage of yours to Aaron Miller."

"I did no such thing—I mean, I learned plenty. Not that it's any of your business. What I want to talk about now is you."

Except for a few folks in the Witness Protection Program, there isn't a soul alive who doesn't want to talk about him- or herself. Lots of people claim they don't, but they'd change their tunes in a Bedford minute if they felt safe with their listeners. Wanda was no exception.

"Well, what do you want to know? It's not like we haven't known each other our entire lives—well, I've known you my whole life, but you, being older—"

"We're the same age, dear."

"Is that a fact? Anyway, Magdalena, I was born at 345 Bontrager Street because Mama—"

"I want to know where you were yesterday morning."

"I beg your pardon?" She whipped her head back so fast her bun started spinning like a hairy tornado. Should it break loose, I would ignore conventional wisdom, which would have me seek shelter under the table. Instead, I'd make a run for it. I may not be in the best of shape, but I probably could outrun all but the fastest of cooties. The airborne diseases I'd have to take my chances with.

Fortunately, the bun held. "Wanda, if you don't want to answer my question here, I can arrange for you to be brought down to the station." It was a truthful statement, just not as easy to accomplish as it sounded.

"Dorothy, cover me," she yelled. Then she slipped into the booth and sat across from me. "Look, I don't know how you found out, but it has nothing to do with the colonel's murder. Leroy and I were seeing each other long before *he* came to town. And Leroy never even met the man. Magdalena, you're not going to say anything to my husband, are you?"

"Well, I—"

"If you were married to Fred Hemphopple, you'd understand. Sure, he's nice enough at church or if you meet him on the street—everyone agrees about that—but behind closed doors he's as cold as yesterday's bacon grease."

It was a relief to learn that she didn't recycle the grease. "This Leroy—"

"He's not married, Magdalena, so it's not like I'm taking him away from his family. I thought of getting a divorce, of course, but you know the church frowns on that. Besides, I don't think I'm brave enough to marry a black man. Not here. We'd have to move to Pittsburgh or someplace like that."

"You're having an affair with an African-American?"

"You have a problem with that?"

"Absolutely none. We're all God's children. How old is he?"

I wouldn't have thought it possible for a bun to blush, but Wanda colored from the tip of her pointed chin to the apex of her teetering tower. Still, never one to run away from a confrontation, she maintained eye contact.

"Twenty-three."

I jiggled my pinkies in my ears to make sure they were in working order. "For a second there, dear, I thought you said twenty-three."

"I did."

My tired brain was having a hard time keeping up with the astonishing revelation. "You mean years, right?"

"Oh, I get it. You're prejudiced. Well, let me tell you something, Little Miss Bigamy—"

"I'm not prejudiced," I wailed. "I'm intrigued."

"Does that mean you won't tell Fred?"

"This isn't even my business. What I wanted to know was, where were you yesterday morning at eight?"

"Magdalena, you always were a little slow, weren't you? It's a wonder they didn't put you in Miss Lehman's special education class. I overslept at Leroy's house. Came straight from there to the restaurant. Fortunately it was Dorothy's turn to open. You even can ask her—but you can't say anything about Leroy. You can ask him, of course, if you still think I need an alibi."

Wanda's affair may not have been my business, but it was the most interesting thing I'd heard in ages. "What about Fred?" I asked. "Where does he think you spent the night?"

"Pffft. Like he even noticed I wasn't there. But to answer your question, I told him I was spending it with my cousin Shirley."

"Whom you've undoubtedly spent a lot of time with lately."

She giggled. "We're a close family."

Lodema Schrock would have a field day with this news, not that I'd ever tell her. The righteous of Hernia would turn their backs on the Sausage Barn in a cholesterol-compromised heartbeat. The next thing one knew it would be turned into a flea market that sold rip-off designer goods made by child labor on some Pacific islands.

"Give me Leroy's number," I said. "If your story checks out, my lips are sealed."

Wanda got up with a grunt. "Don't think you're going to get any free meals just because you know."

"Not even today's breakfast?" Strictly speaking I wasn't asking for a bribe, since it was she who'd brought the topic up. I was merely clarifying what her statement meant.

She sighed. "Okay, just this once, but no extra bacon."

"Deal. Now, be a dear and go fetch Gabriel."

The Babester knew better than to ask about my conversation with Wanda. We made small talk until the meal arrived, and before long we'd fortified ourselves to the point where I could afford to risk an abrupt end to the dining experience.

"Gabe, I've been thinking that maybe this ring, beautiful as it is, might be a bit too much."

By the look on his face, I may as well have said that it was not Zelda Root, but I, who was Jimmy Hoffa in disguise. He dropped his fork, and since he's a slower eater, tiny drops of egg yolk splattered his crisp blue shirt.

"You don't like it?"

"I *love* it. But it's not really me."

His dark brown eyes fixed on my watery blue ones. "It's not *you,* or it's not what others think you should be wearing?"

"Maybe both. But in this community, in my culture, to some extent they're both the same."

"I see." He sure sounded like he didn't.

"Which doesn't mean that I don't want a ring—I just want one that's a little less fancy."

I could see at once that he'd misinterpreted what I'd said, because his eyes softened and he gave me a glimpse of his trademark pearlies. "But you still want to get married?"

"More than ever." I meant it.

He grabbed my left hand, and then gently removed the ring. "Hon, you're one in a million, you know that?"

"Is that all?"

"You're one in a billion. I can't believe my good luck in finding you. As it happens, I'm going into Pittsburgh on Friday, so I'll exchange this for something a little more modest."

"But not *too* modest."

His eyes twinkled. "Gotcha. And I'm bringing back something else for you too."

"What?" I hate surprises. Perhaps that all started with the birth of Susannah, which came as a total surprise. One would think that an eleven-year-old girl would have some inkling her mother was pregnant, but not yours truly. Of course back in those days women didn't get pregnant; they got in the "family way." Since Mama was always in my way, blocking my every move, I didn't think anything of it. Yes, she did put on some extra weight, but on a woman her size it was hardly noticeable.

When the bawling, red-faced Susannah arrived, I was told by Granny Yoder that the baby had been plucked from under a head of cabbage (this was years before my seed talk with Mama). The very next day, while everyone was preoccupied with the demanding brat, I went out to the vegetable garden and poisoned all the cabbages with weed killer. I checked under each one first, so as not to be guilty of infanticide, but yes, I was an early believer in birth control.

Gabe loves surprises. "I'm not saying another word, except that you're going to love this one."

A big cock, an ostentatious ring—I dreaded this surprise already. "Not even a hint?"

"None whatsoever." He got up, and before leaving planted a smooch on my mug that might have gotten him halfway to second base under the right circumstances, or at least a commitment from me to take dancing lessons. "Gotta go, hon," he said, tearing himself away. "You be careful."

"Aren't I always?"

Gabe knew better than to answer with the truth. Sometimes caution has to be thrown to the wind, and I seem to experience more than my share of breezy days.

*   *   *

The first dangerous thing I did after Gabe left was to order another rasher of bacon. Of course this one I had to pay for, but it was worth it. And if Melvin had had the sense to add me to his official payroll, I could have charged it as a business expense, because my waitress this time was Dorothy, who, as it happens, is my cousin Sam's niece by marriage.

"Can I get you anything else, sweetie?" she asked.

Sweetie? This from an urchin who was barely older than my Alison? I gave her my biggest, warmest smile. It is always a risk, because exposing my chompers has been known to scare horses. Although on one occasion it made a stallion amorous.

"A little more coffee when you have a minute, dear. But no rush. I'm more interested in hearing what you have to say about Wanda's you-know-what."

Dorothy slipped into the seat Gabe had vacated. She's a mere wisp of a girl, so I knew it wasn't because she needed to sit.

"There ain't no need to worry, Miss Yoder. I was a-scared of that thing too, but it ain't never fallen. She's got it pinned up with, like, a million bobby pins. Although one time a little dog got into it, which you'd think was kinda strange, except this—oh, that's right, you know all about that. The dog belongs to your sister, Mrs. Stoltzfus."

"The you-know-what I was referring to, dear, was not her hairdo." I waggled my eyebrows, which are, alas, pale and scant. "I'm talking about why she was late to work yesterday and had to get you to open."

"You know about that?"

"Cousin Magdalena knows everything." I tried winking this time. Although that gesture has provoked laughter among two-legged mammals, it has never caused equids to stampede—or come on to me, for that matter.

Dorothy giggled. "Can you imagine taking piano lessons when you're that old?"

"What?"

"It ain't like she's gonna get famous like you and be on TV or nothing. Or in them papers."

I decided that was a compliment. "Wanda takes piano lessons?"

"Every week, Tuesday mornings at eight. Man, now that I'm out of high school I don't never get up that early—well, except for Tuesdays, of course, 'cause that's when she makes me open. Gotta get my butt outta bed and be down by six to let the fry cooks in."

I shook my head in disbelief. "Why are the piano lessons such a big secret? Is she embarrassed? I mean, a lot of adults take piano lessons."

Dorothy shrugged. "Whatever. But Wanda thinks it's a big deal. If she knew I was telling you this, she'd kill me."

Perhaps I was getting distracted. "Why can't the fry cooks let themselves in?"

"Geesh, you're kidding, right? Nah, I can see you ain't. Well, because they ain't as responsible as me."

My head was spinning, which often happens after I've had a vigorous workout of jumping to conclusions. But this time I'd only been gullible and swallowed a pack of lies.

"Your boss," I growled, "told me she was having an affair with a twenty-three-year-old African-American and—"

"Leroy?"

"He's the one."

"He ain't her boyfriend; he's mine—which is *so* not anybody's business. You'd think I robbed a bank or something, when all I did was fall in love with someone of a different color."

I was shocked. Why hadn't I heard this piece of gossip? Was I that far out of the loop? Was I losing my touch? No, it had to be because this Dorothy, being the niece of Sam's Dorothy, was a Methodist *and* lived in Bedford. Had the girl been a Mennonite, or even just a Hernian, I would have been among the first to pass along this juicy tidbit.

Not knowing what to say, I switched subjects. "Where does Wanda take these piano lessons?"

"From Miss Quiring. She used to be the music teacher at the high school."

"I know her well. She was there when I attended."

"No kidding! She must be, like, really ancient."

I gave Dorothy the evil eye and picked up another slice of bacon. "Are these lessons at the high school?"

"Nah, at Miss Quiring's house. Wanda says it smells like the inside of a birdcage."

I sighed. To get from the Sausage Barn to the retired teacher's house, one takes Highway 96 until it hits Augsburger Road, and then one makes a sharp left onto Schwartzentruber. One does not pass my house—not unless one is male and therefore refuses to read his map or ask for directions.

"Well, dear, you've been very helpful, and the bacon was just right. You can count on a nice tip. And speaking of tips, here's a little free advice. If you're sure Leroy is the right man for you, then ignore the gossip and criticism. However, if you're involved with him just for the shock value—maybe to give your parents a hard time—then it's not a good thing, and you're just using him."

"Miss Yoder, I love Leroy with all my heart. It wouldn't matter what color he was."

"Then stick to your guns."

She blinked. "I don't have a gun, Miss Yoder."

"What I meant was, hang in there, or whatever it is you young people say these days."

"Thanks." She got up and looked both ways down the

narrow aisle. "Oh, and there's no charge for the extra bacon. Just don't say anything to Wanda."

You can be sure that Dorothy got a fat tip. You can also be sure that I did not go straight to Miss Quiring's house.

27

The First and Only True Church of the One and Only Living God of the Tabernacle of Supreme Holiness and Healing and Keeper of the Consecrated Righteousness of the Eternal Flame of Jehovah is barely more than a link's throw from the Sausage Barn. Two tosses at the most. When the wind is right, the smell of bacon, pork patties, and authentic imitation maple syrup all vie for one's olfaction. Despite this onslaught of odors, members of this sect refrain from eating on Sunday mornings until after the three-hour service—which, come to think of it, might be why there are so few of them. This might also help to explain why, until recently, the small building had no windows.

Of course my object was not to sniff the air, but to check out the color of the reverend's car. I'd seen it a million times, and my recollection was that it was black. But that was before I had any real reason to notice. It could well be a dark navy. After all, Ivan Yetinsky had said that his form of color blindness made it hard for him to distinguish shades.

Much to my relief the reverend's car was as black as sin—well, those parts that weren't being consumed by rust. I would have wheeled right on out of there, headed for Miss Quiring's, had I not noticed that the door to his trailer was open.

While I'd been inside the church with thirty-two names on numerous occasions, I had never had as much as a peek into the bachelor preacher's living quarters. They say curiosity killed the cat, but since I didn't have one anymore, what did a little snooping hurt?

"Knock, knock!" I called cheerily, although I didn't dare do any actual knocking, because the mobile home was nearly as rusty as the car.

No one answered, so I climbed the rickety wooden steps and poked my horsey head through the door. Boy, was I in for a surprise.

On either side of the entrance, cartons of canned food were stacked to the ceiling. They formed a corridor that made a ninety-degree left turn about six feet into the trailer. The corridor of cans—and they covered all the food groups, from SPAM Lite to diced pears in heavy syrup—led to the far end of the trailer. Every now and then there would be an entrance to a tiny room entirely lined with boxes of food. Inside these rooms were tables and chairs, sofas or beds, just like the ones you might find in a regular room, except they were jammed closer together due to the lack of space. I know all this, of course, because I gave myself the grand tour.

It wasn't until the very last room, at the end of the corridor, that the construction material changed from food to dry goods. That entire wall was built from toilet tissue rolls, the ones that come packaged together by fours. That door was closed.

"Knock, knock," I cried cheerily again.

The door swung open so fast and with such force that the paper wall wobbled. For a second I feared being smothered by an avalanche of Scott double-ply.

"Magdalena!" The good reverend was as pale as the paper around him.

"The front door was open, so I let myself in. I hope you don't mind."

His expression made it clear that he did, even though Richard Nixon is a kindly man who wouldn't hurt my feelings for all the hygiene products in the world. He pointed down the narrow hall.

"The latch needs to be fixed, and I don't usually lock it during the day. Anyway, my sitting room is down there. Come, please, be my guest."

He squeezed past me and led me to the first room, which was arranged as a parlor. A very cramped one, of course. The furniture had been through the Goodwill outlet in Bedford at least once—I think I recognized the end table as something I donated—but one hardly noticed its vintage or wear. It was the walls that grabbed your attention.

The one in front of me contained cans of baby peas, baby peas with onions, both fingerling and sliced carrots, whole-leaf spinach and chopped, tomato sauce with and without onions, tuna fish in oil and spring water, jars of applesauce with cinnamon and without, as well as jars of both creamy and crunchy peanut butter.

"It's almost like Noah's ark," I said. "There's two of each, but they're not quite the same."

The reverend smiled. "That's to give me a little variety."

"Reverend, I hope you don't mind me saying so, but that's an awful lot of food for one person."

"It's supposed to last a year, Magdalena."

"Still, that's a lot. I couldn't eat that in a year—although I probably could use all that toilet paper."

"Well, it's not all just for me. There are some in the church who do not put aside the required food."

"Required? Reverend, what's the story?"

"It's in your Bible, Magdalena. The Book of Revelations."

"I believe there's no *s* on the end—" I slapped my mouth for having corrected a man of the cloth. "Reverend, does it mention stockpiling enough food to feed an army?"

"It talks about the end times, Magdalena. The day of wrath. Do you think the Giant Eagle in Bedford—or even your cousin Sam's little market—will stay open then?"

I shrugged. The Book of Revelation has always made me uncomfortable, and not because I don't feel assured of my salvation. I do. But whereas I view this collection of writings as allegorical, people like Richard Nixon take them literally. I fear that my opinion may be in the minority.

"Believe me, Magdalena, when the time comes, those who haven't planned ahead will wish they had."

"I'll keep that in mind, Reverend." It was time to change the subject. "Did you go to the zoning commission like I suggested? Did you speak to Claire?"

"Yes, and I want to thank you. I've been sleeping much better since then. In fact, that's what I was doing just now."

"Sorry, Reverend, didn't mean to wake you."

"That's all right, Magdalena. It's always a pleasure to see you."

"So what happened? No punishment of any kind?"

He bit his lip. It was obvious he was thinking twice before speaking, a habit I would do well to learn—although it would leave me a very dull gal.

"Come on, Reverend, spit it out. We're friends, aren't we?"

"They fined us fifty thousand dollars."

"They *what*?"

"That was at first. But the Lord provides, Magdalena. I was able to talk them down to twenty."

"I don't mean to be disrespectful, Reverend, but is the Lord going to provide that as well?"

He looked like he wanted to crawl under the Wal-Mart-via-Goodwill coffee table in front of him. " 'And we know that in all things God works for the good of those who love Him,' " he said, quoting Romans 8:28. "In other words, Magdalena, whatever happens is for the best."

That just so happens to be my least favorite Scripture verse—after the one that says "Wives, submit to your husbands." I tried, but I just couldn't keep my yammering yap shut.

"Tell that to the mother over in Somerset whose two-year-old was crushed by the cement truck."

"Magdalena, what are you saying? Are you having a crisis of faith?"

"Absolutely not," I wailed. "But I don't have to like everything in the Bible, do I?"

His look said that I did.

Rather than argue theology, I decided to help the Lord carry out His promise to the reverend. I took out my well-worn checkbook and scribbled out a two and four zeros. Before I get nominated for sainthood, it is only fair that I state, yet again, that I am a wealthy woman. I can afford to be generous. Besides, my accountant would find a way to make at least part of that sum tax deductible. Having said that, by the time I got to zero number four, I felt like I'd put my hand in a blender. It might be better to give than to receive, but that doesn't mean that giving isn't painful.

"Here you go," I said, handing him the check. "Don't spend it all in one place."

He stared at the check with the same wide-eyed wonder with which I'd stared at Aaron Miller on our bogus wedding night. "Is this for real?"

"That's the same thing I said," I cried.

"I beg your pardon?"

"Never mind, dear."

"Magdalena, how can I ever thank you?"

"No need, dear. The expression on your face is enough."

"We'll pay you back, I promise. We can work out a monthly—"

"No need to do that either." I glanced around the room with edible walls. "When the time comes, maybe you will let me have a couple of those cans. But not the peas. With them, it's either fresh or nothing."

"You got it."

Having been promised food during the Apocalypse, I set out in earnest to visit its horse*woman*—not mentioned in the Bible, by the way—Miss Quiring. Next to being chosen last in gym class, the music teacher had been what I hated most about school. In the tradition of Beethoven she was hard of hearing. There is, of course, nothing wrong with that, but it is quite wrong for a teacher to pull a student's ears just because she can't hear you.

It wasn't just my ears Miss Quiring pulled, but those of every student who passed through the doors of Hernia Elementary School. We arrived in the first grade looking like beatific cherubs, and graduated from the sixth grade resembling mules. Jack Rule, who broke every rule in school and perhaps deserved to have something pulled, was the only exception. By the time he entered the seventh grade, he looked like a jackrabbit on steroids.

So it was with fear and trepidation that I rang Miss Quiring's bell. I didn't expect her to answer the door right away and had already made a fist, prepared to bang myself into her consciousness, when the door opened.

"I already belong to a church, thank you very much."

"Miss Quiring, it's me—Magdalena Yoder."

"Yes, I'm getting older, but my church sends a van around to pick me up."

"I know, dear. You go to my church." There was nothing to be gained by telling her I was the one who donated the van.

"We don't drink beer at my church," she said and started to close the door.

One of the benefits of having big feet and wearing clodhoppers is the ability to stop folks from shutting their doors all the way. If I'm really quick and turn my feet sideways, they can't shut them at all.

"Miss Quiring," I shouted, "I'm Magdalena Yoder. Can I come in?"

The woman barely comes up to my bosoms. She'd shrunk a bit since the last time I saw her, but my bosoms had gotten lower, so in that respect nothing had changed. She stared up at my lips, trying to make sense of what I'd said.

"Did you say Magdalena Yoder?"

"As big as life and twice as ugly."

"Ugly, you say? Why, I'll have you know I was Miss Bedford County of nineteen forty—"

"Not you, me. I'm the ugly one, and it's only an expression." Thank heavens I'd had practice talking on a cell phone; otherwise I never would have made myself understood.

"Well, yes, you always were a homely child, Magdalena. Now, what is it you said you wanted?"

"I'd like to come in and ask you a few questions."

For a few painful seconds I saw loneliness and pride duke it out. Loneliness won.

"Come in then, but mind you don't let the birds out."

I'd known the woman my entire life, but I'd never been in her house. I'd never had occasion to. Mama didn't believe in wasting money on piano lessons, not when she could teach me herself. Never mind that Mama played the piano with all the grace of a drunken marionette, and every song she taught me sounded mysteriously like "Chopsticks."

There was certainly no mistaking why Miss Quiring's house smelled like a birdcage. There were only two real birds, canaries both, but they were not confined to a cage. Their names, 1 learned immediately, were Mendelssohn and Mozart. They flitted about the room in a dither, all the while depositing feathers and droppings, like a yellow snowstorm punctuated by hail. I had to brush the sofa with my hand before I sat. Even then it was better to squint.

"Keeping them locked up in a cage would be cruel," Miss Quiring said after I'd shouted myself hoarse asking the question.

I nodded, needing to save my voice for the question I'd come to ask. "Was Wanda Hemphopple here for a lesson Tuesday morning?"

"Gracious me, I hope it won't topple. I've heard there's a rat in there that likes to eat birds. Do you think I should lock up my canaries when she comes? I could chase them into the bathroom."

As much as I would have liked to track down the origins of yet another rumor about Wanda's 'do, I really needed to get down to business. "That was a dog, not a rat," I croaked, "and it was a one-time thing. I wanted to know if Wanda was here yesterday morning? Did she have a lesson?"

"She told you about her lessons?"

"Someone did," I said, hoping she'd heard an affirmative answer.

Apparently she did. "Well, there's no shame in not knowing how to read. It was the school's fault, if you ask me. Not Wanda's."

Already I disagreed. "The school has enough of a job teaching kids how to read words. Reading music, on the other hand—"

"I'm talking about reading words," Miss Quiring said, her hearing suddenly restored. "It's amazing how some folks compensate. Running a business like the Sausage

Barn and not being able to read past a third-grade level—one has to admire the woman."

"Wanda Hemphopple can't read?"

"Well, she can now. What do you think I do, give her piano lessons?"

I was stunned. "Yes, that's exactly what I thought."

Miss Quiring's hearing was on a roll. "Piano lessons to Wanda? Now, that's a good one. Ha! Why, that woman has less talent even than Magdalena Yoder."

"Than who?" Both Magdalena and Yoder are common names in these parts, but to my knowledge there is currently just one—and that would be moi—who uses both monikers.

"Tall skinny girl I taught in elementary school some years ago. Couldn't carry a tune if you handed her a radio and told her to walk."

"Wait a second. When was that?"

"Like I said, it was years ago—but I remember her like it was yesterday. I'd given her a solo to sing in the spring festival, on account of I felt sorry for the big galoot. Was that ever a mistake. She hit so many wrong notes half the audience got up and left before the piece was finished."

"That was because the stupid spring festival was held outdoors," I wailed, "and it had started to rain."

"That's right, she sounded just like a train. But afterwards her mother still had the nerve to ask me if I wouldn't give that tone-deaf daughter of hers piano lessons. And at a discount yet."

"*Mama* asked that?" I had no trouble believing the discount part, but that my penny-pinching progenitrix was willing to part with any of her pennies was music to my ears. Mama's only answer to me had been a flat-out "no."

"Speak up, child—you're not making any sense."

"I'm hardly a child, dear. That was me all those years ago."

"Ears? Yes, I pull ears if children don't listen, and I'm not ashamed of it. Schools have gotten too liberal these days—won't allow corporal punishment anymore. Spare the rod, spoil the child. Says so right in the Bible. That's why I no longer teach, you know."

"For that every child in Hernia should be grateful," I whispered. I said it so softly my left brain couldn't even hear my right brain, much less my mouth.

"I heard that!"

"Uh—I don't think so, Miss Quiring."

"You said children should be grateful I no longer teach."

I stood. "Well, it may have sounded like that, but—oh, before I forget, what time Tuesday morning did Wanda have her reading lesson?"

"Seven thirty, like she always does. The actual lesson lasts about half an hour. Then I make her stay an extra hour to read on her own."

"So she didn't leave here until nine?"

"Wine? I'll have you know I don't even allow beer in this house."

"I didn't say wine—"

"I know what you said, young lady." She was spry for a woman of her years, and apparently a good jumper as well, because the next thing I knew she had me by my left ear and was twisting it like it was nothing more than a piece of dough. Believe it or not, that was a new twist. In the old days, when she was taller than I, she would have merely given my ear a good tug to get me out of my seat, before taking her director's baton to my comely caboose.

"Ow! Miss Quiring, that hurts."

She twisted harder, leading me to believe it was a certain Mennonite woman who invented those sugary treats called elephant ears available at county fairs. And those curious pastries have nothing to do with pachyderms, but once graced the heads of this woman's music students at Hernia Elementary.

There is only so much pain a body can take, even if it belongs to a committed pacifist like myself. When I reached my breaking point, I did the unthinkable and pulled one of Miss Quiring's ears.

28

"Oh Mama," I wailed, "I can't believe I did it!"

Mama couldn't hear me, of course. Ever since she died, her hearing has been worse than that of Miss Quiring. Still, I find it comforting to sit at the foot of Mama's grave—I don't dare sit *on* it—and pour my heart out to a woman I couldn't have said the same things to when she was alive.

But just because Mama can no longer hear with her flesh and blood ears doesn't mean she's not listening. I know she's aware of what I'm saying, because I hear her responses in my head. I can be certain these responses are hers, and not just the figments of my imagination, for two reasons: (a) I don't have an imagination, and (b) even if I did possess some small shred of imagination, it could never come up with the things I hear in my head.

"Magdalena, dear, did you pull both her ears, or just the one?"

"Just the one, Mama."

"That's a shame. While you had the chance, you should have given them both a good hard tug. Maybe even got her in a headlock and given her a few noogies."

"Mama!"

"I never did like that woman, dear. Always picking on you like that, just because you had a tin ear."

"But you were going to buy me piano lessons."

"I was? Oh yeah, well, write it off to a moment of weakness."

"Mama!"

"Magdalena, you sure wail a lot, you know that?"

"You would too if you had my problems."

"And just what would those problems be?"

"For starters, I have a sister who never grows up, a cook who quits at the drop of a saucepan, a hunky fiancé who is not of my faith, a foster child with more holes in her body than a pound of Swiss cheese, and a murder case to solve, which is currently going nowhere."

"Quite whining, Magdalena. First of all, Susannah may not be your ideal sister, but she loves you dearly, which is more than I could say about my sister, Matilda. Not to mention the fact she worships the ground you walk on, which I can't for the life of me—"

"That's because you're dead, Mama."

"Whatever. Now, where was I, before you so rudely interrupted?"

"I think you were about to mention Freni."

"Yeah, Freni. Salt of the earth. So what if she quits? You always get her back. And as for that cute guy you call the Babester, calling off the marriage isn't going to help him see the light."

"Mama! I wasn't even thinking about calling it off."

"Don't lie to me, Magdalena. You know how I hate that."

"Yes, ma'am."

"Now, about that child Alison. You should thank your lucky stars for the opportunity to raise her, as difficult as it might be. You foolishly waited too long to have a child of your own—"

"It's not like I had a choice, Mama."

"Oh, yes, you did. Remember Wilmer Sprunger?"

"The man with two Adam's apples?"

"That extra Adam's apple was a sign of virility. You could be the mother of an entire brood by now if you hadn't been so picky."

"What about the murder case, since you seem to have an answer for everything?"

"Give me a moment, dear. You always were so impatient."

While Mama took her own sweet time thinking, I looked around me. Settlers' Cemetery straddles the crest of Stucky Ridge and has commanding views of the countryside. It is *the* place to be buried in Hernia, and only the direct descendants of the town's founders can be interred there. From Mama's grave site I can look right down on the PennDutch Inn. I barely have to turn my head to see where Freni lives. This is truly the land of the pilgrims' pride, land where the Indians died, or however that song goes. Every time I visit the cemetery I feel connected to my past, and therefore to my future.

"So, Mama," I said, after admiring the view and feeling my roots for a respectable length of time, "what's your theory?"

"Rush, rush, rush," Mama said. "All you ever do is rush me, but okay, here goes. You can cross Sam off your list."

"Reason?"

"He's your cousin, for crying out loud. Besides, Samuel Nevin Yoder is a coward. Always has been. He doesn't have the *cajones* to stand up to his wife, Dorothy, much less murder someone."

"Mama! You used a bad word."

"I'm dead, Magdalena, or have you forgotten? I can say anything I want."

Do you see what I mean? The voice I hear when I visit the cemetery could only be Mama's. I could never dream up such language on my own.

"Go on, Mama," I begged.

"Well, as you found out on your own, Wanda Hemphopple has an alibi. An airtight one too, I'd say. There's not another soul in Hernia who would risk having her ears pulled to contradict that old woman. By the way, how does your ear feel?"

I touched the injured party. "It's still a little sore."

"Do you ever stop complaining? Now, where was I?"

"You'd just crossed Sam and Wanda off my list. That leaves Principal Herman Middledorf and Elspeth Miller."

"Do you want my opinion?"

"Yes?" I asked anxiously.

"Think about it, Magdalena. Don't be such a dummkopf. Miss Quiring had an alibi, but Herman has three hundred and eighty-five."

"He does?"

"Honestly, Magdalena, you can be so slow at times. Students—that's what I'm talking about. And of course teachers. A high school principal has his hands full at eight in the morning."

"Okay, okay. So that leaves Elspeth. But of the four of them, she would be least affected by a five-star hotel. Custard's last stand was not going to take any business away from the feed store. And even if they widened the road in front of it, what's the worst that would have happened? She'd have lost a little of her parking lot, that's all."

"Again, you're not thinking, silly. A wider road means more traffic—the Amish wouldn't have liked that. Too dangerous for horse-drawn buggies."

To my credit, I refrained from calling Mama a dummkopf. But clearly, eleven years of decomposition had not done her brain any good.

"Elspeth could have sold that store to developers and built a new one farther out from town. On Augsberger Road, for instance."

"Unless she had something to hide under that parking lot of hers."

"Hide? Like what."

Mama's sigh of exasperation lifted a stray wisp of hair on my forehead. "Do you really know what happened to her husband, Roy?"

"He took off someplace to escape being abused by Elspeth the Hun."

"Give me a break, Magdalena. He ran away *before* the fishing trip he planned with Sam."

I gasped. "You don't mean—I mean, you think Elspeth killed Roy too?"

"Well, if she was capable of killing the colonel in cold blood for business reasons—think about it, Magdalena. The woman despised her husband for his weakness. After she became a full-fledged U.S. citizen, what else did she need him for?"

"Well—although I guess there is always the Maytag."

"I've been meaning to talk to you about that, Magdalena."

"Not now, Mama, we're on a roll."

"You mean *I'm* on a roll. Now where was I?"

"Elspeth killed Roy. But if that's the case, Mama, how come he never showed up dead?"

"Maybe he will yet, Magdalena. What is it Elspeth sells in that feed store, besides feed, I mean."

"A little bit of this, a little bit of that."

"Be specific."

"But Mama, she sells just about everything a farmer would need, besides livestock and large machinery. You can buy barbed wire, posthole diggers, pickaxes—even cement."

"And why was Elspeth so upset with the water people the other day?"

"They wanted to dig up part of her parking lot on account of a possible leak—Mama, are you saying what I think you're saying?"

But Mama, always one to have the last word, didn't have anything else to say, not even good-bye. Just left me sitting there at the foot of her grave with my mouth open wide enough to catch dragonflies. With no salutation, I was tempted to doubt she'd even been speaking to me at all. Of course that was silly, because I never could have come to those conclusions on my own. Not me, the dummkopf.

I waited patiently for another ten minutes and then picked a handful of dandelions and laid them on her grave. Then I tried to imagine what Mama would say about my thoughtful gesture.

"Is that all you think of me? Weeds?"

The words were right, and so was the tone, but I no longer felt her presence. It was time for me to scoot my skinny patooty back down the ridge and do some serious investigating.

Owls are nocturnal and see best at night, but I knew from experience that Elspeth Miller was the exception to the rule. Therefore, it was with extreme caution that I cased her parking lot. I even went so far as to borrow a black traveling bonnet and cape from Barbara Hostetler, Freni's daughter-in-law. Well, actually I borrowed it from Freni, because Barbara was still not home. Freni was more than happy to lend me her daughter-in-law's things without permission, a fact that did not please me, but what else could I do? My cook is a mere five feet two, while Barbara is six feet in her thick cotton stockings.

Because I wear no makeup, and share a genetic history with ninety percent of the community, I can pass as an Amish woman with just the addition of the bonnet and cape. Although I drove to Miller's Feed Store, I parked in the farthest corner toward the back and didn't don my garb until I was out of the car. There was absolutely no reason for anyone to be suspicious.

Clutching my cape closed to hide a too pale blue dress, I wandered about, unchallenged, in search of Roy Miller's final resting spot. It was a busy day at the feed store and the lot was filled with Amish buggies and cars belonging to more liberal Mennonite farmers. Finding an anomaly was not going to be easy.

I poked about for twenty minutes or so, peering under buggies, and discreetly getting down on my hands and knees on the asphalt and peeking under cars, when I remembered something Mama had said. Elspeth possessed the means of disposing of Roy's body. In other words, she already had everything she needed in the store.

What she didn't have was hot asphalt and a giant rolling machine. How stupid of me to not have thought of that right away. Roy Miller could only be buried on that small portion of the lot that was poured concrete. This was restricted to the sidewalk, the curb, and a narrow strip along the street that had once been a flower and vegetable display bed. Several years ago, about the time Roy disappeared, Elspeth decided extra parking spaces were more important than showing customers the latest varieties of marigolds and pole beans.

"Dummkopf," I cried, and hit myself on the forehead with the ball of my hand. "Magdalena, you are such an idiot."

"That is the truth."

I whirled. It was the bird lady herself, having flown within inches of me on silent wings.

"Elspeth!"

"That is my name, yah. So do not wear it out."

"Not much danger of that, dear."

"What are you doing dressed like the Amish, Magdalena?"

"Practicing."

"For what?"

"Well, you have to admit this cape and bonnet are pretty snappy. If I like the way they wear, I might just consider switching over." The word "might" makes all the difference, don't you think?

Elspeth's beady eyes could bore through steel. She stared at me so hard I was forced to look away.

"You think I do not know the customs because I am a foreigner? The Amish do not drive cars, Magdalena, but you have a foot of lead. You would not be happy with the horse and buggy."

"I'm rich," I said. "I could buy a racehorse and have an aerodynamic buggy especially designed for me." My retinas would have been scorched had I the nerve to be looking her in the eyes.

"Yah, maybe you could do that, but the Amish would not approve. And they will never accept that you marry the Jew." She pronounced the word "chew."

Elspeth wore her anti-Semitism on short English-style sleeves, but she had a point. Reverend Schrock was willing to overlook the fact that Gabriel Rosen was as Jewish as Jesus, but the Amish would not. Conformity to the rules of the Ordnung is what identifies them as a people. You are either Amish or not, and if you are, then you act like one. That includes who you marry.

"Okay, okay," I said, scrambling to think up another necessary lie. "I needed something from the store, and since I know you hate my guts, I decided it would be easier on both of us if I sneaked in wearing a disguise."

Elspeth grunted. "Why did you not send Freni or Mose?"

"What? Use a septuagenarian Amish couple as errand boys?"

"This does not stop you before."

Judging on my past encounters with the merchant of menace, I figured I had about fifteen seconds left before she planted a foot on my bony behind or, worse yet, stabbed me with a pitchfork. It was time to get down to business.

"So, dear, what happened to your lovely display garden? It always made me want to try the various seeds."

"Bullcrap," she said. Actually, being a Lutheran, she was permitted a much worse expression. Unofficially, of course.

I feigned an even temper. "I remember one September you had the most spectacular display of mums—"

"Leave now, Magdalena."

"I beg your pardon?"

"Or I make you leave, yah?"

"Is that a threat?"

She may have thought her smile masked her deadly secret, but it was a wasted use of facial muscles. Still, an itty-bitty murderess—because that's how I now thought of her—who dared threaten a woman of stature in broad daylight was much to be feared. Perhaps she had another gun hidden somewhere on her miniature person.

"Don't get your nasty Nazi knickers in a knot, dear. I'm out of here. But first be a sweetheart and write down the name of those fabulous mums." I fished in my purse for a palm-size notebook that I sometimes use to take notes when I'm working a case but, if the truth be known, is more often used for making grocery lists during Reverend Schrock's less engaging sermons. Before Elspeth could react I thrust the tablet at her. With any luck she'd grab it, thereby giving me a good set of prints.

Her first reaction was to reach for it, but the second her fingers closed on the smooth, shiny cover, she practically threw it in my face. "I am not a fool, Magdalena. I know what you are up to."

I caught the notebook by its spiral binder and dropped it in my purse. "Maybe you do know, or maybe you don't. Either way your gig is up."

Having said that much I had no option but to hustle my bustle up the street to the Hernia Police Station. Halfway to my car I turned and looked, like Lot's wife. Fortunately I did not turn into a salt sculpture. Neither did Elspeth. In fact, she was no longer in sight.

29

Zelda was too busy painting her nails a glossy shade of black to look up when I burst into the station.

"I need a warrant," I gasped.

She finished spreading the goo on her right pinkie and then closed the lid tightly. "You're not authorized to make arrests, Magdalena."

"Then you arrest her."

"Arrest who?"

"Elspeth Miller. Not only did she kill the colonel, but she knocked off her husband, Roy, as well."

Zelda smiled. No doubt it gave her a sense of superiority to be patient with me.

"Elspeth couldn't have killed Roy, Magdalena. Nobody knows where he is."

"I do. He's buried in her parking lot where the flower and vegetable display used to be."

While Zelda mulled over what I'd said, peace came to the Middle East and my size elevens began to sprout roots. When the bulb finally clicked on in her head, both ears emitted a soft glow.

"So that's why she didn't want the hotel built. The road would have eventually been widened and poor

Roy—" Zelda clapped a hand over her mouth, the freshly painted nails gleaming like wet obsidian.

"Mazel tov," I said, borrowing from Gabe. "So you're going right out there to arrest her, right?"

She shook her bleached spikes. "Not without a warrant. And for that I need proof."

"So get it."

"But I need a warrant to search the parking lot." She moaned. "Where is Melvin when you need him?"

"Good point. Where is he?"

"Don't you know? That was a historical question, Magdalena. He's headed out to your place—"

"What?"

"He called and said he had some checking around to do and—"

"Didn't you warn him about the snake?"

"Of course I did. But you know our Melvin. Said he wasn't afraid of a little thing like a snake."

"A twenty-five-foot supersize sneaky snake," I hissed. "An African rock python, one of the most aggressive species in the world."

Fear flickered across her eyes. "You think he might really be in danger?"

"Are those nails of yours the height of fashion?"

"What—oh, he is, isn't he? Magdalena, what shall we do?"

"You call the county sheriff, dear. I'll try to head our bumbling bumpkin off at the pass."

I turned and ran to my car. True to my reputation, I pressed that pedal to the metal so hard it nearly broke through the floorboard. In fact, I made it back to the inn in record time. Sure enough there was the Hernia squad car parked in my driveway, but the menacing mantis was nowhere to be seen.

I'm not a total fool. I checked the barn and the hen-house before turning my attention to the inn. The sheriff was taking his sweet time about showing up, and I doubted if Melvin Stoltzfus had a whole lot of that precious commodity at his disposal. Not if he was indoors battling a snake. The nincompoop Chief of Police is a scrawny man, as befits a mantis. Any creature that could get the better of the bad-tempered Miss Thrope—and I do not mean to speak ill of the dead—would find my brother-in-law easy pickings.

As much as I abhorred the idea, it was up to me to enter the house and rescue my nemesis. If I didn't, I'd have his blood on my hands, and my sister back under my roof. I really had no choice.

"Melvin! Melvin!" I opened the back door to the kitchen just wide enough for my probing proboscis, one eye, and half of a very loud mouth. Surely a twenty-five-foot snake could not fit through a crack that narrow. If it did leap at me and got my nose, I might even come out ahead.

There was no response to my shouts and no sign of a reptile, so I pushed the door all the way open and stepped in. The kitchen was as comfy and inviting as it had always been. Despite the lingering odor of some fancy-schmancy dish prepared by the late Miss Thrope, perhaps one containing that heathen herb cilantro, I could still smell Freni's homemade cinnamon rolls.

I poked my head into the dining room. "Melvin! Melvin!"

Still no answer. Before leaving the kitchen I grabbed a meat fork with eight-inch tines and a can of nonstick cooking spray. Freni uses only butter and shortening to grease her baking pans, like the Good Lord intended, so the no-calorie stuff must have belonged to the deceased. The only reason I picked those two items was that they were both within easy reach.

It would be a lie, and one without an obvious moral benefit, if I were to say I wasn't scared. My legs were trembling, my heart was pounding, and the short hairs on my neck stood out at right angles. Even my bun strained at the bobby pins that held it in place.

"Oh, Lord," I said aloud, "if you get me through this—help me to find Melvin unharmed—I promise to never say anything sarcastic about him. Well, at least not for a week. I'll even try and find something to compliment him on."

My prayer brought me a good deal of comfort, because I had been very generous with the Lord. Hence I found the strength to look in the parlor and my bedroom, both of which are downstairs. There was no sign of Melvin or a giant python. For a second there, I wanted nothing more than to push heavy furniture over the vents, lock my bedroom door, and crawl under the covers. All the way, so that not a strand of hair showed. Add a bedpan and some food—brownies and milk— and I wouldn't have to come out for hours.

It was, of course, a fleeting fantasy. Hiding under the covers was not going to save Melvin's carapace. I fortified myself by repeating my earlier prayer, and even added a clause whereby I promised to be nice to Lodema Schrock for an unspecified period of time.

Having girded my loins with new courage, I faced my impossibly steep stairs. "Melvin, dear, are you up there?"

Again no answer.

"Well, here I come," I called to the snake. "If you value your scales, stay out of my way."

"Help! Magdalena, help!"

I could hardly believe my ears. Someone, or something, was answering. The voice was high-pitched, about what you'd expect from a snake—if one could talk— and it didn't sound a bit like Melvin. Could it possibly be that the Devil really was masquerading as a twenty-five-foot African rock python? The serpent in the Garden of Eden talked up a storm, so there was certainly a precedent for such a phenomenon. But surely Satan didn't know me on a first-name basis.

"Melvin, dear. Is that you?"

"Magdalena, help, help! It's got me!"

It was definitely not Melvin. And unless the Devil had a German accent—always a possibility, I guess . . .

"Elspeth, is that you?"

"Do something, you dummkopf, or this snake will eat me."

I charged up my impossibly steep stairs. Don't ask me why I flew to this woman's aid. She wasn't supposed to be in my house, for crying out loud.

You can't imagine what a twenty-five-foot snake looks like until you've seen one. Who knew that it would be as thick around the middle as Gabriel's thigh, or that its head, which was quite big enough, was small compared to its body? This particular monster was tan with brown spots outlined in black, and had a tan V-shaped mark on its face. Its eyes had the curious quality of being both vacuous and vicious.

The behemoth was coiled in a corner, between the bed and an armoire. Gripped in its death embrace was the tiny frame of Elspeth Miller. The snake's hideous head rested on her shoulder, and all I could see of the woman at first was her head. My first impression was that the reptile had two heads—although one had scales. The other was as pale as rice and sweating profusely.

"Do not just stand there," she panted. "Do something, you idiot."

I looked at the meat fork in my right hand and the can of PAM in my left. The casual observer—one who managed to miss Elspeth altogether—might have surmised that I was about to cook something. Perhaps sweet-and-sour snake.

What was I supposed to do? Stab the reptile? What if I missed and stabbed Elspeth in the neck? Or what if I actually hit the snake, but merely succeeded in wounding it? What if it let go of its ill-tempered dinner and lunged at me? I am prepared to meet my Maker, but prefer not to leave this world as an animal's entrée. If I wasn't discovered in time—Lord knows Elspeth wouldn't try to save me—there'd be nothing left to bury but a pathetic pile of python poop. I wouldn't even need to be cremated. The scat could be scattered in my garden. Talk about a good crop of mums.

"Well, you idiot, are you going to help me or not?"

"Oh, Lord, give me strength," I cried, and raised the hand with the fork.

I must have a simple mind, because indeed, the reptile read it. He lifted his head, uncoiled half a loop, and strained to reach me. "Go ahead," he seemed to say, "make my day. I'd rather eat you anyway."

"Stab him, stab him, you idiot!" Elspeth's voice was stronger now that the distracted snake was loosening its grip.

What is wrong with me that I couldn't even stab Satan's older brother to save a human life? It was all I could do just to aim the can of PAM at the python and spray it in the eyes.

The evil creature didn't even blink, but the head bobbed, and its tongue flickered. It was presumably tasting the nonstick stuff, and must not have liked it too much because the top two coils loosened, exposing Elspeth's neck and shoulders. I don't get credit for what happened next, because I didn't stop to think before acting. I dropped the meat fork, grabbed Elspeth by the hair, and pulled. With my left hand I sprayed PAM in the widening gap between her and the upper part of the snake. In order to do so, I had to get so close to the beast that its bobbing head banged against my left arm. It felt like a striking fist.

"Ouch!"

For the record, that wasn't me, but Elspeth. I ignored both her and the hammering head and sprayed until the can was empty. Then I whacked the python across the snout with the empty can. The beast was not amused and lunged with its jaws wide open. Pythons don't have fangs, by the way, but can inflict painful bites. They also have viselike grips.

Fortunately, as befits a good Christian woman, I was wearing elbow-length sleeves. The powerful jaws ripped off a mouthful of fabric but missed my arm. Finding nothing on my end to support it, the head swung down and away from me, and in that split second I grabbed Elspeth's locks with both hands and jerked for all I was worth. She slid out of the coils like a greased pig and, like the said swine, squealed loudly.

"Damn you, Magdalena Yoder. If my hair is ruined, I will sue, yah?"

"Sue away," I cried. I was too exhilarated by what had just happened to care.

Elspeth's escape had totally confused the reptile. Instead of pursuing either of us, it was rapidly retreating underneath the bed. Where just seconds ago there had been a pile of coils, now there was only a stained carpet and a gun. A gun!

Again, it was my reflexes, not bravery on my part, but I swooped down on that revolver like a hen on a June bug. Elspeth swooped too, and given that she is part fowl, she normally would have stood a better chance of recovering the weapon. Fortunately for me, being almost hugged to death by a twenty-five-foot serpent had left her wobbly, and she collapsed in mid-swoop. But not without a good deal of sound effects, I might add.

For the second time in two days I held a gun in my hand. I wouldn't hesitate to shoot the snake—an action far less personal than stabbing—but I could never bring myself to shoot another human being. Even Elspeth Miller.

The weak-kneed Nazi sympathizer knew that. After all, I was a Mennonite, wasn't I? A dyed-in-the-wool pacifist. The colonel's murderer floundered in my direction, hoping to wrest the gun from my hand. I had no choice but to disable her by connecting one of my size elevens with her solar plexus. My aim was true and she collapsed again, this time as silently as a pile of feathers.

My plan was to drag her from the room by her crowning glory. Once I got her out of harm's way, with the door closed safely behind us, I'd deliver another swift kick. One just hard enough to keep her out of action until I could run, carrying the gun with me, for help.

I had the bird woman halfway across the room when the door to the armoire opened and out tumbled Melvin Stoltzfus. "Give me the gun, Yoder. I'm taking over."

My jaw dropped so far even I could have swallowed Elspeth. "M-M-Melvin," I finally managed to gasp.

"That's my name, Yoder. Don't wear it out."

"B-but were you in that armoire the entire time?"

"I was trapped, Yoder. What of it?"

Elspeth started to moan, so I did my civic duty. Even though my toe still hurt like the dickens, it was able to find its way back to her solar plexus. Anyway, I got her through the door before Melvin slammed it behind us.

"What of it?" I cried. "You let me fight with an African rock python and—"

"Well, I'm here now, aren't I? Besides, like I said, I was trapped. That thing was lying right in front of the armoire."

"But why did you get in it in the first place?"

It was deus ex machina, although Deus was not on my side. As my nemesis and I stood there, he defending his cowardice, and I seeing it for what it was, the front door to my inn flew open and in burst the county sheriff and two deputies. We could only hear them at first, as we were still at the top of my impossibly steep stairs, but even Melvin knew it was the moment of truth.

"Yoder, I'm begging you. Let me tell it my way."

"Upstairs, boys," I shouted. I turned to Melvin. "Give me one good reason."

"So Susannah will respect me."

"But she adores you now."

"Yes, but—" Melvin took a step closer to me and then, because I am indeed a dummkopf, he grabbed the gun from my hand.

When the sheriff and his boys rounded the first landing, it was Melvin they saw standing over Elspeth Miller.

30

Crème Brûlée

"Burnt cream," the richest of all custards, presumably originated in seventeenth-century England, and not France, as one would suspect. The brittle caramelized topping is a pleasing contrast to the soft, cool custard.

2 cups heavy cream
1 vanilla bean, split and
   scraped
5 large egg yolks

½ cup sugar
1 teaspoon vanilla extract
Garnish: Fresh berries of
   your choice

Preheat the oven to 325° F.

Scald the cream and the vanilla bean in the top of a double boiler. Off the heat, let the bean steep in the cream for 10 minutes.

Lightly beat together the egg yolks and ¼ cup sugar. Slowly whisk in ½ cup cream, blending thoroughly. Pour into the remaining cream, whisking as you pour. Add the vanilla, then strain into 4 or 5 flameproof custard cups. Skim off any foam.

Bake in a bain-marie for 45 to 50 minutes, or just until custard is set. (The custard will be wobbly but will solidify as it chills.) Let cool to room temperature, then refrigerate for several hours.

Sprinkle with the remaining sugar and place under the broiler just until the sugar caramelizes. Watch carefully. Let cool for 5 minutes, then refrigerate for 15 to 20 minutes so the custard can firm up again. To serve, garnish with berries.

SERVES 4 OR 5

Variation: Pumpkin Créme Brûlée

Add ½ cup cooked or canned pumpkin puree, 2 tablespoons cognac, ½ teaspoon ground cinnamon, ¼ teaspoon ginger, and ¼ teaspoon ground nutmeg to the cream and egg mixture. Serve with gingersnaps. This is best made the day before so the flavors can blend.

31

"Tell us again, Uncle Melvin." Alison had asked to sit next to her new idol at the birthday dinner I was throwing for myself at my newly liberated inn.

True to his word, Gabe's contact at the pet shop had come out the day after my big ordeal and lured the giant reptile out from under the bed with a live goat. Sure, it took him several days to do it, but the fact that the event made national news should have been payment enough for Harold. But oh no, when the snake handler found out that Charlie the Python was not his to keep—the snake was official evidence—he was anything but charmed. Now I was going to have to pay almost five hundred dollars in pest removal charges, thanks to Colonel Custard's last stand.

"Uncle Melvin," I said through gritted teeth, "has told that story one too many times. In fact, I'd say the first time he told it was one too many."

"You're just jealous, Yoder."

"I most certainly am not!"

"Give it up, sis," Susannah had the nerve to say. "My shnuggy-wuggy is a famous hero."

I rolled my eyes, as did Freni and Mose, who had

joined us for dinner. In fact, Freni cooked the meal, although it wasn't quite up to her usual standard. The dear woman thought it was possible that Charlie had laid eggs during his time down in the floor vents, and that at any minute we could be overrun by baby pythons. Larry from the pet store had tried, but without success, to convince her that the snake was a male. After all, the twenty-five-foot monster lacked any visible appendages.

Our ocular gestures were not missed by Susannah. "I saw you guys roll your eyes. Well, I'll have you know that someone from Letterman's office called this afternoon. They might have him on the show."

"Cool," Alison said, and gazed adoringly at her pseudo-uncle.

"Might?" I asked. "What's wrong? Does Dave have an aversion to praying mantises?"

"Hey," Alison cried, "that's not nice."

"You're quite right, dear. Sorry."

"For your information," Susannah said, "it was all set up, but then I spilled the beans and told the staff about Melvin running for office. They said they're not so sure about having a politician on as a guest, but I don't see why."

"They won't mind when I become President," Melvin said.

My eyes got another good workout.

"Don't laugh, Yoder. Elspeth confessed to killing Roy. She'd beaten him so badly he was going to require serious medical attention. Decided to finish him off and make it look like he'd left town. Then she buried him in the exhibit vegetable garden, just like I suspected—"

"Excuse me. I'm the one who figured that out."

"Whatever," Susannah said. "Go on, sweetiekins."

"But sis," I hissed, "you said you didn't want him to win—"

She clamped a moist hand over my mouth. Her palm smelled of peanut butter.

"That was then; this is now. Please finish your story, pooky-wooky."

Melvin's left eye glared at me, while his right focused on the footprint that graces my dining room ceiling. "As I was about to say before I was so rudely interrupted, she confessed to killing the colonel too, so that her nasty secret wouldn't be uncovered if the road was widened. Made an appointment to meet him here at the inn the morning you were playing tourist with your guests. She left the gun behind on purpose to make it look like suicide."

"Which clearly it didn't," I huffed.

"She was going to kill you, Yoder, on account you knew too much, until I came along."

"But that's just it. It was *I* who knew too much—"

Wet, warm peanut butter covered my mouth again. "Please," Susannah whispered, "I'm begging you. Let it go."

"Thwhy thwould I?"

"Because our sex life has been over the moon since Melvin solved these murders."

"Oh, gross," Alison said. "I heard that."

"Yah?" Freni asked. Her hearing is not as sharp as a twelve-year-old's. "What did you hear?"

"Auntie Susannah said her and Uncle Mel's sex life—"

"Ach!" Both Freni and Mose clapped their hands over their ears. If Melvin would only have covered his eyes, we'd have had all three monkeys accounted for.

It was clearly time to change the subject. I forced Susannah's hand aside.

"Well, Alison, dear. Tell us why you left the door to the chicken coop open."

"Me?"

"It was you, wasn't it?"

Alison stared at her plate, which, by the way, was far from empty. "How did you know it was me?"

I was being unfair, and I knew it. It had occurred to

me that Alison was the culprit and, in fact, had left the door open to support her claim of spotting Bigfoot. This was all part of her plan to get my attention. Her reaction to my question confirmed this. Still, we should not have been having this conversation in public.

"Who knows all the words to 'Pop Goes the Weasel'?" I asked, proving that someone as tall and gangly as I can turn on a dime.

But Alison, bless her heart, seemed relieved to have been found out. "I'm sorry, Mom."

I smiled at my pseudodaughter. "Apology accepted."

"Hey," Susannah said, "that's not fair. We're missing out on something here, aren't we?"

"I'm the one who originally spread the Bigfoot rumors," Alison said. She seemed almost proud of her sin now.

The elderly Hostetlers nodded wisely, but the stubborn Stoltzfus shook his head. "Don't be so sure they're just rumors, Alison. The boys and I found some really big tracks out there in the woods."

"They probably just belonged to Mags," Susannah said. In her own dear way she was trying to make up for depriving me of the credit I deserved for solving the colonel's murder.

Mose, ever the peacemaker, and sensitive far beyond the restraints of his gender, picked up a heavy platter. "Does anyone want more of this suffocated steak?"

"That's 'smothered,' dear," I said. "And please, everyone, have another piece. Just save one for Gabe."

The love of my life, the shining beacon in my darkest hour, had driven into Pittsburgh to exchange the ring and pick up what he promised was going to be the birthday present to top all presents. It was one of a kind, he'd assured me. I'd been expecting him home by six, but it was already going on seven, and still no Babester.

"I tell you what, sis," Susannah said, still trying to

smooth things over, "you're really lucky to have found him."

"Are you implying—"

The front door opened, and there were voices in the lobby. Then Gabe entered the dining room preceded by a woman half his size. For a second there, I thought I was looking at the ghost of Granny Yoder—same grizzled features, same dark beady eyes.

"Hey, everyone," Gabe said jovially, "I want you to meet my mother, Ida Rosen. She's agreed to live with Magdalena and me after we're married."

Susannah giggled. "Or maybe *not* so lucky."

Author's Note

I would like to thank Roark Ferguson of Roark's Reptile Safari in greater Charleston, South Carolina, for his knowledge of big snakes.

Help the outrageous Magdalena Yoder
smoke out a killer in Tamar Myers's
Pennsylvania Dutch Mystery
with Recipes

Thou Shalt Not Grill

An irresistible novel that really sizzles.
Includes a half dozen tasty recipes for
outdoor grilling!

Available from Signet

Turn the page for a special sneak preview....

I had to quit obsessing about Ida Rosen. Just thinking about her was making my skin itch under my sturdy Christian underwear. To take my mind off my misery, I washed the dishes by hand in scalding water. Still unable to rid my brain of frightening images of my future mother-in-law, I started to scrub the kitchen floor. This was, of course, an exercise in futility, since Freni keeps the place so clean that germs die of starvation. Nevertheless, I had worked my way halfway across the room, when the doorbell rang. That's when I discovered, much to my dismay, that I had trapped myself by an expanse of wet floor.

"Would someone please get the door?" I hollered.

No one responded, and the bell rang again.

"Doesn't anyone hear the doorbell?" I bellowed. After all, the front door is much closer to the front parlor than it is to the kitchen.

The bell rang a third and fourth time in rapid succession.

"Darn," I said, which is as bad as I can swear.

Because I was still expecting one last guest, I had no choice but to answer it myself. I was not, however, a happy hostess when I flung open the door. In my mind I saw Ida Rosen, her face screwed up in a disapproving look. It took me a few seconds to adjust to reality. Unfortunately my mouth works faster than my mind.

"Now what is it?" I snapped.

"Is this the PennDutch Inn?" a small voice asked.

I stared. Standing on the porch was a beautiful Japanese girl. I knew her nationality because it was written on the reservation card. What I hadn't known until then was her gender, thanks to a rather difficult name.

"Miss Mukaisan?" I did the best I could with the pronunciation.

She bowed from the waist. I followed her example, which prompted her to bow again. After the fourth round we both gave up.

"My name is Teruko Mukai," she said, "but everyone calls me Terri."

I hate being wrong. "Are you sure? I know there was a 'san' in there someplace."

She smiled. "San is a title—like mister or miss. We attach it to the end of the name. But in English, I think, you would hyphenate it."

"Then you may call me Yoder-san. Velkommen to zee—" I stopped my silly charade. After all, the girl spoke perfect, unaccented English, and she hailed from the other side of the globe. "Yes, this is the PennDutch Inn. And you're a mite late, dear."

She smiled again. "I'm sorry Yoder-san, but this is a very big country. I had no idea Pennsylvania was such a long state. And the traffic out of New York City—"

"New York? Is that where you drove from?"

"Oh no. I took a cab from Kennedy International Airport."

"You *what*?" But there it was, pulling out of driveway and onto Hertlzer Road.

"I'm afraid he was not happy with my tip, but that was all the cash I had."

"Don't worry, dear. I take most credit cards, and there are banks over in Bedford." She was a mere slip of a girl, so it was easy to glance behind her. "Where is your luggage?"

Terri's hands flew to her face. "The cab!"

I was faced with two choices: Hop in my car and chase down the cab, or call the Hernia police. I'm a fast driver for a Mennonite, but what if the cabdriver refused to pull over? Or what if he did pull to the side of the road, and he was armed and still in a cantankerous mood? On the other hand, dealing with the local authorities was less appealing than a liver-flavored milkshake. The chief is my nincompoop brother-in-law, and the only other officer is his spoony sidekick, Zelda Root. Working together they could possibly find their way out of paper bag—if given both directions and a string to follow.

"Darn," I said for the second time that night, and ran inside to make the call.

No one answered at the station, so I called Melvin at home. My sister, Susannah, picked up.

"Susannah! Put Melvin on the phone, please. This is an emergency."

My sister giggled. "I can't, Mags."

"Is he there?"

"Oh, he's here all right, but he can't come to the phone."

There was no time for nonsense. "Then take it to him."

"We don't have a portable, silly. You know that. Besides, he hates being disturbed when he's—uh—you know."

"Put him on *now.*"

Susannah sighed loudly and let the phone drop. Then I heard her voice in the background, followed by a whoosh of water. Finally Melvin picked up.

"Yoder, this better be good. I still haven't read the comics."

"Melvin, listen to me. You need to take the cruiser and chase down a cab."

"You're nuts, Yoder," he said and hung up.

I know I should make allowances for Melvin, given that he was kicked in the head by a bull when he was a teenager—one that he was trying to milk—but not only is he a nincompoop, he's arrogant. Besides, I'm not really sure he's human. He looks just like a praying mantis, with eyes that move independently of each other and a bony carapace. The Bible commands us to love our neighbors, but it says nothing about loving insects.

Still, the man wields power in our small community, and one must give unto Caesar what is his. For the sake of Teruko Mukai I would grovel to the man who once sent his favorite aunt a gallon of ice cream by UPS. I punched redial.

My sister picked up after the first ring. "Susannah's house of perpetual love."

"Susannah!"

"Oh, Mags, I'm only pulling your leg. You know we have Caller ID."

"Put Melvin back on the phone."

"He doesn't want to speak to you."

"This is police business."

"But—"

"I'll cut off your allowance for a month." When our parents died—squished in a tunnel between a milk tanker and a truck full of state-of-the-art running shoes—they left the farm in a trust to me. I was instructed to make sure my sister was cared for, but she was not to be given her inheritance outright until such time that she proved she was a mature adult. That was eleven years ago, and Susannah is now thirty-six. Enough said.

Susannah didn't hesitate. "Milkins," she called, "Mags is insisting."

He got on the line with remarkable rapidity. "Is this extortion, Yoder? Because if it is—"

"Shut up, dear, and listen. One of my guests—a Japanese lady—took a cab from New York. He dropped her off here, but then drove away with her luggage. He was angry at her for not tipping well, and I think he means to keep her stuff. By now he's probably halfway to Bedford."

"But, Yoder, I'm in my pajamas."

"Then throw a coat on. Just think, this time you'll have a good excuse to drive fast with the siren on."

"Hmm. Okay, but you better not be making this up."

It was my turn to hang up. Then I comforted Terri Mukai. The poor woman had been privy to my conversation, and being somewhat brighter than my brother-in-law, she was clearly concerned about his competence.

I'm convinced the Good Lord doesn't mind a white lie if it's meant to comfort someone. "Don't worry, dear," I said. "The man's an expert at what he does." An expert at irritating me, that's what.

The reason there hadn't been a helpful response from the parlor when the doorbell rang is most of my guests had gone to bed early. Freni's cooking has a tendency to produce that effect. Plus, as I've observed, traveling can be very tiring. What surprised me is that Alison had hit the sack as well. I don't have a television—I have long since given away my black-and-white—but that doesn't stop her from begging to stay up late.

At any rate, the Littletons were still awake; I could tell by the light under their door. When they heard me show Teruko Mukai to her room, they popped out to say hello. The Charlestonians were still dressed, by the way. Even though it wasn't their business, I shared with them the sad fate of Miss Mukai's belongings. I thought of it as a preemptive strike, lest the new arrival put an even worse spin on the story. It wouldn't do to have my charming Southern guests think that we Yankees were nothing but a bunch of cutthroats and thieves.

Upon hearing the sad tale, Capers Littleton gave Miss Mukai a hug and then held her at arm's length. "You know, darling," she drawled to the new arrival, "you and I are about the same size. I'm sure I could find a few things for you to wear."

"Please, Mrs. Littleton," the young woman protested, "I do not want to trouble you."

"Oh, it is no trouble. I insist. I always travel with twice as many clothes as I need. Don't I dear?"

Buist nodded vigorously. "That's a fact."

"There then, it's all settled," I said.

Teruko Mukai bowed deeply to show her appreciation. "Americans are very kind," she said.

I waited patiently while Capers retrieved a fresh nightgown and a set of casual clothes for the following day, and then I showed the girl her room. Her basic toiletries I supplied myself. Half my guests leave their brains at home when they go on vacation, along with half the things they mean to pack, so I am well stocked with the essentials. Usually I charge my guests by the item, but in Teruko's case I decided to make an exception in the interest of international goodwill. Finally, the girl was settled in and I was able to totter off to bed myself.

Although Alison complains loudly when she has to share my room, the child is starved for affection and doesn't really mind. Many times she stays in my room a few extra days on her own volition. I enjoy her company too. The only real downside is that she somehow manages to hog my king-size bed—oh, and she thrashes about like a shark out of water.

Sure enough, the girl was sprawled across both sides, snoring as loud as a chain saw. "Move over, dear," I said and pushed her to the halfway mark.

She rolled back to where I'd found her. I pushed her again, and before she could react, I threw myself on the empty spot. A moment later the back of her hand connected with my nose. I have the prominent Yoder nose—one deserving of its own zip code—and I know it's an easy target, but it's just as sensitive as any other shnoz. Being bonked on it hurt like the dickens.

Because I knew the child meant no harm, I gently moved her arm away and then protected my face with my pillow. That turned out to be a good move, because four inches of feathers helped to muffle the sound of her snores. Eventually I fell asleep, although I dreamed I was on the *Nina* with Christopher Columbus. The ship was pitching, and every now and then the yardarm would smack me on some vulnerable part of my body. Just as I was lecturing the famous explorer on how to provide better guest services, his cell phone rang. And rang.

"Chris, dear, pick it up."

"But Magdalena, Carina, it's your phone you hear."

"It is?"

That's when I awoke to find my bedside phone ringing. I glanced at my alarm clock. Five a.m. on the dot. Unlike my sister, I do not have Caller ID. Since the only folks who have my private number are family or close friends and they would all be asleep now—well, except for Babs who, given the time difference, could still be praying—I panicked.

"What happened?" I blurted.

"I didn't catch the cabdriver, that's what."

"Melvin! You woke me at five in the morning to tell me you failed at your job?"

"I didn't fail, because there never was a cab. It's time to face it, Yoder, you're getting senile."

"Good night, Melvin."

"Yoder, I'm not calling about the stupid cab, anyway."

"Susannah? Is something wrong?"

"Something's wrong, all right, but it has nothing to do with my Sugar Boo."

"Spit it out, dear. You've got to the count of three. One—"

"There's been a murder."

National Bestselling Author of *Thou Shalt Not Grill*

TAMAR MYERS

Assault And Pepper

A Pennsylvania Dutch Mystery with Recipes

New American Library

SIGNET   (0451)

TAMAR MYERS
PENNSYLVANIA DUTCH
MYSTERIES—WITH RECIPES!

"As sweet as a piece of brown-sugar pie."
—*Booklist*

"Rollicking suspense."
—*Washington Post*

GRUEL AND UNUSUAL PUNISHMENT
20508-1

THE CREPES OF WRATH
20322-4

THE HAND THAT ROCKS THE LADLE
19755-0

PLAY IT AGAIN, SPAM®
19754-2

EAT, DRINK, AND BE WARY
19231-1

BETWEEN A WOK AND A HARD PLACE
19230-3

JUST PLAIN PICKLED TO DEATH
19293-1

NO USE DYING OVER SPILLED MILK
18854-3

PARSLEY, SAGE, ROSEMARY & CRIME
18297-9

TOO MANY CROOKS SPOIL THE BROTH
18296-0

Available wherever books are sold or at
penguin.com

S314